a writer of penny dreadfuls

a prima ballerina

a coffin maker's daughter

a physician

"For I have all the instincts of ..."

a secret agent

a stockbroker

a trapped miner

a caterpillar

a princess in a tower

a postmaster's daughter

a prized stallion

a junior Sherlock Holmes

a prima ballerina

a Buddhist monk

"For I have
all the instincts of . . ."

a stockbroker

a princess in a tower

a writer of
penny dreadfuls

a five-star general

a coffin maker's daughter

an assistant librarian

a physician

a sedated cow

a caterpillar

a postmaster's daughter

a highland hermit

a secret agent

a startled rabbit

a lion

a trapped miner

a cheese maker's niece

BRING ME THE HEAD OF
Ivy Pocket

By CALEB KRISP

Illustrations by
BARBARA CANTINI

BRING ME THE HEAD OF
Ivy Pocket

By CALEB KRISP

GREENWILLOW BOOKS
An Imprint of HarperCollinsPublishers

Bring Me the Head of Ivy Pocket
Text copyright © 2017 by Caleb Krisp
Illustrations copyright © 2017 by Barbara Cantini
First published in 2017 in Great Britain by Bloomsbury Children's under the title
Bring Me the Head of Ivy Pocket
First published in 2017 in the United States by Greenwillow Books
The right of Caleb Krisp to be identified as the author of this work has been asserted
by him in accordance with the Copyright, Designs and Patents Act, 1988.

The text of this book is set in Spectrum MT Std.
Book design by Sylvie Le Floc'h

⸙

Library of Congress Control Number: 2017937637
ISBN 978-0-06-236440-1 (hardcover)
17 18 19 20 21 CG/LSCH 10 9 8 7 6 5 4 3 2 1
First Edition

Greenwillow Books

For my benefactress, Gwendolyn Greystoke,
who was kind enough to vanish at sea

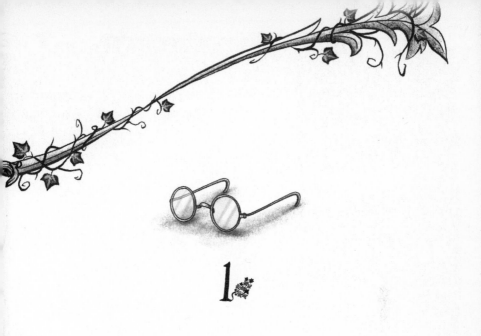

1

"Why are we slowing?"

I wasn't asleep. Just lightly dozing, as young ladies do on long carriage rides. My mouth wide open. My head tilted back in a dainty manner. The odd musical snort escaping from my nose. All very elegant.

"Driver, why are we slowing?" It was a woman. She sounded rather annoyed. "It's *miles* from our next stop. This is highly irregular."

My peaceful nap was no match for such a loud creature. As she prattled on about "unscheduled stops," I was suddenly aware of the rattling windows and the fading roar of carriage wheels coming to a halt.

"Excuse me." I felt a sharp jab to my ribs. "Would you mind moving over?"

I was pushed sideways as someone wedged themselves down between myself and the window. My eyes sprang open. "What are you doing, you mad cow?"

It was the prim-looking American—Miss Finch. The one who had been so appalled that I was making the journey to London alone. "I can't see the road from my seat, and I wish to know why we're stopping all of sudden." She pursed her lips and scowled. "It's *highly* irregular."

I was now squished against a handsome young man, fast asleep with a copy of *David Copperfield* resting against his chest. While on the seat opposite, three white-haired sisters were busy knitting matching yellow-and-blue scarves. (I didn't know their names, but I'm almost certain they were Shorty, Big Ears, and Grumpy.)

"Perfectly understandable," I said, politely ramming Miss Finch with my shoulder. "After all, what are carriage rides for, if not being violently attacked in your sleep?"

Miss Finch pulled back the curtain. "Well, I'm sorry for that," she said, not sounding terribly sorry at all. "Though it was just a little jab."

"True enough," I heartily agreed. "I'm certain it only *felt* monstrously painful because you are blessed with the arms of a lumberjack."

Miss Finch blinked furiously. Looked down at her arms. "I . . . I've always been described as *dainty*."

"Which makes your bulging forearms all the more remarkable." I slapped her knee in the way new friends do. "You should join a circus, dear. You'd make a fortune."

She frowned, shook her head, and snorted. Which was the American way of expressing profound amusement. Then she turned and peered out the window. "It's so dark out there I can hardly see a thing."

Which was very true. Though my watch told me it was two in the afternoon, the view outside was bleak—dark clouds hung awfully low, churning like smoking furnaces.

I sat back in my seat and sighed. Thinking on where I was. And why. The carriage was bound for London. And I was going there for the gravest of reasons. To save Rebecca and bring her home (Winslow Street was the only location that would allow me to cross directly into Prospa House). To find out why those guards keeping her prisoner had seemed to recognize me. And to liberate Anastasia Radcliff from that hideous madhouse in Islington and reunite her with the child she had been cruelly separated from. But right at that moment, the carriage was at a standstill. And for the first time, that struck me as rather odd. "What can you see, Miss Finch?"

"Not a lot," she replied. "Though the driver's climbing down."

"There's something on the road," said Big Ears, peering out her window.

"What could it be?" asked Shorty.

Grumpy clicked her fingers at me as if I were a poodle. "Girl, go and tell the driver to pass around whatever is blocking the road. Tell him my sisters and I must be in London by nine, or we will miss our boat."

While I positively hated doing what I was told—especially by rude old bats—I *did* want to find out what was holding us up.

So I squeezed past Miss Finch and stepped out of the carriage. Thick wheat fields bordered the road, the golden stalks rendered a rusty brown by the brooding storm clouds. I could hear the murmur of agitated voices in the distance—but it wasn't until I walked around the horses and got a clear view of the road ahead that I understood why.

A small wagon loaded with trunks had overturned. The driver lay on the ground, blood oozing from his head. A hefty woman stood nearby, sobbing madly, while our driver, Mr. Adams, was untethering a pair of black stallions hitched to the wagon.

When the horses were free, Mr. Adams bent down and tended to the injured man, who seemed more concerned about his wagon. As the two drivers discussed what had happened, Mr. Adams pointed to a small farmhouse in the distance and said a few extra hands might help.

"Shall I go and sound the alarm?" I said helpfully.

"I could have been killed!" shrieked the chunky woman. "It's a miracle I didn't break my neck!"

"Are you hurt, ma'am?" came a voice behind me. I turned

and discovered Miss Finch looking on with a furrowed brow. "Can I help?"

"I landed on my shoulder," said the woman, clutching her arm, "and it aches something fierce." She sobbed again. "I could have been killed."

"What happened?" I asked her.

She pointed at the injured man. "He was driving like a madman, that's what!"

Above us the rain began to fall, pushed about in all directions by the wind.

"You poor woman," said Miss Finch solemnly. "Come and take shelter in the carriage with us. We will send for a doctor."

"That's very kind," said the woman, "but I should stay here and keep an eye on my belongings." She nodded her head in my direction. "Perhaps the girl could keep me company? I'm a bundle of nerves, I am."

Miss Finch thought that was an excellent idea—pushing me toward the whimpering lady and hurrying back to the carriage. The woman took my hand tightly in hers and repeated how close she had come to death. I noticed that she kept stealing glances at the road behind us.

"It's a bad knock to the head you've taken," said Mr. Adams, pulling the wagon driver to his feet.

"I've had worse," said the driver, wincing in pain. "I just . . . need to rest a spell."

Mr. Adams helped the driver hobble to the side of the road, setting him down gently. But I wasn't paying much attention— for my gaze was still fixed on the blubber guts clutching my hand. She was magnificently beefy for a damsel in distress. Beady eyes, terribly close together. Skin so full of craters and dints it resembled a crumpet. Shaggy eyebrows. A nose that took a sharp right turn about halfway down. The hint of a mustache. All in all, she was tremendously convincing. Just not to me. For I knew *exactly* who was lurking beneath that artful disguise.

"Very impressive, Miss Always," I said, snatching my hand away. "The overturned wagon, the injured driver—it all looks so real."

The villain stepped back, startled. "Whatever do you mean?" she cried. "I nearly died! I could have broken my—"

"Yes, yes, your neck could have snapped clean off your head. But it didn't, for this whole thing is a monstrous trap. Only I am far too clever to fall for it."

"You are delirious." The wicked woman looked to Mr. Adams. "Did you hear what she said to me? The girl is mad!"

The sky trembled violently as Mr. Adams scratched his chin and regarded me. "I can't speak for her mind," he said slowly. "I only know she's traveling alone and has no luggage."

"There!" cried the woman. "What sort of child travels across the country *alone*, with no possessions?"

Hysterical accusations tend to attract a crowd—which is why the three wrinkly sisters had their heads stuck out the carriage door, gawking furiously. "Is there a problem?" said Big Ears rather eagerly.

"This girl has accused me of being an imposter!" shrieked the devious woman.

The three sisters gasped as one.

"Because she *is* an imposter," I declared, pointing to the scoundrel. "Just a few months ago, she was masquerading as a chunky librarian. And now she is wearing another disguise. Beneath this hulking monstrosity is a thoroughly devious bookworm. She is here to capture me and make me her puppet queen."

The sisters gasped again. Mr. Adams shook his head. And the beastly woman in disguise began to sob. What a masterful performance Miss Always was giving!

"What is going on?" Miss Finch was walking toward us, arms folded. "And why is everyone staring at the girl?"

"She's made some *allegations*," said Mr. Adams solemnly.

"What sort of allegations?" said Miss Finch.

I stated my case again.

Miss Finch listened. Then sighed. "I see."

She did not believe me either!

"We must not blame the child," said the disguised scoundrel, shaking her head. "I know a doctor in the next village—you go on your way, and I will take the child there myself and see that she is given the help she needs."

My fellow travelers seemed to think that was a sensible idea. As such, urgent action was required. "Look!" I said forcefully. "I will prove that what I'm saying is true."

I lunged at the imposter and grabbed her crooked nose, yanking it in a winning fashion. Once Miss Finch and the others saw the artificial nose come off in my hand, they would be full of humble apologies.

"What is she doing?" shrieked Shorty.

"Unhand that woman!" cried Miss Finch.

"In a moment, dear," I called back. "Just let me pull her face off first."

I continued to yank the nose. Unfortunately, it was rather stubborn and would not come off, no matter how hard I tugged. With time against me, I left the nose and went for her bushy eyebrows. Determined to rip them off. But they would not budge either.

"Stop!" shrieked the devious trickster, slapping me away. "Get off me!"

Her nose was surprisingly red after all that yanking, and I noticed a small trickle of blood slipping from her left eyebrow. Which was terribly unexpected.

"Leave her be, little one," said Mr. Adams, gently pulling me away. "You're only making things worse."

"She's deranged," said Grumpy.

"And violent," added Big Ears.

"I've never been treated so viciously!" wailed the injured woman. "Not in all my life!"

I felt the smart thing to do was offer a few kind words to smooth things over. "You mustn't blame yourself, dear. Having features so delightfully grotesque that any right-thinking person would assume it was a hideous disguise is hardly *your* fault." I walked over and patted her shoulder sympathetically. "Blame the parents, I say."

The woman's hand flew up and slapped me straight across the face.

"What a wicked tongue," she said fiercely. "A girl like you should be locked away."

My right cheek stung a great deal, but I refused to show it. "If it's any comfort, I was recently held prisoner in a madhouse. Which wasn't nearly as much fun as it sounds."

There was a small amount of chatter about me being bonkers. I was giving an impassioned defense of my sanity and didn't notice the small carriage charging up the road toward us. Or coming to a screeching halt just a few feet away. In fact, I only glanced over as the carriage door swung open and a grim figure in black leaped out, her face a mask of cold determination and wicked delight. The *real* Miss Always fixed her eyes upon me and began to sob.

"Thank heavens I've found her!" She pointed at me, her eyes overflowing like two buckets in a rainstorm. "My darling daughter, my little Ivy, ran away, and I've been scouring the countryside all night looking for her."

"And you want her *back*?" said Grumpy.

I turned and bolted but did not get far. For the sobbing creature I had accused of being Miss Always lunged and ensnared me in her tight grip. "It's a terrible thing you've done," she said, "running away from your poor mother."

"She's *not* my mother, you hefty halfwit!" I looked to Miss Finch in desperation. "Miss Always is a murderous hag from another world—please don't let her take me!"

"You are unwell," said Miss Finch gravely. "You must go with your mother."

The three sisters and Mr. Adams nodded in agreement.

"I just want my darling daughter back!" blubbered Miss Always.

"Of course you do," declared the woman gripping my arm.

I struggled wildly, but could not break free. As she pulled me toward Miss Always, she pressed her head close to my mine and whispered, "The gatekeeper has plans for you."

And in that moment it all made sense. This whole thing had been an elaborate plot to ensnare me. My only hope was to create a moment of distraction. Which is why I stopped struggling. "I'm acting like a lunatic, do forgive me," I said loudly. "Of course I'll go with dear Mumsy. It's only right."

The rain grew more urgent, hitting the road like sparks.

"I thought she was a murderous hag from another world?" sneered the crooked-nose henchwoman.

I shrugged. "Nobody's perfect, dear. Just look at you."

And with that, I kicked her as hard as I could in the shin. She shrieked rather violently and began to hop about, releasing her tight hold. Miss Always stormed toward me. Which seemed like a perfect moment to push the hopping heifer into her. They both tumbled over, hitting the damp road. Glorious! But my victory did not last long. For the wagon driver jumped up (he had never been injured to begin with) and began to charge.

Thunder shook the sky as I turned and ran.

Miss Always let out a treacherous war cry as I darted into the field, the wheat parting and crushing beneath my feet. I knew that cry well and felt certain she had unleashed an army of locks to come after me. This was confirmed when I heard the terrified cries of my fellow travelers—no doubt stunned by what they were seeing.

Rain thrashed the vast field, and the sky seemed to darken by the second.

"Fan out and be quick about it!" I heard Miss Always bellow from behind.

The brutish henchwoman and the driver shouted their obedience. Then I felt the ground rumble and shake as the wheat was trampled in every direction. Which told me the locks were spreading far and wide—ferocious and on the hunt.

Something shot past me in a blur. I pulled up and saw a trail of flattened wheat twisting away. It *had* to be a lock. And as I glanced across the darkened field, I saw dozens of such tracks being carved into the field—each one a tiny hooded beast.

I considered using the Clock Diamond to reach Prospa, but with Miss Always and her goons about, the stone's luminous glow might see me captured before I could cross. So I took off again, rain streaming down my face and clouding my eyes. The field stretched out to the far horizon—I wasn't sure which way to run. Or where I might hide.

"You won't get away, Ivy." Miss Always sounded rather amused. "You are outnumbered and outwitted. Surrender to your fate—you might even enjoy it."

"Never!" I wanted to cry out. But as I wasn't a complete idiot, I held my tongue.

I kept running at speed. Then I heard the sound of loud, ragged breaths. Twisting my head, I glimpsed the wagon driver charging toward me through the wheat stalks. So I swerved left. Which is when I spotted the stone farmhouse we had seen from the road. With no other options, I rushed toward it.

But not for long. A clawed hand shot out, grabbing my ankle. And I tumbled to the ground, my fall cushioned by the clusters of wheat beneath me. I looked up and saw the little robed villain, its face hidden inside that menacing hood. I heard it hiss like a steam train. Then it lunged, its talons unfurling.

With an outpouring of savagery—having all the natural

instincts of a drunken sailor—I unleashed a violent kick. The pint-sized scoundrel was thrown back, hitting the soggy ground and rolling several times. By then I was back on my feet and barreling toward the farmhouse.

"There she is!" shouted the henchwoman. "Boss, she's over here!"

I instantly dropped to my knees. Began crawling between the wheat stalks like an infant. I heard someone whistle and the sound of footsteps close behind. I dropped lower. Kept going. Which is when I noticed the stone well. Just beyond the farmhouse.

"Where is she?" barked Miss Always.

"I've lost her, boss," said the henchwoman.

"Well, find her again, you fool!"

The sky shuddered and the ground trembled. I could hear two or three locks nearby hissing up a storm. So I scurried toward the well. Climbed over the small stone wall. And placed my feet in the wooden bucket. A length of rope was knotted to the bucket and curled around the winch. I grabbed the handle and turned it slowly.

At least, that was the idea. Unfortunately, the winch had

other ideas. The rope began to unspool rapidly as the bucket dropped into the darkness. I was about to close my eyes and pray for a soft landing when the bucket hit the bottom, breaking apart beneath me. It was an impact of the hard and bruising variety. I'm too much of a young lady to record that my bottom ached and throbbed with all the agony of a thousand thrashings.

Water pooled around me, the rain pouring in with nowhere to go. The smell was hideously dank, the rounded wall rather slimy. I heard the henchwoman huffing and puffing up above. Then a shadow passed over, and I guessed she was there. I pressed myself against the wall. Shut my eyes.

"So?" It was Miss Always. "Is she down there?"

"Don't think so, boss," came the wheezing reply.

"Blast! The girl cannot have vanished into thin air."

"I reckon she's crossed into Prospa," said the wagon driver.

"No," said Miss Always, "we would have seen the stone's light if she'd done that." A long silence. Then Miss Always shouted above the rain, "I know you can hear me, Ivy, wherever you are hiding. You might be interested to know that I paid a visit to your little cottage by the sea—your friend Jago didn't give me the warmest of welcomes."

I covered my mouth to trap the gasp that threatened to escape.

"He put up an admirable fight." Miss Always laughed

wickedly. "I'm afraid I may have broken his arm. Terribly unsporting of me. Ivy, if you wish to see Jago again, then show yourself. Show yourself, or the boy is dead!"

How I wanted to give myself up. But could I trust Miss Always to release Jago once she had me? She didn't strike me as one of the more honorable murderous lunatics. For now I had to believe that Jago was of more value to her alive than dead. So I stayed silent.

"Come, we will search the farmhouse," ordered Miss Always.

The rain fell hard. It was relentless. Angry. Even as I huddled against the rounded wall, it came for me. Filling the well until my body began to stiffen and ache. The chill was so sharp and cruel I believed the rain had leached into my skin, cracked my bones, and filled my marrow until it froze. The sky rumbled like an angry giant. The water was up to my waist now. And I could no longer feel my lips.

That is the last thing I recall from my great escape.

2

"She's waking."

The voice sounded faint and far away. So I pretended not to hear it. For I was somewhere else entirely. In a garden overgrown with weeds and wildflowers, playfully leaping from stone to stone. The sun splashing my face. My feet bare. And rather dirty. My arms, pencil thin. My belly rumbling with hunger. Behind me stood a modest white cottage with a thatched roof.

"Quick, Henry, pass me the cloth. Her fever's awful strong."

I heard the door of the cottage opening behind me. That

sound filled me with giddy excitement, though I couldn't say why. But I knew that I had to see who came out of that house. So I spun around. Just as a cold, damp cloth splattered across my forehead. That was all it took. My eyes fluttered open, and I was greeted by a kind and tender smile.

"I was beginning to think you would never wake." The woman was of middle age, with a lean, pale face and stringy blond hair. "How do you feel?"

A persistent ache rippled through my muscles and bones. "Where am I?" I said.

"Harrington Farm," came a voice from across the room.

I lifted my head and saw a tall man with a dark beard and unruly hair. He looked rather sullen as he paced about the modestly furnished bedroom.

"My name is Margaret," said the woman, "and that is my husband, Henry."

"How did I get here?"

"That's a very good question," said Henry. "I went to check my fields after the storm and found you floating in the well. You were limp and lifeless. . . . I was sure you were dead."

"What is your name?" asked Margaret, dabbing my brow again with the cloth.

"Esmeralda Cabbage." It seemed wise under the circumstances.

"What happened to you, Esmeralda?" Margaret sat down on the bed beside me. "How did you end up in our well, half drowned?"

"And what happened in that field?" said her husband. "My crop is trampled, the harvest in ruin—I've never seen anything like it in all my years."

"Funny story, that." I sat up, and a wave of dizziness churned through my head. I shut my eyes briefly to steady myself. "I hitched a ride with one of those charming traveling freak shows. We were stopped outside your farmhouse when the bearded lady made a run for it. As you can imagine, the ringmaster was *furious*. He ordered the two-headed pygmy and six talking chimpanzees into the field to bring her back. I went to help, being a wonderful sort of girl, and as I was looking down your well, I tripped over and fell in."

The farmer and his wife exchanged a look.

"She is still unwell," said Margaret to her husband.

Which was true—but rather odd. I was sure that I *couldn't* get ill, being half dead and remarkable in every way. "How long have I been here?"

"Three days." Margaret looked as if she were about to say something more. But instead, she glanced at her husband again. Which made the knot in my stomach tighten.

"The day of the storm," said Henry, "some folks came to our door looking for a girl. A runaway, that's what they said."

"Then when Henry found you in the well," said Margaret softly, "we figured you were the one they were seeking."

"These folks were awful keen to get you back," added Henry, looking everywhere but at me. "The woman especially. She offered a fifty-pound reward if we were to find you."

Miss Always was coming! I leaped from the bed, and my head swirled more violently than before.

"But we wouldn't do such a thing," said Margaret, helping me find my feet. "Not for all the money in the world. We didn't believe that woman's tears or her promises. Isn't that right, Henry?"

But Henry didn't answer. Instead he pointed at my throat.

"That necklace you wear—looks mighty expensive."

Instinctively I felt for the Clock Diamond—it was still there under my nightdress. "A gift from the bearded lady," I said. "Very pretty, but worthless."

The farmer nodded. "These folks looking for you, are they bad people?"

I decided the truth was my best option. "Yes. Very bad."

"Then I'm sorry, Esmeralda."

Margaret flew to her husband's side. "Sorry for what?"

A loud banging on the farmhouse door provided the answer.

Margaret gasped. "Henry, what have you done?"

The hammering on the door grew more urgent.

"It's fifty pounds, Margaret, and with the crop half ruined." Henry shook his head meekly. "I'm sorry, but what choice did I have?"

"You could have kept your trap shut, you greedy halfwit," I said rather sternly.

The door was taking an awful beating, and I was certain it would soon give way.

"I will tell them I made a mistake," said Henry.

"Stay here, Esmeralda," said Margaret. "No harm will come to you. We will send them on their way."

The poor woman was as featherbrained as she was kind! The farmer and his wife hurried from the room and shut the door. I was already pulling off the nightgown and reaching for my dress (which was folded neatly on the chair). As I slipped it over my head, I heard a great commotion coming from the other side of the door.

"Get out of my way, or you'll be sorry!" It was Miss Always's brutish henchwoman. "Where is she?"

"We do not have her!" Margaret declared boldly.

I was halfway out the window when I heard Margaret scream. Then the sound of furniture hitting the floor. Then the door to the little bedroom broke open. I swung my legs over the window ledge and jumped.

My legs surged with pain as I landed in the flower bed. The farmhouse was set in a small clearing, so the only means of escape was the wheat field. But I knew I hadn't the strength to outrun them.

"Get her!" thundered the henchwoman from the bedroom window.

"She won't get far!" a man yelled in reply.

I looked back and saw the driver coming around the side of the farmhouse, running furiously. I raced across the yard, sweat dripping from my face. And spotted the villain's wagon. It stood empty, two horses happily munching on the grass.

"Leave her alone!" I heard Margaret cry out.

"Hurry, Flanders!" bellowed the henchwoman. "Don't let her get away!"

I jumped up on the wagon. Grabbed the reins. Brought them down hard on the horses' backs. As the wheels began to spin, the driver suddenly loomed beside me. He grabbed the step rail and began to climb up. So I reached for the horsewhip and brought it down viciously on his hand. He squealed like a lost lamb and let go, crashing to the ground.

By then the horses were galloping. I wiped the sweat from my face and turned the carriage onto the main road. All the while, stealing backward glances. Worried that Miss Always was close by. But I saw no sign of her.

As the wagon roared over the dirt road, I tried to calm my mind. Think clearly and whatnot. I had to reach London. To free Anastasia from Lashwood. To journey to Prospa House and bring Rebecca home. The next hour passed slowly, my thoughts still a tangle. The road stretched out endlessly. Pain rattled through my bones. How far until London? Hours? Days? Weeks?

It was impossible to know. Without realizing it, I had pulled the carriage to the side of the road, stopping under a willow tree. The reins went slack in my hands. My eyes shut. Just for a moment. All I craved was rest. A short, delicious rest.

"You all right there?"

I woke with a start. "Pardon me?"

"I said, are you all right?"

"Yes, dear, perfectly fine."

A carriage was pulled up beside me, laden with baskets of vegetables and fruit. The driver was a portly woman with ridiculously red cheeks. "You don't look fine," she said. "In fact, you look sick as a dog."

"It's just a head cold." I waved my hand toward the road. "Now do shuffle off."

"Where are you heading?"

"London."

The woman snorted. "That's a fair way."

"Where am I exactly?"

"Winchester," came the reply. "Why are you driving to London on your own, then?"

"My grandma has taken ill," I said quickly. "Run over by an elephant in the high street—crushed to pieces, poor dear. I'm going to take care of her." I looked at her bounty of vegetables, and it did give me a winning idea. "Are you going to market?"

"I am."

"And do they sell wagons and horses at this market?"

"From time to time."

I used the sleeve of my dress to wipe my damp brow. "Excellent. Lead the way."

The woman shrugged, whipped her horse, and took off— with me following closely behind. The market was a short drive away, just beyond the village square. It was teeming with carts and stalls selling fruits, vegetables, eggs, and cuts of meat. And all variety of pots and pans and tools. At the far end were a few workhorses tethered to a post with a sign saying HORSES WANTED, ONE POUND APIECE. So that was where I headed.

It occurred to me that I hadn't the strength to drive all the way to London. And I was worried about running into Miss Always on the open road. So I needed another way—and a comfortable train ride sounded like just the thing.

Which is why I approached a stockman picking at his teeth beneath the sign and offered him my wagon and two horses. The infuriating man was rather suspicious of my proposition. Quizzed me at length about the particulars.

I pointed out how fine the horses were and that I had my one-legged father's permission to strike a bargain. We haggled for some time (his first offer was criminally low) before reaching a deal—five pounds for the lot.

"There is only one condition," I added, stuffing the banknotes into my pocket. "I need a ride to the nearest train station."

We shook hands and set off at once.

It was dark when the train pulled into Waterloo Station. I had slept the whole way to London, in the comfort of first class. But I didn't wake feeling refreshed. My head throbbed. My body ached. I was hot one moment, then chilled to the bone the next.

I hurried from the station, emerging onto a busy street glowing under gaslight. A slight drizzle glazed the cobblestones. People bustled in every direction. As I looked about for a carriage, I noticed a street urchin across the road—he wore a red coat covered in patches, and he seemed to find me terribly interesting. No great shock there. From around the corner, a carriage rolled into view, and I hailed it.

"Where to, miss?" asked the driver.

"Winslow Street," I replied, climbing in.

"That ain't a nice part of town." The driver lifted his cap to scratch his head. "You sure?"

"Winslow Street," I said again. "And do hurry."

As we drove, my mind returned to the mission. According to Miss Always, Winslow Street was the *only* place that I could cross from if I wished to reach Prospa House—and that was where Rebecca was being held. In that wicked building where all the innocent souls who had put on the Clock Diamond were enslaved. Used as remedies to heal the plague that had raged in Prospa for centuries.

I patted the Clock Diamond beneath my dress. Despite how wretched I felt, it thrilled me to think I would soon see Rebecca. While I wasn't utterly sure how I was going to break her out of Prospa House, I knew that this time I wouldn't leave that world without her.

The driver let me off at the top of the street. It was as bleak and downtrodden as I remembered. A long row of dark buildings, barred windows, and peeling paint. The little pools of gaslight splashing down from the streetlamps were no match for this grim place. There was no one about, save for a passing carriage.

I walked as fast as my aching legs would allow, all the while thinking of Rebecca. Anticipating the moment when the stone sparked into life. Crossing the street, I hurried toward my destination—the empty space between a shoe factory and an abandoned boardinghouse. It had once been a building of some sort, but all that remained now were piles of bricks and a part of the wall. A front door with a frame around it. A tarnished brass plaque.

That was the spot where Prospa House had risen up before me.

"Rebecca," I whispered. "I am coming, dear."

I kept my friend at the very center of my mind. And Prospa House. Waiting for the buzzing to charge the air like a current.

Waiting for the Clock Diamond to heat up against my skin and glow radiantly. Waiting for Winslow Street to bend and melt away like wet paint dripping down a canvas.

But it did not happen. The stone was cold. The only heat came from my fevered skin. I stood there for the longest time, willing the diamond to do its job. The necklace had never let me down before. I scooped it out and looked into it eagerly. But all I saw was a dazzling stone, sparkling in the lamplight. No heat. No light. No life.

Why had the stone stopped working? Might I have worn it out? No, Miss Frost never spoke of such things. My head throbbed and my body ached. And it occurred to me that perhaps my illness had something to do with this mystery. Perhaps I needed to be well, to be *strong*, for the Clock Diamond to come alive and provide passage into Prospa.

With a heavy heart, I wandered over to the shoe factory and sat down in the doorway. It was as good a place as any to rest. The cold wind seemed to crowd around me. I hugged my knees and tried to stop the chattering of my teeth. The situation wasn't ideal, I couldn't deny that. But I was confident that things would be better in the morning. Most things are. The Clock Diamond would work again. It *had* to.

Such thoughts were as welcome as a warm sun. But they did not last. For by then, I had seen him. He stood across the road. The boy from the train station. The one in the red coat covered with patches. And he wasn't alone. Beside him stood a man in a fine white suit and top hat. He was handing the street urchin a few pennies. The boy took off with his bounty. Then the well-dressed fellow shifted his attention to me.

"I've had quite a time looking for you, Ivy Pocket," called the man in white, tipping his hat rather formally. "I have news from an old friend."

An old friend? My blood ran cold. He *must* be one of Miss Always's goons. As the scoundrel stepped onto the road, he quickened his pace. I sprang to my feet, ignoring the ache in my bones, and took off down Winslow Street.

3

"Stop!" His voice was deep and commanding. "Stop, I say!"

Which was ridiculous. Why would I stop when one of Miss Always's henchmen was chasing me down a darkened street? The fever had turned my body into a boiling cauldron; the heat seemed to steam off my skin. But I quickened my pace and turned the corner. Bolting down a narrow street, I passed a crowded tavern and was forced to jump majestically over a sleeping dog.

"Stop, Ivy!" he shouted, his breaths short and rapid. "I don't wish to hurt you!"

"Stuff and nonsense!" I called back.

Despite being on the very brink of some glorious disease, I darted across the street like a stallion. Braved a look over my shoulder. The man in white threw off his hat, charging toward me like a bull. I glimpsed the faintest hint of a smile. The brute was enjoying this little game of cat and mouse! But I wasn't. My chest was painfully tight now, every breath a struggle.

At the end of the street, I took a sharp left. Found myself at the bottom of a steep road—which was beastly. But I ran on, passing an elderly fellow pulling his cart from a small penny-pie shop. With a fleeting glance, I noticed that it was stacked with freshly baked pies of all varieties. Which gave me a magnificent idea.

I stopped and turned back. The man in white was now racing up the hill after me.

"May I borrow your cart for a moment?" I asked the old man.

"Not likely," came the muttered reply.

"Terribly sporting of you," I replied, pushing him out of the way and grabbing the cart.

"Help!" he yelled. "I'm being robbed!"

I took off, pushing the cart down the hill. Right at the man in white. He tried to swerve out of the way, but the footpath was too narrow and the cart too wide. So I was able to smash the cart right into the scoundrel. It sent him reeling back. He hit the ground with a thump. The cart was rather unstoppable at that point and, in a wondrous stroke of good fortune, flipped up, hurling its entire assortment of hot pies over the wicked man's gloriously white jacket.

"My suit!" Then he groaned like a man who'd just been run over by a pie cart. "My back!"

"You horrible imp!" said the old man, shuffling toward me and shaking his fist. "That's a week's worth of pies you've destroyed. I'll have you arrested, I will. Police! Police!"

"Calm yourself, you hysterical nincompoop." I fished out the last of my money (two pounds and some change) and handed it to him. "This should replace most of the pies you've lost."

Which seemed to calm the grumpy fossil slightly.

The man in white was now climbing rather clumsily to his feet—he looked to be in a splendid amount of pain. So I took off again, running up the hill as fast as my tired legs would allow.

"I'll find you, Ivy Pocket!" he hollered. "You can't hide forever!"

"Of course I can, you hideous henchmen," I called over my shoulder. "I have a gift for hiding—possessing all the natural instincts of a lost sock. You tell Miss Always to leave me alone or I'll knock the stuffing out of her too!"

I ran for several blocks, then turned into a narrow alleyway. Ran past a set of stables. Then a barbershop. That's when I stopped—spotting a path running down the side. It was awfully dark, but I followed it and came upon an unkempt yard. A tattered sofa lying on its side. A broken carriage wheel. A maple tree. And that is where I took shelter, sitting with my back against the trunk. I willed my eyes to stay open, intending to keep watch all night. Not to sleep a wink. As luck would have it, I failed miserably.

A dog woke me at first light, barking in an outrageous fashion. My bones still ached. My neck was impossibly stiff. The Clock Diamond felt icy cold beneath my crumpled dress.

All in all, it was a miserable start to the day. I didn't feel even slightly hungry, yet I knew it was important that I eat. The fact that I was ill, *truly* ill, still confounded me. Thanks to the Clock Diamond, I was half dead. Blood no longer coursed through my veins. I supposedly couldn't be hurt or injured as an ordinary girl might. So how was it that thanks to one night spent in a damp well, I was now as sick as a dog? Nor could I fathom why the Clock Diamond no longer worked as it had before.

I got up and headed into the alleyway—looked left and right for any sign of the man in white. Or Miss Always. A young boy was carrying a box full of apples up the road. A woman stood at an open window, drying bedsheets in the cool morning air. She smiled at me. I smiled back, though my heart wasn't in it.

At the end of the narrow lane, I passed into a busy street. But where was I to go? Fortunately, being a marvelous sort of girl, an idea or two was soon bubbling in the wondrous soup of my mind. Which is why I shouted, "Well done, Ivy!"

I waited for a wagon to pass, then crossed the road. While my new ideas were frightfully brilliant, they wouldn't succeed as long as I remained a penniless, homeless waif. Which is why

I quickened my step as I reached the footpath. For I now knew *exactly* where I was headed. Salvation was at hand—and there wasn't a moment to lose.

Returning to Thackeray Street wasn't something I had ever imagined doing. After all, the Snagsbys lived there—and they were the murderous nutters who had adopted me for the very worst of reasons. Yet here I was, standing across the road from their house.

And it was all on account of one thousand pounds. That was my payment from the Duchess of Trinity—that vengeful blubber guts—to deliver the Clock Diamond to Matilda Butterfield on her twelfth birthday. Actually, the amount was five hundred pounds. But the Duchess's lawyer, the grumpy Mr. Banks, had paid me double. I felt a wave of sorrow as I thought of Mr. Banks—who had been as kind as he was stern, and who had died so awfully at the hands of Miss Always.

Mother Snagsby had taken the one thousand pounds when I first came to live in Thackeray Street—for safekeeping, she said. Now I needed it back. After all, it was mine. I had earned it fair and square.

I had another motive for visiting the Snagsbys. Anastasia Radcliff. She had lived with them for a time, after Miss Frost helped Anastasia cross into our world. And they had loved her like a daughter, having lost their own beloved Gretel when she was just a little girl. The Snagsbys believed that Anastasia had returned to Prospa. But if they knew that she was here, in London, locked up in a madhouse—well, they would move heaven and earth to get her out.

As I walked toward the Snagsbys' house, I noticed a carriage parked outside. It was loaded with trunks, the driver fastening them with straps. The front door was open, and Mother Snagsby stalked out, lifting her parasol like a weapon and aiming at the driver.

"Mind my valuables, you clumsy oaf," she commanded sternly. "If anything is broken, I will bill you personally, is that clear?"

The driver looked rather vexed but nodded. Mother Snagsby turned back toward the house. Fearing she would vanish inside again, I stepped around the carriage and blocked her path. "Hello, Mother Snagsby—going somewhere?"

The old crow was a splendid sight. Lumpy skin concealed beneath inches of white powder. The wondrous mole on her upper lip. And that hair—dark as night with a streak of white at the temple. "It's *you!*" she hissed.

It wasn't the warmest of welcomes.

"I realize we had a small falling-out," I said, "on account of you being a crazed fossil with a deadly secret. But I was rather hoping—"

"What were you hoping?" she snapped. "That we would take you back?" Her lip curled into an unsightly sneer. "I'd sooner cut my own throat."

"What a glorious idea. But actually, I'm here about the money."

Mother Snagsby lifted her imperious head. "Money?"

"That's right. The one thousand pounds you've so kindly been keeping for me." I put out my hand in a winning fashion. "I'd like it back now, please."

The old woman's eyes sparkled darkly. "Living with *you*, young lady, was an experience of unspeakable suffering. And do you know what the price for that suffering is?" She took a deep breath, then let it out slowly. "One thousand pounds."

Which was monstrously unfair!

"I sincerely hope," Mother Snagsby went on, "that you are as destitute as you look."

I made no reply.

"In fact, I hope you . . ." Then Mother Snagsby paused. Glanced quickly at the carriage, then back at me. Her craggy face softened. A smile bloomed on her lips. She put a hand around my shoulder, which was *most* unexpected. "If it's money you need, perhaps you would be open to a business arrangement?" she purred. "Something that would benefit us both?"

What a smashing idea! "Spit it out, dear," I declared.

"Sell me the necklace," she whispered, gazing hungrily at the top of my dress (fully aware that the stone was hidden beneath it). "I will return your one thousand pounds and pay another on top of that. Just think of what you could do with *two* thousand pounds."

"Have you lost your mind?" I spat. "There is no amount of money that would convince me to give you the Clock Diamond. You would use it to kill even more innocent souls!" I folded my arms. "Besides, it's not working as it used to."

It was as if a light had been switched off in her eyes. "Then we have nothing more to discuss."

"All done, Mrs. Snagsby," said the driver. "You ready to go?"

The old bat gave me a final withering look, then strode toward the waiting carriage.

"Wait," I said quickly, "I wish to speak to you about Anastasia."

Mother Snagsby stopped. Her glare was ice cold. "What about her?"

I looked at my former mother for a moment or two. Then I shrugged. "It's not important."

Mother Snagsby had loved Anastasia, I knew that. But I suspected that her love, rather like her loathing, would be awfully hard to take. The old goat entered the carriage. As she did, I caught sight of Ezra. He had been sitting there the whole time. He looked older than I remembered. Frailer too. He did not look at me. Not even a glance.

Mother Snagsby pounded on the roof with her parasol. "Away, driver!" As the carriage took off, she stuck her head out of the window. "I hope you get what you deserve, young lady!"

"What a coincidence," I called after her. "So do I!"

I was about to set off, in search of a place to sit and think about what to do next, when I heard it. The distinct sound of weeping. Coming from inside the Snagsbys' house. So I stuck my head in the doorway and found poor Mrs. Dickens on her hands and knees, scrubbing the hall floor. "Mrs. Dickens, whatever's the matter?" I asked.

The housekeeper looked up, and there were tears falling down her pudgy cheeks and mucus oozing from her purple nose. She jumped up and greeted me like an old friend. "It's good to see you, lass," she wailed. "Oh, but what a day!"

I glanced into the darkened hall and saw that it was bare— the carpets were gone; so was the chair by the stairs and the portraits of Gretel that Mother Snagsby had painted. "The Snagsbys have sold up?"

This made the poor creature weep like a spinster at her younger sister's wedding. "Gone for good," she cried. "They shut the funeral home after . . . after that business with Mr. Grimwig. The house has been bought by a rotten lot from Scotland." Mrs. Dickens blew her nose loudly. "They have a housekeeper of their own, so I'm to be out on the street in three days' time!"

"Haven't you got a new position?"

"Not yet, lass." The housekeeper wiped her eyes. "No one wants a woman my age, half worn out and slow on her feet."

"That's true enough," I said tenderly. "What will you do?"

She shook her head. "I'm not rightly sure. I haven't two pennies to rub together." Then Mrs. Dickens gasped. "You look a fright, lass—are you ill?"

"Horribly so," I replied. "Moments from death, I should think. Homeless too."

Mrs. Dickens looked me over and nodded her head. "You'd better come inside, then."

We sat in the empty kitchen on the only two chairs remaining. Mrs. Dickens served me a glorious bowl of broth, and I forced myself to eat it.

"Where have they gone?" I said between spoonfuls. "The Snagsbys, I mean."

"Arundel," said Mrs. Dickens, getting up to stoke the fire.

She didn't need to say anything more. I had once followed

the Snagsbys to Arundel, thinking they were up to some underhanded business. But what I discovered was that their beloved daughter Gretel was buried in a churchyard there. They visited her every week and sat by her grave. It made sense that the Snagsbys had chosen to settle there and live out their days.

As night rose up around us, Mrs. Dickens and I talked of many things. I told her of my adventures. Of Miss Frost. And Anastasia. She was shocked by what she heard, but did not seem to doubt my fantastic tale for a moment. Delightful creature!

When I had said all there was to say, Mrs. Dickens stood up and announced, "You must stay here with me."

Which was a great relief. But not exactly a solution. Which is why I said, "Are you not being tossed out in three days?"

Mrs. Dickens nodded sadly. "But let's not fret about that tonight. Besides, a girl your age has no business wandering the streets."

After supper we retired to Mrs. Dickens's bedroom—it being the only sleeping chamber with any furniture left in it. My fever had returned, and the kindly housekeeper settled me in her bed and placed a cold cloth upon my forehead. Then she lit a candle, opened a drawer in the bedside table, and pulled out a clock. "I kept this for you," she said, placing it beside me.

It was silver. Dented and scratched. And it had belonged to Rebecca—a relic I had rescued from her bedroom at Butterfield Park. I could still picture that room in glorious detail, filled

with hundreds of clocks of every shape and size. I let my hand rest upon the cold metal and felt such yearning for my friend. "Thank you, Mrs. Dickens," I whispered.

The housekeeper arranged herself in a tattered chair by the window, a blanket over her legs. She reached for her cup of tea—which was flavored with a drop or ten of whiskey—and sighed. "Sleep tight, lass," she said. "Though I can't guess what tomorrow will bring."

"I can," I told her. "We are going to a madhouse."

"A *what?*"

"Drink your whiskey, dear. We'll talk in the morning."

Then I blew out the candle.

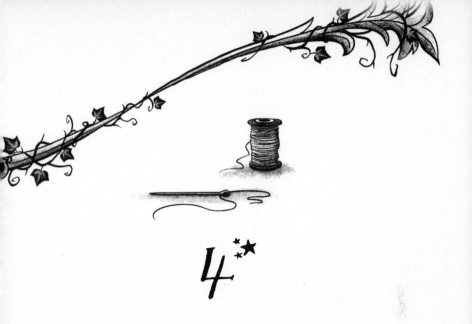

4

"I can't do it, lass."

"Well, of course you can, you lily-livered dingbat."

Mrs. Dickens stared fretfully at the grim building and wiped her bulbous nose. "But what will I say when I get in there?"

We had walked all the way to Islington the following morning, arriving around noon. I was feeling slightly better after a good night's sleep (though I was rather disappointed not to have dreamed of that thatched cottage again, or the garden of weeds and wildflowers). Mrs. Dickens and I were standing across the road from Lashwood. And she was being violently uncooperative.

"You will say that you are here to visit Anastasia Radcliff," I said calmly. "Tell them you are a distant relative who has just returned from America."

"But what if they don't believe me?" she cried.

"Why shouldn't they believe you? You look like a perfectly upstanding woman. They won't be able to tell that you have a fondness for hard liquor, horse races, and violent detective novels just by looking at you." I gave her a gentle shove. "Hurry along, dear."

Lashwood was the most feared madhouse in all of London, so I didn't entirely blame Mrs. Dickens. I would have gone in her place, but as I had only recently escaped from that hideous asylum (with Jago's expert help), I didn't think it wise to show my face.

Mrs. Dickens gulped loudly. "I'll do my best, lass."

"Anastasia knows you, Mrs. Dickens—she will be overjoyed to see a familiar face. Tell her that help is at hand. Tell her we will find a way to get her out."

I watched from behind a lamppost as the kindly housekeeper crossed the busy road and passed through Lashwood's menacing iron gates.

It had been a busy morning. After breakfast, we had gotten

to work baking rhubarb tarts. It was my idea. I chose rhubarb because it was the only fruit Mrs. Dickens had left in the larder. She was frightfully curious when I wrapped three of the delicate and delicious treats into a cloth and shoved them in my apron.

"What are you up to?" she asked.

"You'll know soon enough," I had said as we hurried out the door.

The minutes passed painfully slowly as I waited for Mrs. Dickens to come out of Lashwood. When she finally did, I saw from her face that it hadn't gone well.

"The matron was awful stern," said Mrs. Dickens, puffing. "She said they had no one by the name of Anastasia Radcliff at Lashwood. She kept asking my name. Wanting to know who had told me that Miss Radcliff was an inmate there." The housekeeper took a shallow breath. "Then she told me to stay put and hurried away. I took off as soon as she was out of view."

"Anastasia must be there under another name," I said. "That would make it easier for the Dumblebys to keep her hidden away, I suppose."

Which was all rather beastly. Luckily, I had already

considered such a possibility. That was why I kept my eyes trained on the main gates of Lashwood. After an hour or so, a group of guards and kitchen hands came out all at once. I knew from my time in that monstrous madhouse that the workers changed shifts shortly after lunch was served.

From among the miserable crowd, I found my target. She wore a grimy uniform of black and white, her pudgy jowls shaking with every heavy step—and as I had once tried to bribe her with a shoemaker from Bristol, I remembered her well. At my instruction, Mrs. Dickens called her over. "What you want with me, then?" she grumbled, sticking a finger up her nose.

I stepped out from behind the lamppost. The kitchen hand recognized me instantly.

"You're the brat from cell twenty-four who never stopped yapping." Then she frowned and pulled the finger from her nose. "Hold up—aren't you the one who escaped?"

"Yes, dear, and you're the halfwitted nose picker who fed me gruel twice a day. Now that we are reacquainted, let us get down to business."

She sniffed. "What sort of business?"

Which is when I pulled the folded cloth from my apron and flashed the rhubarb tarts at her. In an instant, her putrid hand was reaching for the delectable goodies.

"Not yet, you greedy goose," I said, pulling them away. "First, I want you to pass on a message to one of your inmates."

"Do you now?" She sniffed again. "Which one?"

"The woman who hums day and night."

She shrugged. "Can't."

"Why not?"

"She's gone, she is."

"Lord have mercy," muttered Mrs. Dickens.

"Gone where?" I said next.

"Dunno. She was moved a few days back—in the dead of night and all. Chained up well and good, she was, then bundled into some fancy carriage." She laughed gruffly. "Took four guards to load her in." She fixed her eye on the rhubarb tarts. "That's all I know."

Like a rattlesnake, her hand darted out, snatching the tarts from my hand. Then she stomped away. All that remained was the cloth in my hand. And a very great mystery.

"How unexpected," was all I could think to say.

Mrs. Dickens summed up our predicament perfectly. "What do we do *now*?"

I spent the walk back to Thackeray Street thinking. Trying to figure out where Anastasia had been taken. Or how I might discover the location. I looked at the problem from every angle. Turned it inside out. Upside down. Shook it around. Slapped it about the head. But nothing. Which was a *huge* surprise, as I'm usually an exceptional problem solver—possessing all the natural instincts of a Russian chess master. Or at very least, a Mongolian checkers player.

It was Mrs. Dickens who provided the solution. At dinner that night.

As she served me the last of the potatoes, demanding that I eat something or I would waste away to nothing, she said something rather stupendous. "I found myself staring at the empty larder just now, thinking I'd have to go to market tomorrow and stock up." She sat down and sighed sadly. "I don't have a house to run anymore—that'll take some getting used to. Old habits die hard, don't they, lass?"

At which point I jumped up and kissed the purple-nosed nincompoop. If Mrs. Dickens was a creature of habit, so too were the Dumblebys. Hadn't they spent the past twelve years visiting Anastasia at Lashwood every week and demanding she tell them what had happened to their Sebastian? And now that Lady Dumbleby was dead, didn't Estelle go in her place?

Wherever Anastasia was being kept, I felt utterly certain that Estelle would continue to visit her each and every week, seeking the answer that would always elude her.

So the next morning, I set off for Highgate. Bound for the Dumblebys' grand villa. Mrs. Dickens was against me going for three reasons. One, Estelle was rather dangerous. Two, there were more important things to worry about—like the new family moving into the Snagsbys' house tomorrow, leaving us homeless. And three, I had been coughing all night and looked paler than a sack of flour.

But I went anyway—after all, the Clock Diamond was still cold and lifeless, so reaching Prospa was not a possibility at present. I took precautions, of course. Was stupendously sneaky—wearing a large straw bonnet that belonged to Mrs.

Dickens and hiding in the alcove of a handsome building directly across from the Dumblebys' grand residence.

I was prepared for a long and tedious wait. But I needn't have been.

Just ten minutes after I took up my position, a carriage pulled up outside the Dumblebys' villa. Then the front door opened, and Estelle glided out as if on a cloud of old money. She was ravishing in a pale pink dress with matching feathered hat and parasol, her golden locks tumbling down her back. She didn't look even slightly demented.

The young woman stepped into the carriage after a quick word with the driver. Which is when I made my move. With the elegance of a gazelle, I dashed silently across the road and leaped onto the back of the carriage. I gripped the luggage rack just as it took off. Holding on wasn't easy, but luckily I was an old hand at this form of transport.

Excitement coursed through my aching bones as the carriage turned left at the end of the street. I was on the trail of Anastasia Radcliff! Though where we were headed, I hadn't a clue.

My disappointment was of the most violent kind.

"Yes, Miss Dumbleby, your order is ready," said the shopgirl, gawking in awe at the pink-feathered goddess. "Shall I carry the box out for you?"

Estelle smiled shyly. "There is no need," she said, her voice hardly more than a whisper. "My arms work well enough."

This made the shopgirl giggle like a halfwit.

The carriage had driven to Mayfair. I jumped from the back of the carriage, my arms heavy and sore, and scooted around the side—just as Estelle hopped out and headed into the nearest door. My heart sank. Instead of being led to Anastasia Radcliff, I had hitched a ride to a dress shop. It was an outrage!

Then a thought occurred to me. Perhaps the dress shop led to a secret passageway that led to a door that led to a set of stairs that led to another door, on the other side of which was a windowless cell. And it was there that Anastasia was being detained. With that in mind, I sneaked into the store while Estelle and the shopgirl were deep in conversation, and hid artfully behind a well-dressed mannequin.

Sadly, Estelle's business there seemed to be entirely about

clothes. The shop was full of gowns of every shape, style, and size. Plus an array of coats, shawls, wraps, and stoles. It wasn't busy. The only other customer was a tall woman wearing what looked like an antelope on her head. She gave me disapproving glances from time to time, and I responded by sticking out my tongue and pointing accusingly at her hat. I would have left if not for the fear of discovery. Which, as it turned out, was extremely fortunate.

For the conversation got *terribly* interesting.

"Is the dress for a special occasion, Miss Dumbleby?" gushed the salesgirl.

Estelle paused for a moment. Turned her head slightly. I held my breath. Had she seen me? Did she know I was there? I froze with all the commitment of an icebox. Keeping utterly still.

When Estelle answered, her voice had grown louder. Which was a great help! "I am going to Suffolk tomorrow," she announced. "I have some business there—and there is a ball being thrown by a most important family."

Some business there? Could she mean Anastasia?

"How exciting," said the woman with the antelope on

To the Dress Shop

her head. "I am acquainted with some of the oldest families in Suffolk—where is the ball being held?"

Estelle paused. Patted her hair. I had to repress the urge to cry out, "Answer the question, you beastly cow!"

After what felt like an eternity, she gave her reply. And it stopped me cold. "Butterfield Park," she said merrily. "The ball is at Butterfield Park."

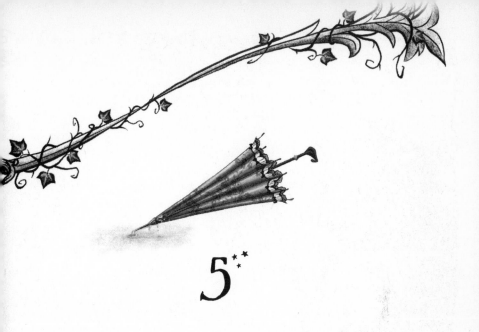

5

She was in no hurry to leave. Estelle lingered at the counter, talking to the shopgirl about hats and gloves and coats as if they were the most important things in the world. I was desperate to get away—to share with Mrs. Dickens what I had just learned. Estelle Dumbleby was bound for Butterfield Park! That could not be a coincidence, could it?

"I'm sure you'll be the belle of the ball," said the shopgirl when Estelle picked up the large box tied with red ribbon. "Those other young ladies will be green with envy."

"What a lovely thing to say," said Estelle with a giggle.

"Though I'm sure there will be many pretty girls at Butterfield Park."

The shopgirl declared Estelle would be the prettiest of the lot. When the devious Miss Dumbleby *finally* left the shop, I prepared to make my exit. In fact, I was poised rather like a tiger, waiting for her to step into the carriage so I could steal away. But that is not what happened.

"Can I help you?" It was the shopgirl. Who was now standing directly behind me.

I pulled the oversized bonnet around my face. "If you could go away, that would be a tremendous help."

"Why are you staring out the window? What are you up to?"

"Just waiting for my aunt Patricia to come. She is helping me pick out a dress for my coronation."

"I do not think you are in the right shop," said the girl haughtily. "There is a seamstress at the end of the street who caters to the *working* class."

At that, I was forced to turn around. "I'm not here for a dress, dear—I came to pick out a new horse for the big parade. You do sell horses, don't you?"

She looked appalled. "*Horses?* This is the finest dress boutique in London."

"My apologies," I said brightly. "I just assumed this was a stable, what with all the manure you shovel at your customer's feet."

"You *horror!*" she spat.

Fortunately, at that exact moment, the lady with the antelope on her head called the girl over to enquire about a pair of gloves. "Leave at once," the girl hissed at me, before departing, "or I will call for the constable."

When she was gone, I turned back to the window, fully expecting to see Estelle's grand carriage rolling away. Instead, it was still parked outside the dress shop. Estelle stood with the carriage door open, deep in conversation with a woman. The unidentified stranger had her back to me and wore a rather sad-looking tan dress. Her hair was matted in the style of a vagabond. And she had a shabby bag in her hand.

Estelle's face had lost much of its sweetness. She seemed to be giving the woman a thorough talking-to—pointing at the stranger in a most unpleasant manner. Perhaps the vagrant was a beggar asking for money? Whatever the case, when Estelle turned to enter the carriage, the woman grabbed her arm. Then dropped to her knees. The poor creature appeared to be pleading.

Estelle responded by hitting the woman over the head with her parasol. The woman slumped to the pavement, using her arms to shield her head. And all the while, the well-dressed people

of Mayfair strolled by with barely a sideways glance. I couldn't bear it a moment longer. Even at the risk of exposing myself, I had to stop that monstrous cow from inflicting such a brutal beating!

I charged across the shop and threw open the door. As I ran out onto the pavement, the bright sun hit my face with such heat it made me woozy. I blinked several times, and when my eyes cleared Estelle's carriage was roaring away. Her victim lay in a ball upon the ground, hiding her face in shame and sobbing like a lost child. I crouched down beside her and gently touched her hand—there were red welts upon it. "Are you all right, dear?"

She was all a-tremble. "Miss Estelle was the only one who could help." Then another violent sob exploded from behind her hands. "I'm ruined. Ruined!"

"Codswallop! As long as you are breathing, there is hope. Now quit your sniveling and tell me what business have you with Estelle Dumbleby."

My kind words seemed to work their magic. She lowered her hands, and I got my first glimpse of her face. Which is why I let out a small gasp.

"Bertha?"

We sat down on a bench outside a chocolate shop.

"Oh, miss, how could she be so cruel?" Bertha heaved another sob and blew her nose with great commitment. "I'm no beggar—I only wanted a reference."

From my limited experience with Bertha, it was clear she was prone to dramatic outbursts. But on this occasion, she had good reason. Her story was indeed a sorry one.

"My ma was awful sick," she said.

"Yes, I remember you mentioning that the night I escaped from Lashwood. Has your mother's health not improved?"

Bertha shook her head. "Ma died."

"I'm very sorry, dear."

"I had to take a day off work to tend to her funeral," said Bertha solemnly. "When I returned, Lampton, the head butler, told me my services were no longer required."

"He fired you?"

"Miss Estelle fired me."

I wiped beads of sweat from my fevered brow. "But why?"

Bertha did not answer right away. She looked sideways at

me. Seemed to be struggling with what to say. Finally she said, "She guessed I'd been talking to you—about when my ma worked for the Dumblebys and about Anastasia and that woman with red hair."

Bertha *was* a monstrous blabbermouth, but as a result of telling me about Miss Frost's visit to the Dumblebys in search of Anastasia, she was now out of a job. Though barely twenty, the poor creature had the sort of wilting features that made her look eternally disappointed—and now fate had given her a life to match.

"The funeral ate up all the savings I had," she went on. "I'm behind on my rent, and the landlady says she'll have her brother round today to turn me out." She looked at the bag sitting on her lap. "This morning I packed up what I had and left."

"And that is why you were begging Estelle for help?"

"I'm no beggar, Miss," said Bertha firmly, wiping her eyes. "I was asking for a reference so I could gain another position somewhere else." Bertha shook her head slowly. "But Miss Estelle said I deserved to be homeless. She said she would make sure I wasn't given a position at any decent house in London."

"The devil!"

"I think you're right about that." Then Bertha looked at me with the eyes of a frightened child. "What am I to do?"

"Fear not, dear. I will help you."

Exactly *how* I would help wasn't clear. After all, I was penniless and soon to be homeless myself. I might have given the problem some serious thought, were it not for the man I spotted on the crowded footpath just twenty feet away.

He stood out from the subdued frock coats and somber day dresses of the pedestrians around him. In fact, he looked rather dashing in his white suit and top hat. Either the pie stains had been expertly removed, or he had more than one white suit. Whatever the case, he had me in his sights, a boyish grin upon his lips.

"I am in a spot of danger," I said quickly, jumping to my feet. "Nothing too serious, just a violent hag's well-dressed henchman. Are you with me, dear?"

Bertha nodded without a moment's hesitation. "Course I am."

Then she leaped up, and we bolted into the crowd.

Running for your life can be a tricky business. Especially when you're ill. My head had begun to churn again. The bright sun hurt my eyes. The footpath was teeming with pedestrians as Bertha and I zipped through the crowd. A crowd that seemed to swell and multiply the deeper we journeyed into it—a great ocean of frock coats and boots, wool skirts and raised parasols.

I stole a backwards glance and saw the man in white coming up behind us.

"It's awful crowded." Bertha was panting beside me, struggling with her bag. "Shouldn't we cross the road where there's less people about?"

"No, dear," I called back, pulling the sluggish girl along. "We are safer in a crowd."

"Who is he, miss?"

"No idea!" I shouted. "But he works for a dangerous woman who has wicked plans for me."

A spark lit up in Bertha's dull eyes. "He won't get you if I have anything to say about it!"

We ran past a theater—the entertainment must have just ended, for a crowd erupted from the doors, swarming the pavement. People stepped in front of our path, or crisscrossed, or stopped suddenly to chat. It involved a tremendous amount of sidestepping and spinning to keep moving forward.

I felt the perspiration dripping from my face and neck. The heat pressing in on me like an oven. Glancing back, I looked for the man in white. He was nowhere to be seen. I checked again. No sign of him. Bertha, despite huffing and puffing like an exhausted donkey, was keeping up admirably. In fact, she was slightly ahead of me. For my legs had begun to slow now, stiff and heavy as two blocks of stone.

"You're burning up, Miss," shouted Bertha. "Your face is awful damp!"

I leaped over an impossibly selfish gentleman tying his shoes, but landed heavily. The straw bonnet blew off my head as a shiver of pain rushed from my feet up to my skull. "Stuff and nonsense," I wheezed. "I think . . . we have lost him. Let us keep going just a little longer."

"Miss, watch out!"

Something flashed to my left. Then an arm seized mine, gripping me like an iron shackle. I was pulled to a sudden stop.

"You're a hard one to catch, Ivy Pocket," said the man in white.

Bertha gave a startled cry. I lashed out—though all the strength seemed to have left my body—pummeling my attacker about the chest and head with my free hand. I heard gasps coming from the crowd. Strangely, as I looked at him, the man in white appeared to be shooting up above me. Too late, I realized that the one moving was *me*. I was falling to the ground. In an instant, the dazzling shimmer of daylight vanished, as if the world had pulled the curtains shut.

The darkness swallowed me whole.

6

The first thing I saw were the bluebirds. A flock of them—feathers glistening, wings extended—flying across a pale sky scattered with heavenly clouds. The bluebirds weren't moving, though. In fact, they were utterly still. And stuck on the ceiling. Painted in glorious detail around a perfectly elegant lantern. Exactly *whose* lantern, I didn't know.

As such, I shot up. Which was a mistake, for my head seemed to spin off my neck and fly across the room. At least, that's what it felt like.

"Calm yourself, miss." Bertha got up from the chair, which

was positioned at my bedside. "You're safe, safe and sound—though your fever's been fierce."

I allowed her to ease me back down—only after checking that the Clock Diamond was still around my neck. It was, but ice cold. "Where am I?"

Bertha giggled. "It's grand, isn't it?" Which didn't answer the question at all. "I'll fetch you some water, miss. You sound awful parched."

As Bertha hurried out of the door, I glanced around the room. Still utterly baffled about where I was. Miss Always's finely dressed goon grabbing me was the last thing I recalled. Thank heavens there was no sign of *him*. The room was delightfully furnished—a mahogany desk, velvet-covered sofas, and a long mirror. On the table beside me were an oil lamp and a silver box full of cufflinks. A marble fireplace stood to my left. Above it, a portrait of a rather pretty girl playing by the seaside. The curtains were drawn, casting the far side of the room in gloomy shadows. Where on earth *was* I?

"You look rather confused, Ivy. Perhaps I can help."

The voice came from across the room. It was deep and

commanding—and it gave me chills. So I wasn't completely surprised when he stood up, slipping out of the shadows where he had been sitting the whole time. His white suit blindingly crisp. His top hat in his hand.

"How are you feeling?" he said next. "Can I fetch you something to eat?"

I responded by picking up the silver cufflink box and throwing it at his head. The scoundrel ducked just in time, and it smashed against the far wall.

"You can't keep me here!" I leaped out of bed and picked up the lantern, holding it like a weapon. "I will fight you to the death if I have to. And let me warn you, dear, I have a gift for vengeance—possessing all the natural instincts of a jilted bride."

"It's all right, miss," said Bertha, hurrying back into the room with a glass of water. "Mr. Partridge means you no harm."

"You know his name?" I gasped. "You two are working together?"

"No, miss, it's not like that," said Bertha.

The man in white chuckled. "You are just as Mr. Banks described."

I frowned. "Mr. Banks?"

"That's right. I have been seeking you out on his account."

"He has good news," said Bertha, "the *best* kind."

"You are wrong, dear," I said firmly. "I do not expect you to understand—you are a trusting sort with all the good sense of a sea slug. But believe me, this man is a wicked fellow who works for an equally wicked woman by the name of Miss Always."

"Perhaps you will allow me to explain, before you fight me to the death?" Mr. Partridge walked over to the desk and picked up a thin volume of papers. "This apartment belonged to Mr. Banks."

I looked around for some sort of proof. Mr. Partridge seemed to read my mind.

"The portrait above the fire is Mr. Banks's sister, Caroline. She died when Mr. Banks was just a young man. The cufflink box you threw at my head belonged to his father; he wore the gold ones every time he appeared in court. He believed they brought him luck."

I sat down on the bed. Rather dazed and confused. "Why am I here, Mr. Partridge?"

He walked over and placed the papers in my hands. "Mr.

Banks was my mentor and my friend," he said gently. "He spoke of you a great deal in the weeks before his death. I think . . . perhaps you reminded him of the sister he lost."

I recalled Mr. Banks saying much the same thing. So it seemed Mr. Partridge was telling the truth. But that only raised more questions. "How did you find me?" I said. "*Why* did you find me?"

"How did I find you? I had an excellent description of you from Mr. Banks, and I spent a small fortune hiring urchins to scour the city looking for you. I was aware that you were incarcerated in Lashwood, but after that the trail went cold . . . until a few days ago when you were spotted at Waterloo Station."

Which made sense.

"*Why* did I find you?" said Mr. Partridge, grinning mischievously. He had a pleasant face. Brown hair, slicked back. Large brown eyes. Narrow nose. Dimpled cheeks. "The papers you have in your hands are the last will and testament of Mr. Horatio Banks."

I looked down at the dreary-looking document. "What has that to do with me?"

"Everything, as it happens," said Mr. Partridge. "The day Mr.

Banks left for Suffolk, bound for Butterfield Park on some secret business, he handed me his new will. In it, he left his entire estate to one Miss Ivy Pocket."

Bertha clapped her hands. "It's a miracle, it is!"

It was stunning news. An utter shock. I wiped my brow and felt the beads of sweat on my skin. "I . . . I don't understand. He left me his estate?"

"Aren't you happy?" Then Bertha's smile faded. "Oh, miss, you look awful pale."

"I will send for the doctor," said Mr. Partridge. "I should have done it hours ago."

"No need," I said quickly. "I feel perfectly fine. Fit as a fiddle. Strong as an ox."

Being half dead and no longer able to bleed, I felt a visit from the doctor would be dreadfully unwise. Besides, I had more pressing concerns. "What *exactly* have I inherited?"

"Mr. Banks's estate isn't especially complicated," said Mr. Partridge. "There is this apartment, of course, which now belongs to you, some bank bonds, a few paintings . . . and the sum of five thousand pounds."

Five thousand pounds! I lunged at Mr. Partridge, squeezing him with the sort of violent force normally used to dislodge a peanut. "That *is* good news, you eccentrically dressed wonder! And dear Mr. Banks. If he weren't dead, I would kiss his enormous forehead a thousand times!"

"If he weren't dead," said the lawyer with a grin, "he would hardly be giving you his estate."

Bertha looked at me with tears in her eyes. "You're an heiress, you are."

"Naturally, there are arrangements to be made." Mr. Partridge put on his top hat. "As the executor of Mr. Banks's affairs, I must ensure that you are well cared for. You will need a guardian, and there is school to consider."

"Stuff and nonsense," I said. "School can wait—I have far more pressing concerns. Missions and plots by the dozen."

"Missions?" said Mr. Partridge doubtfully.

"I'd explain, dear, but it's terribly private. Hidden lunatics. Cursed necklaces. Other worlds. Lost friends."

"I see."

Then I asked Mr. Partridge if he would be able to track down a missing child. I gave him the particulars, without mentioning the otherworldly Anastasia Radcliff. He said it would be most difficult, but he would see what could be done.

"Now as to a guardian," said Mr. Partridge as he prepared to leave, "I have an aunt in town who might be willing to step into the role."

"What a hideous thought," I said tactfully. "No, Mr. Partridge, I have no need for a guardian."

"You cannot mean to live here alone?"

"Of course not." I smiled like a newly minted heiress. "I shall have all the company I need."

"It's a fine kitchen," said Mrs. Dickens.

We sat at a round table by the picture window, which offered a lovely view over Berkeley Square—me, Mrs. Dickens, and Bertha.

"And it's all yours?" said Mrs. Dickens in wonder.

I nodded. It didn't feel completely real. Mr. Banks had actually made me his heir. The apartment was enormous. Polished wood floors. Fine carpets. Elegant French furniture. Five bedrooms equipped with comfy brass beds. Paintings aplenty.

"I'm very happy for you, lass," said Mrs. Dickens warmly. "Seems to me you deserve a stroke of good fortune such as this." Then she sighed. "I don't expect you'll be returning to Thackeray Street again?"

"Certainly not," I replied. "Though I hope you can fetch Rebecca's clock for me."

"Thirty years I've lived in that house," said Mrs. Dickens softly, "and after tonight it'll be someone else's home."

"Where will you go?" asked Bertha (who was homeless herself).

"Well, I'm still deciding," said Mrs. Dickens as confidently as she could muster. "I have a friend in Dover who might put me up."

"You'll do no such thing," I said firmly. "Either of you. This house has five bedrooms, so there is ample space for the three of us—with room enough for Anastasia when I find her."

The ancient housekeeper and the glum maid were positively bug-eyed.

"Live *here*?" cried Bertha. "With you?"

"Why not?"

"You want me to run the kitchen?" said Mrs. Dickens.

"If you'd like," I said.

The silly woman's eyes began to mist. "You really mean it, lass?"

"Of course I do. Please don't blubber, dear, it makes your nose glow like a lantern."

"And I'm to be the maid?" asked Bertha, now sobbing madly. "With . . . with my very own room?"

"Yes, dear. Though let's not get bogged down with who does what. It seems to me we can all muck in together."

I was then hugged rather savagely. There was a great deal of chatter about brighter days and me being the most wonderful girl who ever lived. All very true. But it was Mrs. Dickens who noticed the worry playing upon my face. "You're thinking of those not with us, aren't you, lass?"

I nodded. "The Clock Diamond is quiet as the grave. Without it, how am I to reach Rebecca and bring her home?"

"I'm not sure I understand any of it," offered Bertha, "but if anyone can find a way, it's you, miss."

"Thank you, dear," I said. "But even I'm at a loss."

"As for poor Anastasia," said Mrs. Dickens, shaking her

head, "now that she's been moved from Lashwood, I don't think there's any hope of finding her."

On that front, I had some cause for hope. So I told them about what I had learned from my adventure in the dress shop. "There is to be a grand ball at Butterfield Park, though I know for a fact that Estelle has other reasons for going to Suffolk." I turned to Bertha. "Does she even know the Butterfields?"

"Not sure, miss. They never called at the house that I can recall."

"Something is afoot, I can feel it," I said. It was impossible to imagine that Estelle Dumbleby's connection to the Butterfields did not involve Anastasia—after all, both families had locked perfectly innocent people in Lashwood. Could it be a coincidence? I was practically positive that Estelle's trip to Butterfield Park had *something* to do with Anastasia.

"Half of London is going to that ball," said Mrs. Dickens, getting up and putting some water on the stove. "It's the one hundredth anniversary of the park, so they're making a great show of it. I heard a few maids talking at the market—the ball is in four days, and all the servants from the Butterfields' London house are going to Suffolk to serve. Three hundred guests are attending, that's what I heard."

The first hint of a smile broke across my face. "Three hundred and *one*."

Later that afternoon, Mrs. Dickens went back to Thackeray Street to collect her things (and Rebecca's clock), while Bertha insisted that I go to my delightfully elegant bedroom and lie down. Thanks to a small advance from Mr. Partridge, she was off to the market to buy food, then across town to select some new dresses for me to wear.

I told her I felt perfectly fine, but she didn't believe me for a moment. So there I was. Lying in my comfy new bed (which was Mr. Banks's old bed). While my body was weary and sore, my mind spun at great speed, thinking about the Clock Diamond. And Prospa. And in the elegant surrounds of this new life, a brilliant notion found its place. I had struck upon a way to reach Rebecca!

But that wasn't why I sat up in bed with a start. Rather, it was the enormous ball of blue gas that dropped from the chimney into the fireplace and rolled swiftly across the floor. When it hit the chest of drawers, the ball bounced awfully high into the air before landing at the foot of my bed. It hit the floorboards silently, and in an instant a rather chunky ghost, glowing violently, unfurled and hovered before me.

"Hide me, child," said the Duchess of Trinity with some urgency, her bloody nightdress rippling as if she was in a windstorm.

I might have insulted her. Or asked a dozen questions. But I could see the look of desperation on her luminous face, and I recalled that not too long ago this wicked ghoul had saved me from Miss Always and her army of locks. So I shrugged and pointed. "The water jug's over there."

"No, she will look for me there," said the ghost, starlight swirling about her hair like fireflies.

At that exact moment I couldn't help but notice flakes of smoldering ash raining down from the ceiling. The ghost had noticed it too. "Say you have not seen me." Then she lunged at me, vanishing inside my dress. My rather grubby frock began to swell quickly, expanding as if I were a helium balloon about to take flight. Sadly, I didn't. Nor did my dress split at the seams as you might expect—instead, it grew and stretched as the Duchess took up residence.

"What are you doing, you blubbery barnacle?" I shouted, jumping from the bed.

"Don't give up the ghost," I heard her whisper. "*Please*, child."

"Give you up to *who*?"

The answer was to be found in the falling ash. It did not scatter about the room. Rather, it collected in a single spot just a few feet in front of me. Piling up at great speed. Taking shape. Filling out. When it was done, a woman stood before me. She was largely transparent, her skin a mottled collection of molten flakes. Rather tall. A stiff, dark dress with a high neck. A glorious head of white hair.

She looked me up and down. "I'm sorry to intrude," she said grandly, "but I must ask . . . have you seen the Duchess of Trinity?"

"Who, dear?"

"The Duchess of Trinity," she said again. "I believe you are acquainted."

"Highly doubtful."

The imperious dead woman seemed rather preoccupied by the fact that I was stupendously fat. "Please forgive my directness, but you appear rather *bloated.*"

"Oh, yes. I ate a huge breakfast—half a pony and three barrels of vanilla custard." I gestured to my majestic surroundings. "As you can see, I'm monstrously rich and therefore off my rocker. What business have you with the Duchess?"

She didn't answer at first. Then she sighed. "Some ghosts choose the wrong path. They seek to visit vengeance and bloodshed on the living, and when that happens they are no longer allowed the privilege of an earthbound existence."

"She is in the gray lands," I said, well versed in the Duchess's dilemma.

"She *was.*" Her dark eyes shimmered sadly. "Now she must move on, for it is time she came home. If she stays here . . . if she stays, it will be a great tragedy."

"Why? What would happen?"

The ghost began to come apart before my eyes, the embers breaking off piece by piece and floating up toward the ceiling.

When there was barely a trace of her left, I said, "Did you know the Duchess?"

The regal old woman, nearly gone, allowed a sad smile. "She is my sister."

Which was unexpected! Once the last ember had floated up and vanished, I ordered the Duchess to vacate my dress immediately. She burst out with a rather loud pop, looking terribly pleased with herself. "You did well, child," she purred.

"Don't ever hide inside my clothes again, you ghoulish blubber guts." I patted down my nightdress, which had returned to its previous size. "It's plain bad manners!"

"As you wish."

"Why were you hiding from your own sister, anyway? Though I am stunned that you have one—I just assumed, being a bloodthirsty tyrant, you were an only child."

"She is *one* of my sisters. There are seven in total." She growled like a lion. "All dead."

"Do you not wish to see them again?"

"Don't be absurd. Besides, I have one last great mission to attend to."

"What sort of mission?"

"Well . . ." She paused. Licked her lips, her black tongue slipping out like a serpent. Then said, "I am haunting an old friend who is selling the painting I left to her. It was a sentimental gesture that she had little regard for. I visit her every night, making a great racket." She smiled menacingly. "It warms my dead heart to watch her tremble."

"You'll give her a heart attack."

"Undeniably."

"Must you try and murder *everyone* who displeases you?"

The ghost shrugged. "It passes the time."

Before the Duchess departed, I pressed her for any information on Rebecca. She claimed to have none. "I concern myself with *this* world and no other."

"Very well—what of Jago? Miss Always took him. Do you know how he is? Do you know *where* he is?"

The ghost closed her eyes, great wafts of blue gas lifting from her enormous body. "The boy lives," she said at last. "And before you ask, *no*, I do not know where."

Which wasn't very helpful at all.

"It would seem," said the Duchess of Trinity, floating close to my face, "that without the Clock Diamond, your friend Rebecca is beyond your reach."

"You're hideously wrong, dear," I said. "While traveling to Prospa with the help of the Clock Diamond was my preferred plan, just before you came rolling out of the fireplace, I struck up with an outstanding plan B."

Her dark eyes crackled. "Which is?"

"None of your business, you bombastic fatso. By the way, do you know when the next quarter moon is?"

"In four days, I believe. Why do you ask?"

"No reason at all."

The ghost growled. "Insufferable child."

The first dinner in my new house was a very grand affair. "My new house"—what a thrilling set of words! Bertha laid the table beautifully; Mr. Banks's fine china plates and silverware sparkled under candlelight. Paintings of the English countryside looked down from every side.

Mrs. Dickens had cooked up a storm. The roast chicken

was burned to a crisp. The potatoes baked until they had all the delicious fluffiness of a crab shell. The beans appeared to have been tortured. The gravy was a horror show of lumps. But for the first time in an age, I felt rather content. My throat still hurt. My bones were stiff. But I had a few winning plans—one for Rebecca and one for Anastasia. There was hope!

Eating a hideously burnt chicken

When Mrs. Dickens had finished overseeing the serving of dinner, she ordered Bertha to the kitchen so that they could clean up before eating their supper. The two women were hastening out of the dining room when I ordered them to stop.

"Why shouldn't we all eat together?" I said.

Mrs. Dickens gasped. "Whatever do you mean, lass?"

"Just what I said." I picked up my napkin and arranged it on my lap. (I was wearing a lovely pale green dress that Bertha had selected for me in town.) "Mrs. Dickens, it's true that your only real talents are afternoon naps and hiding whiskey bottles—but you cooked this hideously burned chicken, and it seems to me you have as much right as anyone to sit down and enjoy it."

The housekeeper was startled. But when she saw that I was as serious as a funeral, she hurried over and took a seat beside me. "It's most improper," she muttered, already shoveling a potato into her mouth. "But bless you, lass."

Bertha suddenly curtsied (strange girl!). Then began to back out of the dining room. "I best get to cleaning the pots."

"You'll do no such thing," I declared.

"I won't?"

"Bertha, you weep like a burst boil at least eight times a day, but you're a good egg—and if two maids can sit at such a fine table, why shouldn't three?"

She blushed. Giggled. And took her seat. The talk soon turned to my fantastical plans—well, *one* of them anyway. When I announced that not only was I going to attend the anniversary ball at Butterfield Park in four days' time, but that while there, I was determined to uncover the whereabouts of Anastasia Radcliff, both Bertha and Mrs. Dickens were stunned stupid.

"You can't do it, lass!" said Mrs. Dickens. "That awful Lady Elizabeth will have you locked up again."

"It's true, miss," cried Bertha. "The minute she claps eyes on you, you're done for."

"That's why I won't be going," I told them.

"I don't understand," said Mrs. Dickens, putting down her knife and fork. "If you're not going to be there, how can you attend the ball?"

My grin was triumphant. "As Esmeralda Cabbage, that's how."

7

The gentleman with the furrowed brow and bright blue vest looked me up and down. "An actress, are you?"

"Oh, yes," I answered. "Painfully gifted. Stupendously talented. You might have seen me in such productions as *The Girl Who Slapped Her Majesty*, which ran for nearly a year, or *Lady Vivian's Rabbit*, a play so heartbreaking the theater flooded most evenings."

I stood in a vast and rather shabby second-story workshop. The home of BUZZBY'S STAGE EMPORIUM—FOR ALL YOUR THEATRICAL NEEDS. I had once followed Miss Always to this very place—her wickedly brilliant transformation into Miss Carnage was the work of Alfred Buzzby. Which is why I had come to see him.

Naturally, I couldn't tell him the *real* reason I needed a convincing disguise. So I posed as an actress about to take the lead role in a brilliant new production.

BUZZBY'S STAGE EMPORIUM - FOR ALL YOUR THEATRICAL NEEDS

"The lead role, you say?" Mr. Buzzby was wiping down a mirror, mounted on the wall behind a long table filled with powders and glues and molds of every shape and size. "I've got two musicals, three plays, and a pantomime on my plate. Why would I take on *another* job, missy?"

At which point I produced a roll of pound notes from my pocket (now being fabulously wealthy and whatnot). "Because you will be ten pounds richer if you can turn me into a convincing aristocrat."

Mr. Buzzby moaned. "I suppose you want me to make you look pretty?"

"Don't be stupid," I declared. "I'm playing an *aristocrat*. Make me look like the daughter of a pair of chinless first cousins. A nose so stubby it points toward the sky. Blotchy skin smothered in freckles. And a set of buckteeth that could chew through a fence post."

I saw the possibilities dancing in his hazel eyes. So I went in for the kill. "Perhaps you haven't the skills to transform me?"

"Haven't the *skills*?" he shouted, spit flying.

"Not to worry, dear," I replied, stepping away. "We can't all be brilliant."

He lunged, practically pushed me into the makeup chair, and turned my face toward the large mirror. "Watch and learn, missy."

"Heavens!" cried Mrs. Dickens.

"I didn't even recognize you!" offered Bertha.

"Of course you didn't, dear," I said, pulling off my nose.

Mr. Buzzby had done a wonderful job. With a blond wig, freckles by the dozen, a stub nose, and a wondrous set of teeth, Esmeralda Cabbage had come to life. The entire process had taken most of the day, but I had studied Mr. Buzzby's methods carefully so that I could complete the transformation myself when the time came.

"The ball is in three days," I said, popping out the false teeth and placing them on the kitchen table. "If all goes according to plan, Bertha and I shall leave tomorrow."

Bertha looked startled. "I'm coming with you?"

"A fine young aristocrat like Esmeralda Cabbage can hardly travel without a maid, now can she?" Using a damp cloth I began to remove the layer of freckles from my face. "Besides, while I hunt for clues among the gentry, you can snoop belowstairs."

"Like a regular detective," said Bertha dreamily.

"But what do you expect to find at Butterfield Park?" said Mrs. Dickens, who was energetically deboning a duck for supper.

"Anastasia," was my simple reply. "While I can't say for certain that she is being kept in that house, we know that she is no longer at Lashwood. And we know that Estelle has *business* in Suffolk. There must be a connection, don't you see?"

The housekeeper didn't look at all happy. "If they discover who's lurking about under all that makeup, they'll have you locked up."

"How could they possibly find out?" I pulled off my wig. "You saw my disguise, it's brilliant. And my acting skills are the stuff of legend—they'll never know it's me."

"I think you're right," said Bertha, nodding eagerly.

"How does a girl who doesn't exist get invited to Butterfield Park?" challenged Mrs. Dickens, her purple nose twitching up a storm. "As you say, the ball is in just three days—all the invitations will have already been sent."

I informed my housemates that I had taken a small detour

on my way to Mr. Buzzby's theatrical emporium—dropping into the law office of Mr. Partridge. Where I convinced him to wire a message to Butterfield Park on behalf of Lady Morag Cabbage.

"Who's that?" said Bertha.

"My mother," I replied. "Well, *Esmeralda's* mother."

"Lord save us," muttered Mrs. Dickens.

"Mr. Partridge's cable," I continued, "said that Lady Morag's young daughter Esmeralda, who has lived in India these past seven years, was back in England for the season and was very keen to make the acquaintance of the *right* sort of people."

"That's awful clever," said Bertha. "And they said yes?"

"Not yet," I replied. "Mr. Partridge promised to send Lady Elizabeth's reply as soon as it came to hand." I sat down at the kitchen table and smiled knowingly. "But I am *awfully* confident."

I didn't feel the need to add that I *may* have browbeaten Mr. Partridge into adding that Esmeralda was the second cousin of the King of Spain. And that she would be very keen to invite Matilda to meet the King and his family when they visited London in the coming spring. While I was carefully packing away my new face, there was a knock at the door. Bertha hurried from the kitchen to answer it.

"Lady Elizabeth sounds like a shrewd and dangerous woman," said Mrs. Dickens somberly, slicing into the dead duck's breast. "I don't imagine she'll throw out invitations to her fancy ball as easy as that."

Perhaps she was right. In my excitement, I hadn't really considered the possibility that an invitation to Butterfield Park wouldn't be forthcoming. So when Bertha entered the kitchen with a note from Mr. Partridge, I was suddenly rather nervous. I opened the letter and read it through carefully—three times.

"Well, what does it say?" said Bertha.

"The answer's no, isn't it, lass?" said Mrs. Dickens.

I slapped the note down on the table. "We're in!"

Mrs. Dickens packed sandwiches for the train. She was full of doubts, as you might expect. Bringing up every little thing that might expose my real identity.

"Bertha worked for Estelle's family for years," she bellowed as we hopped into the carriage bound for the station. "She will take one look at the girl and smell a rat."

"Nonsense, you silly woman," I said, closing the carriage door and sticking my head out the window. "Esmeralda Cabbage is new to England, so it makes sense she would seek out a local maid. And Estelle knows full well that Bertha is unemployed and destitute—so it makes perfect sense that I would hire her."

"With so many guests around, she might not even notice me," said Bertha hopefully.

Lady Elizabeth had fallen right into my trap. Not only had she issued an invitation for Esmeralda to attend the ball, she had invited the girl to stay at the house as her special guest.

The journey to Suffolk was smooth and without incident. We were in first class, and my disguise was working a treat. I was in a perfectly lovely pale blue dress with lace trim, a white ribbon fixed around my golden locks—and the worst of the aching had faded from my bones. We were nearly in Suffolk (just a few stops from Butterfield Park's nearest station) when Bertha hit upon a bright idea. "Why don't you show off that necklace of yours?" she said eagerly. "They'd believe you were a regular toff if they saw a diamond that huge."

I explained to Bertha that if any of the Butterfields got a glimpse of the Clock Diamond, the jig would be up. "I must be inconspicuous, dear. My aim is to become a close friend and confidant of Estelle Dumbleby. That is the key to finding Anastasia."

It was raining lightly when we stepped off the train. Wishing to make something of an entrance, I hired a carriage and four horses to spirit us to Butterfield Park. As the carriage curled up the long drive, past the schoolhouse and the gardens, I must admit to a few nervous butterflies.

The horses pulled up under the portico, and a footman was there to open the carriage door. "Here we go, dear," I whispered to Bertha, checking that my nose was still stuck in place.

We exchanged a secret look and a nervous grin. Then Esmeralda Cabbage and her maid stepped out of the carriage.

Pemberton, the head butler, greeted me formally as our bags were unloaded from the carriage. He stepped aside as I glided into the great hall. Memories of my last visit rushed at me.

The opulent chandelier that I had swung from. The grand iron staircase that Rebecca had pushed me down (for perfectly good reasons!). And just down the hall was the imposing two-story library where my lost friend had put on the Clock Diamond and withered before our eyes.

"Welcome to my home, Miss Cabbage."

Her voice was like a snake slithering into my ear—slippery and dangerous. I turned with a smile fixed upon my rubbery face. "You are Lady Elizabeth, I presume?" I said rather grandly.

The old bat walked toward me, cane in her hand, her head as craggy and crinkled as a walnut. "Who else would be welcoming you to this house?"

Behind her, Lady Amelia came rushing down the stairs, fixing a brooch to her splendid bosom and apologizing for being late. The old woman shot her daughter-in-law a withering glance.

"I'm very pleased to meet you both," I said.

"It's been years since I was in India," said Lady Elizabeth. "Where *exactly* is your family's tea plantation?"

That was one detail I hadn't given a great deal of thought

to. But I knew it was *vitally* important that I dazzle her with my local knowledge. "Bombay," I declared with confidence. "You've probably never heard of it. Terribly small. Hard to find on a map. My great-uncle, Beelzebub Cabbage, discovered the place under a fallen banana leaf."

"What the blazes did she say?" barked Lady Elizabeth, squinting furiously.

"I was off my chops with excitement when I received an invitation to your ball, Lady Elizabeth," I said quickly. "By the way, shall I call you Lizzy?"

"Certainly *not*."

"Quite right too." I gazed up at the chandelier. "I was just telling my maid, Bertha, what a lovely little house this is. Having lived these past seven years in the grand splendor of our Indian palace, it's such a comfort to be staying somewhere so snug and cozy."

"Oh, my . . . ," muttered Lady Amelia.

"You have a lot to say for yourself, Miss *Cabbage*," said Lady Elizabeth sharply. "Though how much sense you make is another matter."

I was acting up a storm. Convincing these blockheaded aristocrats with every word and gesture. "It's rather daunting to be so far from my family, but I already feel as if you're my very own granny." I beamed at Lady Elizabeth. "While we've never met, your strength of character and hardy spirit are legendary."

Lady Elizabeth grunted. "Are they indeed?"

"Oh, yes!" I continued. "Which is all the more remarkable, given that you resemble a leather glove left out in the rain."

Lady Amelia clutched her bosom and began to pant.

"A feather dove left *where*?" said Lady Elizabeth, cupping her ear.

"It's not important," said Lady Amelia hastily.

"The journey has tired my lady," said Bertha, trying to yank me away. "She will be more herself after a bath and a lie-down."

What was the silly girl *talking* about? Did she not see how well I was doing? I leaned close to Lady Elizabeth and yelled into her good ear. "I was just saying that you are magnificently young at heart for a shriveled-up bag of bones!"

The old woman's beady eyes tightened, causing wrinkly fault lines to buckle all around her face. She lifted her cane and then brought it down swiftly, hitting the stone floor like a gunshot. "Outrageous!"

"Nonsense, Lizzy," I said, pinching her sagging cheek. "You are a medical marvel, and I won't hear a word of protest." I smiled in a humble fashion. "I'm not one to blow my own trumpet—did I mention I'm magnificent on the trumpet?—but I am known throughout India for my lavish compliments." I slapped a passing butler in a noble fashion. "Show me to my quarters, good fellow, and have the kitchen send up whatever dead bird they have handy. I'm positively famished."

Lady Elizabeth glared at me in admiration while Lady Amelia stood utterly speechless, looking at me with a mixture of awe and profound confusion. I bid them good day, called to Bertha, and followed the butler up the grand staircase.

8

That night I dreamed of the garden of weeds and wildflowers again. Only this time I was inside the tiny thatched cottage. Sitting on a stool by the kitchen table. Looking out at the yard, my skipping rope curled around the trunk of a tree. Winter had come, I knew that much. There was a woman with me. Working some lumpy dough with her hands.

From my position by the window, I couldn't see her face. Not properly. Just her profile—brown hair flecked with gray. Pink cheek. Her neck pale and spotty. She sniffed, wiping her nose with a floury hand. And I noticed she was crying.

"They won't answer my letters." She coughed violently. "We'll . . . we must look for somewhere else to live. The money's gone, and the landlord has a heart of stone. I told him so too."

The sun washed through the frosted windows, blinding my eyes.

"They won't answer my letters," she said again. "Come, Ivy, my fingers ache—help your mama knead the dough."

Knock knock. A distant squeak. Then footsteps.

The kitchen vanished like a snuffed candle.

"Time to wake up, miss." It was Bertha.

I was frowning before my eyes even opened. "Why did you wake me?" I groaned. "I was having a frightfully important dream."

"What about, miss?"

My mother. My very own mother. But I didn't say that to Bertha. "What time is it?"

"Time you were heading down to breakfast." Bertha threw off the bedcovers in a brutal fashion and ordered me to stand. "The house is busy as a train station this morning. All the important guests have arrived. I've never seen so many duchesses in one place before!"

I stood up, yawning—feeling stronger than I had since hiding in that beastly well. Looked about the bedroom. It was a charming suite in the west wing, with a carved four-poster bed and a lovely view of the woodlands. How different it was from the attic Lady Elizabeth had stuck me in the last time I had stayed at Butterfield Park.

I removed my nightdress and put on the yellow muslin frock Bertha had laid out, my mind busy with thoughts of my mother. I had no real memories of her—recalling nothing of life before Miss Frost took me to the Harrington Home for Unwanted Children. But now, thanks to the dreams, I had seen her—well, a glimpse or two anyway. While she wasn't *exactly* as I had imagined, it was my mother, and that was all that mattered.

"I've already started digging about," said Bertha, turning me around and tying the pale yellow ribbon around my waist. "Miss Estelle was expected early this morning, but her train's running late and she mightn't arrive until after breakfast."

"Then I'd best get started," I declared. "First, I will chat with Lady Elizabeth and see what I can unearth, then I will set my sights on Matilda."

I turned and headed for the door.

"Stop, miss!" whispered Bertha rather fearfully.

"What's the matter, dear?" I said, turning around.

"Your face," she said in an accusing fashion. "You haven't put it on!"

Which was utterly true. I had removed my disguise before retiring to bed the night before—sleeping as Esmeralda could damage my artificial nose and leave an awful mess on the pillow. So I'd packed it away under the bed and locked the door so no one would come in uninvited and discover my secret. (Bertha slept in a small anteroom off the closet.)

"Well spotted, dear," I said, diving under the bed and pulling out my box of materials. "You're a great deal smarter than you look, and that's a fact."

"Oh . . . thank you, miss."

When I had transformed into the blue-blooded Esmeralda Cabbage, my stub nose glued on, my wig firmly in place, Bertha and I set off for the breakfast room. As we came down the stairs, she filled me in on some of the fancy guests. Only one name caught my attention. "Who did you say?"

"Countess Carbunkle," said Bertha bitterly. "I was

just fetching a fresh jug of water so you could wash before breakfast when I accidentally ran into her on the landing. She told me I was a blundering fool and stormed off—awful rude, she was!"

"Her bark is worse than her bite," I said as we crossed the great hall.

"You know Countess Carbunkle?"

I nodded. "I was her maid in Paris."

Bertha and I separated outside the breakfast room. She went to the kitchen to snoop and eavesdrop, while I headed for the breakfast room. A duke and a baronet passed me, bidding me good morning. I was nearly at the door when I came to a halt—suddenly struck by memories of walking these same halls with Rebecca. It felt wrong. Being in her home without her. But the shroud of gloom soon lifted. While the Clock Diamond hung lifeless beneath my yellow dress, I still had an excellent plan B. And my mission to find Anastasia Radcliff had had its beginnings in the very breakfast room I was poised to enter. With that in mind, I took a deep breath, and stepped into the fray.

Breakfast was a grand affair. Platters of food, fresh flowers, and butlers by the dozen. While my appetite hadn't returned, I managed a boiled egg and some crispy bacon. I would have preferred a slice of raw pumpkin—but Ivy Pocket's peculiar eating habits were well known to the folk of Butterfield Park, so I thought it best not to eat like a dead girl.

"Are you not hungry, darling?" It was Lady Amelia, her voice ringing with maternal devotion. "What about a lovely cup of tea?"

"If I want a cup of tea, I will kick a maid and demand one." Matilda Butterfield's arms were crossed, her dark fringe falling over her eyes. "There are sixty guests staying in this house and not one brought me a gift. Not one!"

"But it's not your birthday, my sweet," implored Lady Amelia.

"Well, it should be," snapped Amelia. "My birthday ball was ruined, and now that Grandmother has *finally* agreed to hold another, she makes it about Butterfield Park's birthday, not mine! And why did Grandmother insist that my ball be held in the dreary hall, while *this* party is to be thrown in the grand ballroom? It's not fair!"

"Lower your voice, darling," said Lady Amelia meekly. "People are staring."

"Well, let them!" the hideous brat bellowed. "Sixty guests and not a single gift!"

With a look of thunder upon her face, Matilda stomped out of the room, straight past where I was sitting. She was a beastly girl, but I couldn't forget that without her assistance, I might not have been able to escape Lashwood.

"Lady Amelia," barked Lady Elizabeth from across the room, "stop loafing about like you're waiting for a carriage and get over here—my bacon won't cut itself!"

Lady Amelia let out a faint groan. "Of course, Lady Elizabeth."

"The fruit is delicious," a woman exclaimed.

I looked over and wasn't completely surprised to see Countess Carbunkle taking a seat beside me. She was eating a strawberry, a trickle of juice bleeding down her largely nonexistent chin. It took all my self-control not to tilt her head back and wipe it off.

The grand creature was quite a sight. Hair piled up on her head like a crown. Wrinkles aplenty. A large and drooping bottom lip. She leaned close to me. "I recently returned from a long journey abroad and let me tell you, there is no finer hostess in all the world than Lady Elizabeth."

It was a remarkable coincidence that Countess Carbunkle knew the Butterfields. But then, I supposed that most aristocrats knew one another. "You were in Paris, were you not?" I said, scratching at my wig (it was painfully itchy). "Then you set sail for South America, if I recall."

Countess Carbunkle threw me a sharp look. "And how would you know that, Miss . . . ?"

"Cabbage," I said quickly. "Esmeralda Cabbage. As for how I knew, I must have heard it somewhere. What with you being monstrously important and whatnot."

The Countess seemed to find my face stupendously interesting. "What a charming girl you are, Miss Cabbage," she said, her watery eyes twinkling. "I think we are going to be *great* friends."

The glorious blockhead was utterly fooled by my disguise!

"I have read about you in the newspapers many times," I said, slapping her on the back as dignified ladies do. "And they are quite wrong—you don't look *anything* like a bloated walrus." I shrugged. "Well, apart from the fish breath and unruly whiskers."

Countess Carbunkle's puffy face turned bright red. She bared her teeth and hissed at me. Which I assume is the European way of acknowledging a glorious compliment. Then a smile slithered across her face, and she patted my hand. "What *refined* manners you have, Esmeralda." Then she sighed. "As for the newspapers, you must have been reading that awful gossip column written by the equally awful Miss Anonymous. She took great delight in reporting the *incident* in Paris."

Oh, yes. The *incident*. During a rather grand dinner for the French President, Countess Carbunkle's tender-hearted maid (me) had tried to relieve her brain fever by pushing her head into a bowl of fruit punch. But instead of being overcome with gratitude and adopting me on the spot, the Countess had run screaming from the room, abandoned me in Paris without a penny, and sailed on the next boat to South America.

"I hadn't the courage to return to England after that," she said sorrowfully. "What happened in Paris haunts me still."

"And why shouldn't it?" I said, patting her hand. "You are filled with shame about abandoning that wondrous junior lady's maid who saved your life."

"I have a great deal to say about Ivy Pocket," whispered Countess Carbunkle. Her eyes narrowed, latching on to mine.

"In fact, I have dreamed of the day when we might meet again and I could tell her *exactly* what I think of her."

Strangely, the pompous woman didn't look especially pleased. "Did you not adore and worship this magical maid you call Ivy Pocket?" I said with tremendous subtlety.

"*Adore* her?" shrieked Countess Carbunkle. Then she looked across the table, right at Lady Elizabeth. Something passed between the two of them, for her cold expression suddenly dissolved and was replaced with a painful smile. "Of course, I adored her! Never will I have a maid as enchanting as darling Ivy."

Now that made sense!

"Will you excuse me?" The Countess got up and joined Lady Elizabeth by the terrace doors. I might have wandered over to join them, but I saw Bertha loitering in the hall outside. She waved at me rather excitedly. So I sprang up, my chair toppling over, and slipped discreetly out of the breakfast room.

"She's here."

"Who is?"

"Miss Estelle—I saw her maid in the kitchen." Bertha gulped. "She's really here, miss."

"Don't look so anxious, dear. Estelle is the key to finding Anastasia Radcliff."

"But what if . . . what if she knows what we're up to?"

"Why would she? I have just come from the breakfast room where Countess Carbunkle was practically eating out of my hands—I was once her favorite maid, yet she did not recognize me for a moment. Now, do you have anything to report from the kitchen?"

"Not a lot, miss," said Bertha, looking about nervously. "The house has an awful mouse problem—all the maids are scared silly of the little rodents, but apparently Lady Elizabeth is too stingy to get the problem tended to."

"Well, that's of no interest. Was there no other scuttlebutt about strange comings and goings? Or singing lunatics? Or secret hideouts?"

"Sorry, miss," was Bertha's feeble reply.

"Lady Elizabeth has invited Estelle to a ball celebrating the one hundredth anniversary of Butterfield Park," I said, tapping my freckled chin. "Why would Estelle care how long this dusty old house has been standing? There must be *another* reason she is here."

"The servants are scared stiff of Lady Elizabeth," muttered Bertha. "Her chambermaid looks terrified, she does. The poor girl's exhausted too, what with being up half the night bringing extra supper to Lady Elizabeth's bedroom. Eats like a horse, that's what I heard."

"Does she?" During my previous visit to Butterfield Park, the old bat had hardly touched her food. "How interesting."

Bertha looked deeply confused. "Is it, miss?"

"Excuse me, have we met?"

I turned and came face to face with Estelle Dumbleby. She practically glowed in a white dress, her fair hair fixed elegantly around her heart-shaped face.

"I don't think so," I said. "Perhaps you have been to India?"

"I have not," she said. "But I confess, your voice is rather familiar."

I smiled sweetly. "What an awful thing to say."

Estelle released a glorious laugh. "Very true. I do apologize."

We introduced ourselves. I couldn't help but notice Estelle

throwing scornful glances at Bertha, who was cowering behind me like a lamb before the huntsman's axe.

"I believe I am acquainted with your maid." Estelle spoke as if Bertha wasn't in the room. "If I may ask, wherever did you find her?"

"The poorhouse," was my quick response. "The dear girl won't name names, being monstrously discreet and whatnot, but she worked for a mad cow in London who fired her on the very day her mother died."

Estelle glowered. But just for a moment. "I'm sure she had her reasons."

"Wickedness would be my guess," I said. But I instantly regretted it when I saw the ferocious spark in Estelle's eyes.

"Please excuse me," said Estelle coldly, "I was just on my way for a walk in the woodlands."

I did not want her to get away before I could slyly press her about Anastasia.

"What a terrible idea," I said diplomatically. "These woodlands are teaming with feral pigs. I have it on good authority that they ate the vicar and his wife just last week."

Estelle kept stealing glances out of the window. I turned and looked—Lady Elizabeth had walked out onto the terrace and was shooing a maid away. It was a rather cold morning, so that struck me as strange.

"I will take my chances," said Estelle. "Besides, I should pay my respects to Lady Elizabeth. She is a great woman, is she not?"

"Oh, yes. Terrifically great. Stupendously grand. Outrageously bonkers."

She giggled musically. "What a funny thing to say, Esmeralda."

The rotten girl was falling for my charms. But I knew better than to fall for hers.

"Have you known the Butterfields long?" I asked casually.

"Not really," she said, opening the front door. "We have a mutual acquaintance."

Ah-ha! How blindly she had walked into my trap!

"Who might that be?" I asked artfully.

Estelle smiled sweetly. "No one you would have heard of all the way over in India."

"Are you only here for the anniversary ball?" I said next. "Or have you other business in Suffolk? I only ask because it's an

English custom in India to be offensively curious about things."

The question seemed to startle her. But just for a moment.

"Yes, as it happens."

"Oh?"

"Nothing that would interest you, I'm sure." The young woman smiled softly. "Just a small family matter."

Then she walked out of the front door and hurried to Lady Elizabeth's side.

I went hunting that night. My investigation thus far had been a tremendous success. Estelle had practically confessed the whole villainous scheme. Well, not *exactly* confessed. But as I was an expert at jumping to conclusions—having all the natural instincts of a village gossip—I felt supremely confident that my hunches had been right.

Estelle had practically run out the door to conference with Lady Elizabeth. What could those two—one young and devious, the other old and feral—have to discuss so urgently? Was it really so far-fetched to think that their mutual love of locking people in Lashwood had forged a bond, and now Lady Elizabeth was complicit in hiding Anastasia away?

While I wasn't entirely sure what Lady Elizabeth had to gain, I knew in my gut that dark deeds were at play in this house. And it wasn't just *my* dazzling instincts at work. Something Bertha had said about Lady Elizabeth struck me as very interesting.

The old bat was having food delivered to her bedroom chamber in the dead of night. Now *that* made no sense. Which is why I slipped out of my bedroom just before the clock struck midnight—my disguise still in place—and tiptoed across to the east wing, taking up position around the corner of a long, dark hallway. Even in the dim light, I had a clear view of Lady Elizabeth's bedroom door.

Falling asleep wasn't part of the plan. But I did. Waking up with a start in the wee hours of the morning as a rather exhausted-looking maid came down the hall carrying a tray covered by a silver lid. My timing was perfect! She put the tray on a table beside Lady Elizabeth's door, making a great deal of racket—which was rather foolish of her. Knocked three times loudly. Then scurried away.

A few minutes ticked by. Then I heard the handle squeak as the door swung open. Lady Elizabeth, in a long robe and nightcap, stepped out, coughing up a storm. I jumped to my feet and chanced a look around the corner, just as Lady Elizabeth was hurrying down the corridor carrying the silver tray.

I took off after her—as hushed and unnoticed as a shadow. I reached the top of the landing and looked down as Lady Elizabeth was crossing the great hall. She passed the drawing room and turned toward the east wing. Taking two steps at a time, I bounded down the stairs, the hall a tapestry of pale moonlight and gloom. Without a candle, it was a rather tricky business. My bare feet skidded across the wooden floor as I flew into the passageway, hot on the wicked bat's trail.

Lady Elizabeth must have been headed for the library. Which is why I stopped suddenly. For so had Lady Elizabeth. But instead of opening the library door, she put the tray to one side and unlocked the large carved doors of the ballroom. Then she picked up the tray again and slipped quietly inside. The doors closed. A crisp *click* broke the silence as the lock snapped into place.

The situation was urgent. With the ballroom door locked, I had to find another way in. Lady Elizabeth had some clandestine business in that room, and I was certain it had to do with

Anastasia. What possible reason would a dried-up fossil have for carrying a tray of food into a ballroom at four o'clock in the morning?

Which is why I slipped furtively into the kitchen. The cooks were busy over the stove, already boiling up pork and beef for breakfast. So I passed through and darted out the kitchen door (it being the only one unlocked at that early hour).

The damp ground chilled my toes as I hurried around the side of the house. The ballroom was just a short distance from the kitchen, and I intended to access it through a window (I prayed they were unlocked). I stole frequent backward glances to ensure no one was following me. As a result, I ran smack into a deliveryman.

He wore a thick wool coat, a checkered cap, and a patch over his right eye. And he carried, hoisted on his shoulder, a large package of fresh cheeses for the ball.

"What you scurrying about for?" he said with a twinkle in his eye. "Running away, is ya?"

"Certainly not, you ridiculous pirate."

He looked rather hurt. "I lost my eye in the war, I did."

"I should hope so, dear." I put out my hands. "If you *must* know, I was sent out by Cook to collect the cheese. We have a great ball happening tomorrow, and we are preparing madly, as you might expect."

He looked at me rather uncertainly. Then he shrugged, placing the heavy package in my hands. "Just be sure this lot goes in the icebox, you hear?"

"Consider it done."

When the one-eyed fellow had returned to his wagon, I got moving again. Precious time had been wasted! So I bolted to the long bank of windows running along the side of the ballroom. Stopped. Peered in. All was darkness. The sun had yet to rise, dawn throwing little light into the vast chamber. I ran from window to window, trying each one. All locked.

I was despondent as I reached the final window. Pushed on it, expecting disappointment. I wanted to shout for joy when it slid up. I climbed in, dropping the parcel of cheese on the floor beside me. I was concealed behind a thick velvet curtain that bunched together at either end of the windows. I pushed the drapes to one side and sneaked a peak.

The enormous gallery, with its vaulted ceiling and eight

splendid chandeliers, was a tangle of darkness—webs of inky black, twisted around others in shades of mottled gray. There was no sign of Lady Elizabeth. The ballroom appeared to be an empty tomb.

I decided to chance a look around. As I stepped out, I heard the lock snap. Then the large doors began to open. I jumped back behind the curtain, leaving just a sliver for me to peek through. Soft light spread across the parquet floor as the door opened. A girl entered the room, locking the door behind her.

She carried a glowing candle, her silky blond hair loose around her shoulders. The girl was halfway across the ballroom when the wind suddenly picked up, blowing through the open window behind me and fluttering the heavy curtain.

Estelle Dumbleby stopped. "Hello? Is someone there?"

I kept utterly still. Waited for the sound of her footsteps hurrying toward me. Certain I was done for. But the girl never came. Perhaps a minute ticked by before I dared to peek around the velvet curtain again. And when I did, the chamber was empty. The door was still locked. No one had come or gone, for

I would have heard them. With great courage, I stepped out and charged around the melancholy ballroom, trying to make sense of it. And after I was done, only one thing remained certain. Estelle Dumbleby had vanished into thin air.

9 ✳✳

"**V**anished!" I declared. "Into thin air no less!"

The ballroom had me baffled. Though I had searched the vast chamber, high and low, I could not solve the mystery. Estelle had disappeared. So had Lady Elizabeth. The ballroom was shaped like a chocolate box; along one wall was a bank of windows; along the other, a row of paneled mirrors. There *had* to be a hidden door somewhere. But I could not find it.

With the sun creeping up over the woodlands, spilling early morning light into the ballroom, I climbed out the window (the ballroom door was locked), sneaked back through the kitchen, and went up to my bedroom chamber. Where I promptly woke Bertha and told her what I had witnessed.

"What a strange business," she said, adjusting my wig in the mirror (my disguise was in need of refreshing after the long night). "People creeping about in the night and vanishing without a trace—gives me the chills, it does."

"If I had any doubts that Lady Elizabeth and Estelle are in cahoots, last night settled the matter. The tray of food had to be for Anastasia. What a fiendish pair they are!"

"What are you going to do, miss?"

"That's the easy part, dear," I said, fixing a dab of glue to my nose and sticking it back on. "I shall return to the ballroom before breakfast and snoop about until I find the secret door."

"Shall I come with you?" said the maid hopefully.

"No, thank you, dear." I threw on a white dress with a lovely silk collar. "I want you to stay as close to Estelle as possible today—see where she goes, what she does, who she talks to."

Bertha nodded. "Yes, miss."

With no time to waste, I set off for the ballroom again. But my hopes of having the place to myself were dashed. As the ball was tomorrow, the servants were swarming like locusts, setting up the long banqueting table where the food and drink would be served.

In fact, I didn't get much farther than the ballroom's carved oak doors. For it was here that I came upon Matilda and her mother having a rather heated discussion. About the sort of entrance Matilda wished to make at the ball. Namely, that she wanted to be carried in on a gilded throne.

"That seems rather excessive, darling," said Lady Amelia meekly.

"Excessive?" Matilda stomped her foot. "I'm to inherit this

great pile when Grandmother kicks the bucket. Don't I deserve a little respect?

"Of course you do, my sweet." Lady Amelia began to fan herself manically. "But I fear that Lady Elizabeth might object if you are carried in by eight footmen."

Matilda folded her arms. "Doesn't she want me to feel special?"

"Aren't entrances marvelous things?" I said, butting in helpfully. "I once saw Queen Victoria arrive for morning tea on the back of twelve eagles—smashing stuff." I smiled at Matilda. "But perhaps Lady Elizabeth would prefer you didn't enter the ballroom like an Egyptian princess riding her slaves."

"Who asked you?" snarled Matilda.

Before I could answer, Lady Elizabeth's voice came bellowing down the hallway. "Where is my blasted daughter-in-law?" she thundered. "Lady Amelia, come and rub my bunions, you indolent woman!"

I saw Lady Amelia's petite nostrils flare. Just slightly. The smallest flash of irritation shadowing her round face. Then she groaned wearily. "Coming, Lady Elizabeth!"

"Lady Amelia," I said, "I'm not one to stick my nose in where it doesn't belong."

"Liar," snapped Matilda.

"But you really should stand up to Lady Elizabeth. Show her you won't be pushed around." I patted her fleshy arm. "The old bat will thank you for it."

"No, she won't," said Matilda with a grin.

"You really think so, Esmeralda?" said Lady Amelia meekly.

"Why ever not?" I asked. "The only way to defeat a bully is to bash them senseless."

"Oh, *my*," whispered Lady Amelia. "What a thought!"

Lady Elizabeth bellowed again, and her daughter-in-law took off down the hall like a puppy. As she departed, I felt Matilda glaring at me with terrific interest. Studying my face as if it were a wall hanging. I prayed she had not recognized me.

"You're the ugliest girl I ever saw, Cabbage," she declared at last. "Are you *really* related to the King of Spain?"

"Most certainly," I said. "We're violently close. Practically sisters."

"That doesn't make any sense," said Matilda. "But as all of

my friends hate me, I suppose you'll have to do."

"If it makes you feel any better, I'm practically positive I'll end up hating you too."

Matilda frowned. "You remind me of someone."

"I'm sure she was glorious. And violently misunderstood."

"She was unhinged." Matilda glanced in at the ballroom. "Do you know why we haven't had a party in this house for ten whole months, Cabbage?"

I nodded. "It was in all the papers—about your cousin Rebecca's sudden death."

Matilda undid and retied the ribbon in her hair, her hazel eyes sparkling. "She shriveled up right before our eyes and died. At least, I *think* she did."

"You're not sure?" I said gently.

"Of course I am." Matilda glared at me again. "Follow me, Cabbage. I want to show you something completely bonkers."

Matilda unlocked the door and ushered me inside. It was just as I remembered, yet it still made me gasp. A neat bedroom with a pretty brass bed—and a wonderland of clocks. They crowded the walls and the floor, the tables and drawers and cabinets. Brass clocks, silver ones, cuckoos and carriage clocks. Each timepiece ticking as one, like the heartbeat of this abandoned bedroom.

"Are you shocked, Cabbage?" said Matilda.

I wasn't shocked. I was sad. Horribly sad. Thinking of how my friend was suffering in Prospa House. A place without hope, that's what she had told me. I didn't know all the grisly details, but her life as a remedy was beastly—curing those in Prospa dying of the Shadow and, with each healing, fading a little more until there would be nothing left of her.

"Whose room is this?" I asked.

"My cousin's," said Matilda.

"And the clocks?"

"Some foolishness about her mother." Matilda wandered between the clocks toward the window. "But then, this is a strange house. Things happen here."

"How thrilling!" I cleared my throat. "Such as?"

"I'm not really sure." She gazed out at the parkland below. "But I have my suspicions."

I had wondered whether Matilda was in on the wicked

scheme involving Anastasia. After all, hadn't she conspired with her grandmother to trap me at Lashwood? The girl was certainly capable of skulduggery. Yet she seemed to be as mystified as I was about the goings-on at Butterfield Park.

"Grandmother hated the clocks," said Matilda. "Yet after my cousin died, she ordered this room to be locked up like a vault." She walked back toward me. "Everything is just as my cousin left it."

Except that wasn't completely true. The last time I had been in Rebecca's room, after the awful events of the birthday ball, the clocks had been knocked over and scattered about. And that wasn't all. The timepieces had no longer ticked as one—they had been horribly out of sync. Yet now all of the clocks had been put to rights, just as Rebecca kept them, and they ticked with a single beat. Which begged an interesting question. "Someone is keeping the clocks ticking," I said. "Is it *you*, dear?"

Matilda reached out and touched a gold carriage clock on the table beside her, her pretty face etched with melancholy. It only lasted a second. Then it was gone. "Don't be stupid, Cabbage." She turned and stomped out of the room. "I'm bored, let's go."

When Matilda tired of my delightful company shortly after lunch—muttering something about me being too nosy for my own good—I returned to the ballroom. It was unlocked and wonderfully deserted. I slipped in and closed the door behind me. A long banqueting table ran down the middle of the room. I walked around it, making a beeline for the wall of mirrored panels. Each mirror was surrounded by a gilded frame, and between every third panel was a candelabra wrapped in gold ivy.

I started at one end and moved down, pushing and poking each panel, looking for any sign of a secret door. Or a handle. It wasn't a great success. The glass did not budge. There was no sign of a concealed entrance. But not willing to give up, I walked quickly back to the first panel and started again.

"Miss Cabbage?"

I jumped, startled. Lady Elizabeth was standing at the far end of the banqueting table. Which was rather odd, as I was just a few feet from the ballroom door—it was still closed. And I would surely have heard her come in.

"What are you doing in here, Miss Cabbage?" she said next.

"I was just admiring your glorious ballroom. But I must ask, Lady Elizabeth—how did you get in here?"

"Well, I didn't fly in on my broomstick, if that's what you're worried about," she barked.

"Of course you didn't," I said, moving toward her. "I never imagined for a *moment* that you were the sort of witch that used a broom."

She huffed. "Is that what passes for flattery in India these days?"

"Oh, yes. It's all the rage." I stopped a few feet from old Walnut Head. "I'm still rather puzzled about how you got in here—I was standing right by the door."

It made my blood boil to think that Anastasia was somewhere close. I was tempted to call out her name and pound on the mirrors. But if I did, the game would be up—and I might never secure that poor woman's freedom.

"Puzzled, are you?" said Lady Elizabeth. "Well, don't trouble yourself, Miss Cabbage. I was here long before you entered the room."

"But I did not see you."

"Then I suggest you consult a physician." Then she pointed with her cane. "I was over there, inspecting the rostrum. Tomorrow night there will be a full orchestra playing for my guests."

It was true there was a stage at the far end of the room, but I would surely have noticed if Lady Elizabeth had been up there. She didn't fool me for a moment. The ballroom had been empty when I walked in. Which could only mean one thing. And Lady Elizabeth knew it.

"Do you imagine," she said softly, "that I have some *secret* way of popping in and out of this ballroom?" Her beady eyes, lost in the folds of her wrinkly flesh, seemed to gaze into my very soul. "Is that what you think, Miss Cabbage?"

"Heavens no." If this were a game of chess, I would have to move my next piece most carefully. "Though if you *did* have a secret entrance, where do you suppose it might be? If you don't wish to say it aloud—for fear of your life and whatnot—just point with your stick or shake some of the dust from your hair and carve an arrow into it, showing the way."

"Dust from my *what*?" Lady Elizabeth cupped her ear and huffed again. "Gibberish, that's what you talk!"

The old bat was getting rather testy, so I felt it best to make a hasty retreat. I would return for another look around the ballroom at the next opportunity. As I turned to depart, I glanced out the window and noticed something odd. *Someone* odd, to be more exact. A woman. She was dressed in black, a veil covering her face. And she stood at the mouth of the woodlands, facing Butterfield Park. Perhaps she was a ghost. I'd seen Rebecca's mother haunting that same woodland on my last visit. So it was something of a shock when Lady Elizabeth fell in beside me and said, "Who the blazes is that?"

"I haven't a clue." And between the time it took for me to glance at Lady Elizabeth and then back at the window, the veiled woman had vanished. "But it's frightfully interesting, don't you think?"

"Claptrap! What are you up to, Miss Cabbage? Why were you lurking about my ballroom as if you were *looking* for something?"

"I could ask you the same question, Lizzy."

"Wretched girl!" she thundered. "My *name* is Lady Elizabeth."

"Of course it is, you poor, delirious fossil." I spoke loudly, as one does to a halfwit with poor hearing. "And this is Butterfield Park—your *home*." I began nudging her toward the door. "What about some fresh air? It might clear the cobwebs from your mind. Though I think it would be wise if I tethered you to a tree—so you don't wander off and fall in a hole."

"Poke me again," she said, raising her cane to my throat, "and I will have your head, Miss Cabbage."

And I could tell she meant it. But at least I had succeeded in derailing her interrogation. The last thing I wanted was for Lady Elizabeth to realize I was on to her.

I made a dignified exit—offering a cheery wave and then cartwheeling out the door (which felt like something Esmeralda Cabbage would do). Then I set off to find Bertha, eager to share what I had learned. Lady Elizabeth's sudden appearance in the ballroom confirmed my deepest suspicions. There was a secret doorway somewhere in that room. The only question—*Where?*

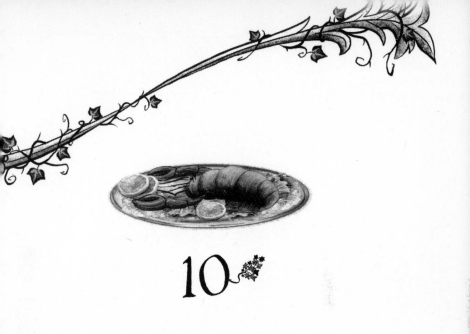

10

No one visited the ballroom that night. I kept watch, peering through the keyhole of the library door (the two rooms were opposite each other). As the hours ticked by, I took a risk and decided to enter the grand chamber myself, hoping to discover that elusive hidden door. I was relieved to find the ballroom unlocked—how wondrously convenient! I searched the vast chamber, without success, until I heard the servants waking up and moving about the house. Defeated, I returned to my bedroom chamber for a few hours' sleep.

Bertha woke me in a great state of excitement. The ball was

that very night, and the house was teeming with activity. I sat before the dressing table, listening to her babble about all the details, as I carefully put on my face.

"I sneaked a peek at the ballroom," she said eagerly, picking up my wig and running a brush through it. "And what a sight! I've never seen such splendor. Though the kitchen's in an awful panic—the cheese never arrived, and they've had to send for another lot."

A note had come by the early morning post. It was from Mr. Partridge. He asked how I was enjoying Butterfield Park and reported that as yet he had been unable to locate Anastasia's missing child. He wondered if perhaps McCloud had put the infant into an orphanage—and said that he would start making enquiries. But that was unlikely. Hadn't Baron Dumbleby told me that McCloud had always wanted a child of her own? Why then would she give it up?

"Miss Estelle was up early this morning, taking a stroll," said Bertha. "She gave me such a *look*. She hates me, she does."

The poor lump had followed Estelle for much of yesterday,

but had come back with nothing of interest to report, apart from the fact that the awful girl spent much of the day lazing about the conservatory. I twisted my braid into a tight bun and pinned it. "I wouldn't worry, dear. Estelle has more on her devious mind than you."

"She has a black heart." Bertha slipped the wig over my hair and made a few adjustments. "There, miss, all done."

Esmeralda Cabbage looked back at me in the mirror. But for once my reflection didn't fill me with hope. For the day of the ball was here. I had been thoroughly convinced I would find Anastasia within hours of reaching Butterfield Park. But I had failed. Nor was I completely certain about my ingenious plan to reach Rebecca. Time was fast running out.

"What's wrong, miss?" said Bertha uneasily. "You look awful serious."

I stood up. Paced around the room like a prisoner awaiting sentence. "Bertha, I need you to listen to me very carefully."

The maid sat down on the bed and gulped. "Yes, miss?"

"If we do not find Anastasia by the end of the ball tonight, I fear we never will." I stopped in front of the quivering maid. "But if we do find her, and we *must*, it's very important that you follow my instructions."

"But why must it be tonight? We are to stay on at Butterfield Park for another two days."

"I will not be here beyond tonight," I said. "At least, I hope not."

Bertha jumped like a startled bunny. "What do you mean, miss?"

"Only this. I have a plan that I hope will take me to Prospa without the stone's help. Tonight is the only night it can happen."

"I don't understand," said Bertha, beginning to sob.

"Bertha, listen to me," I said gently. "I must go to help a friend who needs me even more than Anastasia."

"You mean Rebecca?"

I nodded, my thoughts flying to the mysterious veiled figure I had seen looking at Butterfield Park from the woodlands. "I have a plan. As yet the pieces are not in place, but I have high hopes." I reached into my pocket and pulled out an envelope, handing it to Bertha. "There is money inside and an address in Weymouth. When I find the secret door, we must get Anastasia away from this house—tonight. Take her to that address. Take her there and keep her safe."

Bertha's hands were trembling as she took the envelope. "Isn't Weymouth the very place you ran away from?"

"That's right. It is the very same cottage by the sea."

I could see the fear blooming in Bertha's eyes. "And didn't you say Miss Always went to that house looking for you—and that she took your friend Jago as her hostage?"

"Yes."

"What if Miss Always comes back?" she cried. "You said she's awful dangerous."

"Miss Always wouldn't think I'd be stupid enough to go back to Weymouth." I smiled triumphantly. "She doesn't know me at *all*. So, will you do as I have asked?"

"I will," said Bertha, hugging her arms. "But I'm awful scared, miss."

"Stuff and nonsense," I replied brightly.

Though I couldn't deny the shiver creeping through my bones.

Esmeralda Cabbage wore a peach-colored dress made of silk. Her flaxen hair hung loose around her shoulders, fixed with an auburn ribbon. And her face, held in place by a little glue, had the noble glow of a piglet. She would fit right in among three hundred aristocrats.

The ballroom was as glorious as Bertha had described. The vast room glowed like a jewel beneath the eight chandeliers, each one flickering with a hundred candles. The windows were now covered by the red velvet curtain, which shimmered in the soft light. As I entered the room, the orchestra was playing a waltz, and already a great many guests were dancing about. There were lords and ladies as far as the eye could see. With dukes in tails and top hats and duchesses sparkling with embroidered gowns of brocade silk, feathered hats of every shape and size, and frills and flounces everywhere you looked.

Servants milled about in starched uniforms, filling empty glasses, pulling out chairs, and anticipating the guests' every whim. The banqueting table was a triumph, running down the middle of the ballroom—it was decorated with fresh orchids and candelabras and laden with silver trays teeming with sweetmeats and potatoes, fish, crab and lobster, and every kind of game. There were puddings and tarts and cakes in a rainbow of colors. And the centerpiece of the table was an enormous red-and-blue jelly at least ten feet long—a wonderfully wobbly replica of Butterfield House itself, with the words ONE HUNDRED YEARS carved into the top.

I ventured over to the windows, parted the curtains, and took a peek outside. And noted with a rush of excitement the half-moon etched into the sky, throwing pale light over the park.

"You look lovely, Esmeralda."

It was Lady Amelia. *She* looked like a pound of butter squeezed into a sparkling red sock. "Thank you, Lady Amelia. So do you."

She giggled. Then took a large gulp of her wine. "I've never seen the house so full—Lady Elizabeth will be most pleased."

"I can't think why," snapped Matilda. "It's utterly boring, that's what it is."

Across the ballroom I saw Estelle Dumbleby make her grand entrance. She didn't look even slightly wicked in a blue-and-white dress, a stunning ruby necklace at her throat. She immediately caught the eye of Lady Elizabeth, who was standing beside Countess Carbunkle (who wore a hat positively bursting with peacock feathers). The three of them huddled together and talked for some time.

It was an astonishing coincidence to see them all gathered under one roof. Thank heavens for my brilliant disguise and my staggering acting skills. Here I was, right under their noses, and those clueless chumps didn't suspect a thing.

"Who on earth is *that*?" said Matilda, pointing rudely.

I looked over and saw the object of her disapproval. A woman had entered the ballroom. She wore a long black dress, black gloves, and a small hat, and a veil covered her face.

"It's probably Mrs. Winterbottom from the village," said Lady Amelia. "Her husband died in a shooting accident last spring, and she is still in deep mourning." Lady Amelia sighed. "Poor woman. Her suffering must be hard to bear."

"Who's suffering?" Lady Elizabeth had joined our little group.

"Mrs. Winterbottom," said Lady Amelia. "She is in grief."

The old bat squinted and cocked her ear. "Mrs. Winterbottom's in Greece? I saw the blasted woman at church yesterday morning!"

Matilda laughed heartily.

"I'm surrounded by idiots." Lady Elizabeth huffed.

I peeled away from the group and walked about the ballroom. Stomping on the floor. Pushing on the mirrored panels. All very *discreetly*, of course. The wall behind the orchestra was rock solid, so there was no possibility of a hidden door. Which only left the wall of mirrors. The secret door *had* to be there.

"What are you doing, Esmeralda?"

Estelle had slithered up beside me as I was examining a panel of mirror.

"Just admiring the craftsmanship," I said casually. "They don't build houses like this anymore, what with the empire crumbling and whatnot—I blame the poor, don't you?"

"I rather thought you were looking for something," said Estelle sweetly. "You seem *terribly* preoccupied by these mirrors."

"Well, I'm rather fond of my own reflection," I said, glancing at Estelle through the glass. "Though I find it strange, what with so much to see and do at this great ball, that you choose to spend your time watching *me*."

Estelle blushed and giggled. "I confess I have a rather curious nature—do you think it terribly vulgar of me to wonder about what people are really up to?"

"I'm sure you've done worse," I said brightly.

The smile slipped from her face. She turned on her heels and swanned away.

There was a foul smell wafting about the ballroom, and it was hard to miss.

Countess Carbunkle certainly hadn't missed it. She stood by the banqueting table, munching with great enthusiasm on a lobster claw, her peacock feathers fluttering about as she spoke. "What on earth is that *odor*?"

"Countess Carbunkle," I said, with a wave of my upper-class hand, "what you smell is the stench of moldy aristocrats— gout, mothballs, a fondness for horses and whatnot. My grandmother stinks to high heaven, and *she* is first cousin to the King of Spain."

"Is she indeed?" said the Countess with an arched eyebrow. "Who is this grandmother of yours?"

"Lady Ophelia Cabbage," I said grandly. "A very great woman. She was the toast of London before she set sail for India."

"I very much doubt that." The Countess smeared some buttery cheese on the lobster and took another hearty bite. "Why have *I* never heard of her?"

"It is a great mystery," I said. "Grandmother was a terrific snob. As a chinless countess with bad manners and appalling teeth, you would have been just her cup of tea."

For some reason, this caused Countess Carbunkle to cough suddenly—sending a piece of lobster shooting across the room, where it landed in the hair of a baroness from Gloucester. Just at that moment, the lady in the black veil passed by. Countess Carbunkle took an instant dislike to her. "Probably that wretched *Miss Anonymous*," she grumbled, pointing with her lobster claw. "It would be just like her to slink about looking for gossip to put in that beastly column of hers. I would gladly tear her limb from limb." Then she laughed unconvincingly. "Just a little joke."

I felt the moment was right to tell the Countess she had a chunk of lobster hanging from her chin hair. Countess

Carbunkle gasped, blushing furiously. "I do?"

"Yes, dear. If it were any longer, you could lower it into the river and catch a salmon."

The Countess grabbed a napkin and wiped her chin, and in doing so smeared the buttered lobster claw across her gray dress. That made her gasp again. "Just look at the stain," she cried. "How beastly! How humiliating!"

"Nonsense," I said, feeling rather sorry for the silly creature. "I can remove that in a flash."

I grabbed the napkin from her hand and dipped it in a glass of champagne. Then dunked it in a bowl of cranberry sauce.

"What are you doing?" said Countess Carbunkle, beginning to back up.

"Saving the day," I said with a winning smile. "This mixture will take that stain out in no time. For best results, I usually require a spoonful of crushed beetle wings, but there isn't time."

"This dress cost me a fortune!" she shrieked.

"Well, that's not your fault, dear," I said, attacking the stain with gusto. "I'm sure it looked perfectly lovely on the mannequin."

The Countess backed up toward the banqueting table in an effort to escape my reach. Though *why*, I couldn't say. "Get off me!" she snapped.

At that point, things took a turn for the worse. For some *strange* reason, Countess Carbunkle did not want my help. In fact, she seemed to view it as a form of sabotage! Which is why she was pulling away, her buttocks pressed against the table, her back arched. Which is also why the enormous peacock feathers sprouting out of her hat made contact with a flickering candelabra. And caught fire. The flames roared to life and spread across her feathers like a forest fire. Within seconds her entire hat was burning up.

A pair of dames standing nearby began to shriek.

Countess Carbunkle sniffed the air. "What on earth is burning?"

"You are, dear," I said.

The Countess straightened up and caught sight of herself in the mirrored panels. Which is when she began to scream like a woman whose hat was on fire.

Naturally I was happy to assist. By then the fire was spreading rapidly toward her hair. So I had to act quickly. I looked around for a suitable method of quelling the flames. And found it the moment my eyes flew to the banqueting table. "Brace yourself, Countess Carbunkle!"

"What for?" she shrieked.

Rushing at her like a bull, I pushed hard on the Countess's shoulders, sending her flying back onto the table. Her landing wasn't especially elegant; gravy boats and pheasant went hurtling into the air. Then I leaped onto the table top and slammed her head into the centerpiece—and her hat, indeed her entire head, splattered into the gigantic red-and-blue jelly of Butterfield Park.

The delicious dessert smothered the flaming hat. As Countess Carbunkle's head sank deeper into the jelly, it squished around the sides of her face and spluttered over the top of her dress and up her neck. It had worked a treat! The entire ballroom fell silent. Even the orchestra stopped playing.

"You . . . you . . . stupid girl!" thundered Countess Carbunkle.

"Help her, you fools!" barked Lady Elizabeth, directing two gawking footmen toward Countess Carbunkle. They hurried over and pulled the Countess off the table. Great chunks of jelly were stuck to her hat and the sides of her face. But she arranged herself with great dignity. Head high. Jelly falling from her ears. There was a small amount of sobbing. And some rather unkind accusations.

"There is a jug of water!" she bellowed at me. "Could you not have thrown the water at my hat instead of pushing me into the centerpiece?"

"Now *there's* a thought," I replied. "Countess, you looked awfully rattled. Perhaps you'd be more comfortable lying back on the banqueting table with the other desserts?"

The Countess responded by grabbing a baked potato and throwing it at my head. I dropped down just in time. The potato sailed over me and hit a violinist in the nose. He went flying back—and as he did, he reached for anything to halt his fall. The closest thing was a candelabra mounted on the wall. So he grabbed it.

But no one was paying the violinist any attention. It seemed the whole ballroom had gathered around Countess Carbunkle, trying to sooth her distress. But while the guests and the waiters fussed over a jelly-covered aristocrat, I had my sights set on the violinist. It seemed that only *I* had noticed the candelabra bend when he grabbed it, then snap back into place as he fell to the floor. Bend and snap back. Rather like a handle. And that right after, the mirrored panel closest to the orchestra had popped open—just a crack. To the untrained eye, it might seem like nothing at all. But I knew *exactly* what it meant.

"The door," I whispered.

11

"I am ruined!"

Countess Carbunkle was sitting on a chair, wheezing a great deal, as a horde of noblewomen fanned her face and assured her that *of course* she could show her face in high society again. Though a short exile in Romania might be just the thing. But I was barely paying attention.

A door. There was a door. And I was certain Anastasia Radcliff was somewhere on the other side of it. So I headed toward it at speed.

"Making a run for it, are you, Cabbage?" shouted Matilda.

"Just checking on the injured violinist," I called back. "They are a fragile bunch."

The violinist in question had found his feet. And was about to rejoin the orchestra as they began playing again. I stopped at the side of the stage. Stole a glance at Matilda. She was now ordering Bertha to cut her a slice of cake. With the music playing, and the dancing resumed, I crept over to the mirror. It was just as I had thought. The panel was open just a crack, a seam of darkness etched around the mirror.

I opened it and prepared to slip inside. Now, the trouble with opening a door is that the light from the other side floods in. Which has a terrible habit of startling bats. When I stepped through the door, I found myself in a narrow, dim passageway. What I *didn't* see were the beams running along the ceiling or the three bats hanging from it. That is, until they squawked violently as the light flooded in, flapped their wings, then flew straight out the mirrored door and into the ballroom.

Bats do a few things remarkably well. They flap about, making a great racket. And they scare people half to death. As the bats swooped and swerved, flying in tight circles over the banqueting table, the guests began to scream violently.

"Bats!" cried a chunky duchess.

"Run!" shouted a lord, pushing his wife out of the way as he raced for the door.

"Fetch my musket!" barked Lady Elizabeth. "I'll blast them to bits!"

A great many guests seemed to run for the door all at once. Which created something of a jam. That led to a small amount of panic. A touch of pandemonium. I felt slightly responsible for the chaos. So I quickly came up with a solution.

The bats were circling madly, looking for a way out. So I would give them one. I charged across the room, mounted the banqueting table, and leaped between slices of pork and duck, then jumped down the other side. "Fear not!" I shouted. "The bats will soon be away!"

I bolted to the red velvet curtain, found the thick cord at the far end, and pulled it as fiercely as I knew how. The curtain parted in the middle and flew toward either end. Which was brilliant. I was about to start opening the windows to give the bats an escape when I looked down and made a rather unexpected discovery. It was the source of the odious smell that filled the ballroom. The package of cheese that I had dropped behind the curtain during my late-night visit was still there. Only now it had been torn open and was being fed on, rather rabidly, by what appeared to be several hundred mice.

I wasn't the only one who noticed the rodents. The mayor's wife gave a bloodcurdling scream, then took the top hat off her husband's head and threw it at the mice. Which was a great mistake. The mice, up to their ears in rancid cheese, scattered like the wind, darting across the ballroom.

"Mice!" cried one woman, then another. Panic spread about the ballroom rather rapidly—as did the mice. At least fifty of them scurried up the tablecloth and began feasting on the food, while others darted about causing bedlam.

With the bats swooping and the mice scurrying, the ballroom had taken on the atmosphere of a sinking ship. Several women were overcome with the vapors, while a group of men threw chairs and fruit at the pests. The whole place was in an uproar. Women panicked. Men pretended not to. One of the maids attempted to climb the curtains. And

Lady Elizabeth waved her cane in the air and called again for her musket.

"Why must *every* ball we have end in complete disaster?" howled Matilda to her mother.

That felt like the perfect moment to make my exit. I dropped down, scurried under the table with several of the mice, and jumped to my feet. Then headed straight toward the secret door. When I reached it, I glanced about. Spotted Bertha in the crowd. She nodded her head. I nodded back. Then I slipped unnoticed from the unruly ballroom.

The tunnel was narrow. Bare brick walls. Dirt floor. Apart from a sliver of light slipping in from the ballroom, all was darkness. I felt my way along until the floor dropped away. A steep staircase loomed before me. A faint glow shimmered below. I hurried down.

At the bottom was a large chamber. The floor was damp and pungent. A torch hung from a bracket, throwing scarlet light at the darkness. At one end, a wooden peg stuck out from the wall. On it was a key. At the other end were two lengths of chain and two shackles. One had a woman fixed to it—fastened at the wrist.

Anastasia Radcliff was squatting on the floor, hugging her

knees. A tangle of dark hair concealed her face. Her nightdress was stained and tattered. She rocked back and forth. And hummed that familiar lullaby.

"It's all right, dear," I said softly.

My words startled her. She stopped humming. Sniffed the air.

"I have come to get you out of this place," I whispered.

The madwoman squeezed her legs tighter and began to hum again. I looked about. Saw the key again. While the length of chain was too short for Anastasia to have reached it, I had no such restriction. Grabbing the key, I hurried back to her. While there were a great many unknowns spinning through my mind, of one thing I was sure—there wasn't much time.

"I have a friend, her name is Bertha," I said as I slipped the key in the lock. "She is going to take you somewhere safe. Somewhere far from here."

I turned the key, and the shackle snapped open. I wanted to shout with joy! Instead, I looked through that tangle of hair, hoping to reach the woman inside. "Anastasia, I know who you hum to day and night, and I promise that if you go with Bertha, we will find your child, and the two of you will be together again."

Anastasia Radcliff fell silent. Her hand reached out—her fingers caked with dirt—and grabbed my arm. "My . . ." Her voice was small and wounded. "My . . . baby?"

"Yes, we will find your baby. But right now we must get you out of this house."

"Well done, Miss Pocket."

As I leaped up, Anastasia scrambled into the corner. Lady Elizabeth stood at the bottom of the stairs. And beside her was Countess Carbunkle. And Estelle Dumbleby. They all looked terribly pleased with themselves.

"We hoped you would discover this little dungeon before tonight," said Lady Elizabeth. "We did everything but draw you a map, yet still you couldn't find it." She smiled wickedly. "But better late than never."

How did they know who I was? My disguise had been a smashing success.

"After you escaped from Lashwood," said Estelle, stepping toward me, "I realized that Lady Elizabeth and I shared a common enemy—you." She reached out and ripped the nose from my face. Then pulled off my wig, throwing it aside.

"Miss Dumbleby agreed to assist us in luring you to Butterfield Park," said Lady Elizabeth, "in return for accommodating Miss Radcliff. The dungeon has room enough for two lunatics, so we struck a bargain."

I was stunned. The whole thing had been an elaborate trick? A scheme to bring me to Butterfield Park on the trail of Anastasia? In short, a trap? The awful truth must have carved its way across my face.

"*Now* she understands," said Estelle, her voice ringing with delight. "You have been played for a fool, Ivy. How does it feel?"

I made no reply. Behind me, Anastasia had begun to hum again.

"Silence!" shouted Estelle.

I looked at this trio of villains, and only one of them had me puzzled. "What have you to do with this, Countess Carbunkle?"

"Need you ask?" she sneered, pulling a piece of jelly

from her hair. "You ruined my life, Ivy Pocket—made me a laughingstock from Paris to London! And tonight you have done it again. The only balm for my humiliation is to witness your destruction."

"That's rather unkind, dear," I said, pulling out my false teeth and letting them drop to the ground.

"Your residence at Butterfield Park is only temporary." Lady Elizabeth walked across the dungeon, the torch throwing hideous shadows across her wrinkled flesh. "In a few days, when things calm down, you will be taken to a house in the north—a cell has been prepared for you there that will make this place look like a palace."

"The house is mine," said Countess Carbunkle. "When Lady Elizabeth wrote to me in Spain detailing her plans for you, she hoped I would be willing to provide suitable accommodation."

"That way," chimed in Estelle, "there is nothing connecting you and Anastasia to either Lady Elizabeth or myself."

"The perfect crime," said Lady Elizabeth. "You brought that wretched necklace to Butterfield Park, Miss Pocket, and filled my granddaughter's head with nonsense. She is dead because of you, and for that you must pay.

"You cannot do this," I declared. "I won't let you."

"What choice do you have?" chuckled the Countess. "You will live as a prisoner until you have paid for your sins."

"She will rot there!" hissed Estelle. "They both will."

"Grandmother?"

We all looked over and saw Matilda coming down the stairs. The girl was gawking at us with wonder and unease. Then her eyes fell on me. "Pocket . . . what are *you* doing here?"

I said nothing.

"Grandmother, what is going on?" said Matilda with growing urgency.

"I am restoring the Butterfield name," said the old bat proudly.

"And felling a public menace," declared Countess Carbunkle.

Matilda pointed to Anastasia. "Who is that?"

"A poor, wretched woman who has been horribly mistreated," I said, rushing to Matilda's side. "Locked in a madhouse for no other reason than that she fell in love with Sebastian Dumbleby."

"She killed my brother!" shouted Estelle, her eyes blazing with hatred. "Killed him and then spun a web of lies about other worlds and mystical necklaces."

"It was all true, you mad cow!" I thundered. "Every word. And instead of believing her, you took away her baby and locked her in a lunatic asylum—when you're the one who's barking mad!"

Estelle scooped up one of the shackles and lunged at me. Trying to fasten the chain around my wrist. But I was full of fight, yanking the shackle from her grasp and throwing it aside. She responded by pulling my hair and scratching my face. And I responded by slapping and kicking for all I was worth. We ended up on the ground, rolling about like two quarreling schoolgirls.

"Liar!" cried Estelle, biting my hand.

"Nutter!" I hollered back, pinching her arm.

"Stop it at once!" barked Lady Elizabeth.

"Knock her block off, Pocket!" offered Matilda.

As we tumbled across the dirty floor, a strange buzzing began to charge the dank air. No, not strange. Familiar. My heart was pounding, and the blood tore through my veins, making my body tingle. Estelle rolled over and pinned me with her arms. As she did, I felt the Clock Diamond waking up—the stone suddenly warm against my skin. The angrier I got, the hotter it became. Then it began to glow, giving off a pulsing golden light that pushed through my dress and filled the gloomy dungeon.

There were several gasps. But the most violent was from Estelle. I pushed her off me with great force and stood up. Then fished the Clock Diamond from under my dress. Held it out toward her. "This is the stone Anastasia spoke of," I said, panting. "It is real."

"It c-c-can't be," she stammered, her eyes swelling in astonishment. "It can't be true."

I crouched down beside her. "It can't be, yet it is." The diamond churned and cleared, leaving in its heart a quarter moon high over Butterfield Park. "All of it."

Estelle looked bewildered. Then horrified.

"You have to stop this, Estelle," I said. "Your brother died because he followed the woman he loved to her world. They shared a few happy months, and a child was born from their union. It is cruel and ghastly what your family has done. You must let it go before it consumes you."

"Claptrap!" thundered Lady Elizabeth. "This necklace has *always* been cursed. It changes nothing."

From behind me, Countess Carbunkle lunged, grabbing my arms and dragging me back. "The girl must pay for her crimes!"

"Enough!" Lady Amelia had found her way down to the dungeon—perhaps looking for Matilda. How long she had been there, I wasn't sure. But there was a strength in her plump face I'd never seen before. She looked at me with a certain amount of confusion. "Ivy?"

"It's a long story, dear," I said, elbowing Countess Carbunkle in the belly and pulling away. "This pack of deranged jackals is involved in a wicked conspiracy to lock myself and this poor woman away."

"We were wrong," sobbed Estelle, covering her face with her hands. "We were wrong."

I hurried over to Anastasia. She was rocking back and forth.

Humming. All I could do was pat her hand, though she flinched at my touch. The Clock Diamond began to dim and cool against my dress, so I tucked it away.

"I won't stand for any more vengeful plots," said Lady Amelia.

Lady Elizabeth stared daggers at her daughter-in-law. "*What* did you say?"

"It ends tonight," said Lady Amelia with calm certainty. "Ivy and this sad creature will go free, and I won't hear a word of opposition—that you planned to lock them away like animals is vile and shocking. Do you imagine this vengeance will bring back the dead? Do you imagine it will bring you peace?" Somehow she found the strength to look squarely at Lady Elizabeth. "A very wise girl told me I should stand up to you, and although the thought made me tremble, now that I am here, I can't imagine why it took me so long."

The old bat pointed her cane like a pistol. "Think carefully before you say anything more, Lady Amelia. You may not appreciate my methods, but you certainly enjoy my money."

"Matilda and I shall leave tonight," said Lady Amelia. "We have been under your roof and under your thumb quite long enough. As for your money—if being cut off is the price we must pay for our freedom, then I consider it a bargain."

"Mother, let's not be too rash," said Matilda with a mad grin. "I know this all looks slightly mental, but I *am* to be heiress of this house."

"We will make a home of our own, darling," said Lady Amelia. "You can be heiress of that."

"What a revolting thought," said Matilda, folding her arms.

"You can't *leave*," said Lady Elizabeth.

"We can and we shall," said Lady Amelia firmly.

That might have been the end of it. But the evening was not done with us yet. The sound of boots upon the stairs rolled down into the dungeon. I saw the hem of her dress first. Black as night. Then her gloved hands. Her tightly buttoned collar. Finally her head, concealed behind a veil. The woman in black stepped silently into the damp cell and walked toward me.

"Who in the blazes are you?" Lady Elizabeth demanded to know.

The veiled lady gave no reply. She stood perfectly still and silent.

"Actually, Lady Elizabeth," I said, walking around the mysterious figure, "this woman was once a guest in your house." I stopped and stared into the dark veil. "Weren't you, Miss Always?"

At that, the woman in black lifted her shroud. While her face was wretchedly plain and unremarkable, her eyes sparkled as she gazed at me. "You knew?"

"Oh, yes," I said. "I've been expecting you all night."

"What's *she* doing here?" snapped Matilda. "Has she come back to bore us to death?"

"Who is this woman?" asked Countess Carbunkle.

"A writer," huffed Lady Elizabeth. "As if this evening wasn't bad enough!"

"I confess, Ivy, I am terribly impressed," said Miss Always, adjusting her spectacles.

"You weren't hard to spot," I replied. "I first saw you watching

183

the house yesterday, and then when you turned up in the ballroom, prowling about, I knew there could only be one bloodthirsty hag under that veil." I allowed a satisfied smile. "Besides, tonight is a half-moon—the perfect time for you to strike."

Miss Always had always been my plan B. I knew she was on the hunt for me, seeking to drag me into Prospa and prove that I was the Dual, and I was confident she would try to make her move on the next half-moon—the ideal time for the gatekeeper to cross between worlds. So I had intentionally walked about London, hoping she would be on my trail and that she would follow me to Butterfield Park—even as I assumed the ingenious disguise of Esmeralda Cabbage. And my plan had come off rather perfectly.

"I demand to know what in hickory is going on!" snapped Lady Elizabeth.

Miss Always ignored her. For her attention was elsewhere. She stalked slowly over to the corner of the dungeon and looked down at Anastasia Radcliff. The poor creature was humming and hugging her knees. "What have we here?" she said. "*Who* have we here?"

"No one important," I said, rushing over. "Clearly you came here to drag me into Prospa. So let's get to it, dear."

Miss Always crouched down. Her gloved hand reached out and parted the curtain of matted hair covering Anastasia's face. The madwoman cried out and pulled away, curling up in a tight ball, her body pressed into the corner.

"Could it be?" whispered Miss Always.

"No it couldn't, you bloodthirsty, book-writing, blackguard!" I shouted. "The woman you are looking at was once the mistress of Butterfield Park, but she lost her marbles after her husband fell into a pot of chicken broth and sank to the bottom. All very tragic. Her name is—"

"Anastasia Radcliff," said Miss Always with a faint grin. "How you ended up here, I cannot imagine—but what a lovely surprise."

"How does she know that lunatic's name?" barked Lady Elizabeth.

Miss Always stood up, still fixed on Anastasia. "You will make quite a trophy! Justice Hallow isn't terribly fond of me at present, but when she sets eyes on *you*, she will be forever in my debt. They say nobody loves more ferociously than a mother." She laughed icily. "What fun."

"Ivy, what is Miss Always talking about?" said Lady Amelia.

Estelle wiped the tears from her eyes and made a sudden dash for the stairs. In a flash, Miss Always blocked her path. "Going somewhere?"

"I wish to leave," said Estelle, her face pale and afraid. "Please, let me pass."

"But things are just getting interesting," said Miss Always.

Plan B had taken a turn for the worse. While I intended for Miss Always to drag me into Prospa, I hadn't figured on Anastasia being ensnared in the scheme. I knew nothing of Justice Hallow, but from the way Miss Always spoke of her, I doubted that it would be a pleasant mother-and-daughter reunion. My heart was pounding madly. I could feel the Clock Diamond begin to warm against my chest again—and it occurred to me that I would no longer need the gatekeeper's help in reaching Prospa. Miss Always noticed it too. Which is why she began walking toward me.

"Well, well," she said playfully, "I gain Ivy Pocket, Anastasia

Radcliff, *and* the Clock Diamond in a single evening. The gods must be smiling upon me."

Luckily, an idea popped into my head.

"Miss Always, please leave this poor family alone!" I said, looking suitably distraught. "The Butterfields will be *ruined* if you write about what you have seen here in your new book."

"What book?" huffed Lady Elizabeth.

I sidestepped Miss Always and ran to the old bat. "Miss Always is doing top-secret research for a book about Butterfield family history." I spoke loudly into Lady Elizabeth's good ear. "She intends to dedicate an entire chapter to the tragic love triangle between you, the Duchess of Trinity, and the doomed Nathaniel Farris."

"Blasted writer!" thundered Lady Elizabeth.

"What *are* you talking about?" said Miss Always with some amusement.

"Am *I* to be in the book?" asked Matilda hopefully.

I spotted Bertha coming down the stairs, looking thoroughly alarmed. "That is not the worst part," I said, this time directing my attention to Countess Carbunkle. "Making a living as a writer is frightfully difficult—most are irritable hacks who will do anything for a hot meal." I patted the Countess's burned hat. "You might be familiar with her work, dear, for she has written about *you*—though not under her real name."

Countess Carbunkle gasped. *"Miss Anonymous?"*

I nodded. "The very same."

It was all nonsense. But terribly helpful in my current pickle.

"Enough of this," declared Miss Always, grabbing my arm. "You are coming with me, and so is—"

But she never got to finish her sentence. For Countess Carbunkle had snatched the cane from Lady Elizabeth's hand and was bashing Miss Always about the head and body with it. "Shame on you!" she bellowed.

Miss Always tried to shield herself, but after one particularly harsh whack to the head, she stumbled to the ground. By which point Lady Elizabeth began kicking her rather savagely.

"You'll write that book over my dead body!" she thundered.

"Ivy is lying, you fools!" shouted Miss Always.

"Stop it, all of you!" demanded Lady Amelia.

But they did not. While the pummeling was taking place, I called to Bertha. We hurried over and gently lifted Anastasia Radcliff to her feet. She struggled at first, but we did not let go.

"You must trust me, dear," I whispered. "Bertha is a good soul, and she will take you somewhere safe. Go with her and we will find your child, I promise."

Anastasia made no reply.

"I'm scared, miss," said Bertha.

The Clock Diamond began to glow brightly under my dress. "I know you are," I said, pushing them both toward the stairs. "But follow my instructions, and all will be well. There is a carriage waiting out front. Go to the cottage in Weymouth. I will meet you there."

"But what if Miss Always follows us?" said Bertha, gulping.

"Miss Always will come after me, dear. Now do hurry!"

Bertha nodded, grabbed hold of Anastasia, and took off up the stairs. The air was buzzing relentlessly now. The stone pulsed, throwing honey-colored flares around the dim cell. I knew what was happening. And so did Miss Always.

Still on the ground getting pummeled, she threw back her head and gave a wild cry. And as she did, Lady Elizabeth and Countess Carbunkle were thrown sideways. The locks flew like shadows from the folds of Miss Always's dark dress, hissing viciously. There were horrified screams. Estelle made a run for the stairs, but a lock rushed at her, spinning furiously—the wicked girl was flung against the wall most violently. I was already running by then. Matilda grabbed my arm as I took off up the stairs.

"Find my cousin, Pocket," she whispered. "Bring her home."

I saw the hooded locks churning around the dungeon like a tempest. I was halfway up the stairs when Miss Always leaped to her feet. She charged after me, but Countess Carbunkle was quick, thrusting the cane forward and catching her ankles. I wanted to cheer when Miss Always fell on her face.

"Get her!" she thundered to her little henchmen.

The stone's urgent rhythm synced with the beats of my pounding heart as I reached the top step. The narrow passageway was now heaving like a boat on a stormy sea. I felt a lock grab my leg. But not for long. The walls of the narrow passageway began to slip away with all the force of a mudslide. The ceiling seemed to melt, falling around me in a torrent of drips. I heard Miss Always scream with rage again. Then Butterfield Park dropped like a curtain. I closed my eyes and let go.

12

My landing was something of a blur. The air buzzed. The
ground trembled. And as I fell toward it, the dark soil cracked,
and a great swarm of trees breached the ground. Trees the color
of snow. They rose up like a ghost army, their branches bare,
until an entire forest loomed before me. Then a thick blanket of
vibrant green moss bled up, covering the forest floor. I tumbled
along the ground at great speed, using my hands to try and stop
myself. But a tree trunk did the job for me. I hit it with a violent
thump, groaning loudly.

I sat up and looked about for any sign of Miss Always—but

the night forest was strangely quiet. The half-moon glowed emerald high above the treetops, lighting the woods in shades of green and blue. While I was confident that I had reached Prospa—exactly where I was, I hadn't a clue.

I got to my feet, my back aching, and began to walk. It seemed rather foolish to hang about. I had only traveled a short distance when I felt the air around me thicken. A faint buzz echoed through the white trees. It didn't take a genius to work out what was happening. I took off. Running through the woodlands as fast as my legs would carry me. The buzzing became a roar, and the air seemed to crackle and pop.

"Find her—she cannot have gone far!" It was Miss Always. No great shock there. Then she gave a savage war cry. The ground trembled. Then I heard the unmistakable sound of locks, an army of them, trampling the forest in every direction. But I pushed on, running at speed until . . . until the ground was no longer beneath my feet. Something flew around me, catching me in its web. Before I even had time to scream, I was rising rapidly toward the treetops.

Being caught in a net is a nasty business. You are wrapped within a cage of thick rope, hanging from a frightfully high tree branch. Which wasn't ideal. But there were advantages. I was able to look down and see Miss Always and her locks roaming the woods, hunting for me.

"She *has* to be here," declared Miss Always, turning her head this way and that. "Find her!"

The locks swept through the white woods, darting between the trees at tremendous speed. As I swung back and forth above their heads. I had feared it was Miss Always's net that I was entangled in. But if it was, she seemed to have forgotten.

It occurred to me that if the net didn't belong to Miss Always, then perhaps I should be more concerned about who it *did* belong to. An ill-willed giant perhaps. Did Prospa have giants? I wasn't sure. There was a steady breeze blowing through the treetops, making the net sway rather hypnotically. After a while, Miss Always and her pint-sized goons departed, off to search deep into the forest. By then my eyes had grown rather heavy. So I shut them for a spell.

"Get ready."

I awoke with a start. The sun was coming up. And through the net, I saw a girl perched beside me. "Get ready," she said again.

"Get ready for what?" I asked, rubbing my eyes.

It was then that I saw the blade in her hand. It was raised overhead, right where the net knotted together, fixed to the tree branch. The girl sliced the rope like butter. And I was plummeting toward the ground, the net tangled around me. My landing was sudden. And firm. But not fatal. In fact, the ground beneath me was rather supple.

I did not realize it at the time—for I was too busy kicking and struggling to free myself from the wretched net—but I had landed in a cart loaded with straw. Another set of hands appeared from overhead and helped untangle me from the rope.

"Who are you?" said a boy rather sternly. "Where are you from?"

"I'm from a place where it's frightfully rude to set traps." My orange dress was soiled, a tear on the left sleeve. "Speak up—do you deny trapping me?"

"It's my net," said the boy proudly. "But it's for catching food, not girls."

"Pigs and rabbits, mostly," said the girl who had cut the rope. She jumped from the tree onto the cart. "That sort of thing."

As I caught my breath, I peered at the pair standing above me. They *had* to be brother and sister. Both were whip thin with large brown eyes. Bronzed skin. Wiry hair the color and texture of a hay bale. The boy looked slightly older. The girl had longer tresses.

"Who are you?" said the boy again. "Why are you here?"

"My name is Ivy Pocket, and I am here on most important business," I said, getting to my feet. "Just point me toward Prospa House and I'll be on my way."

"You've escaped, haven't you?" said the girl gravely.

"We'll have to report her," said the boy to his sister.

Then he lunged, grasping my wrist, and pulled me from the cart. I reached for the only weapon in sight—a short rake at the side of the barrow—and whacked him in the arm. He yelped, and a valley of blood rose up on his skin. "That hurt!" he hollered.

"I should hope so," I said, flicking straw from my dress. "What sort of boy goes around trying to report perfectly innocent girls? It's unseemly."

"If you've escaped from Prospa House, we have to tell," said the girl. "If we don't . . . we just have to, that's all."

"I'm not running *from* Prospa House," I told them. "I'm running *to* it."

The boy narrowed his gaze, looking me up and down. "You don't look like you've got the Shadow to me."

"That's because I don't, you trap-setting scallywag." The wound on his arm looked rather severe—he had his hand clutching the cut, blood oozing from between his fingers. "I'm sorry for hurting you, though it's entirely your own fault." I sighed. "But I can help."

The boy looked doubtful. "Help how?"

"If you'll assist me in collecting a few ingredients, I'll show you."

There was some reluctance to trust me. A small amount of hostile suspicion. But eventually my trappers saw sense and agreed to help gather the necessary ingredients. As we walked through the woods, which shimmered a golden brown in the morning light, I told them of my natural remedies. I had considered mending his wound the same way I had healed Miss

Always's wrist back at Butterfield Park, but I felt the less they knew about me, the better.

I collected the necessary ingredients—the stems of a dozen wildflowers, a pinch of moss, the sap of a tree. It was something of a surprise when the girl pulled out her knife and pierced one of the white trunks and I saw sap, rich and red as blood, seep from it.

"Now all I need is half a spoonful of curdled milk," I declared. "For best results, I usually require a small handful of unicorn droppings, but we will just have to make do."

The girl frowned. The boy grabbed his cart.

"Come," he said.

I discovered that the pair were indeed brother and sister— and their names were Lily and Amos Winter. We walked for a mile or two, past a stream and into a clearing. There I found a modest farmhouse and stable. As luck would have it, Amos's cow had dropped dead two weeks before, and they were still using the last of her milk—which was delightfully lumpy.

We sat in the cool of the barn, sunlight slipping between the wood panels, and I told Amos to stick out his arm as I mixed the ingredients together. With the addition of the milk, it made a wondrously thick ruby-colored paste.

"Smells rotten," said Amos.

"Sure does," said Lily, holding her nose.

I heaped a generous helping onto his arm, covering the wound completely. Then I told him to leave it for ten minutes and prepare to be astounded.

"What made you think I had escaped from Prospa House?" I asked, taking a seat atop a barrel of oats.

"The girl," said Lily.

"The girl?"

Amos nodded. "We found her in the woods about six months back. She'd escaped from Prospa House—was being hunted by them locks."

"We hid her here in the barn," said Lily, biting on her bottom lip. "But they found her and took her back." She shook her head. "I've never heard someone scream like that before."

I gasped suddenly. The vision. The one I had seen in the stone—of Rebecca being chased by a pack of rabid locks through the white woods. "Did this girl tell you her name?"

Lily nodded sadly. "Rebecca. Her name was Rebecca."

"Blimey," I heard myself say. "I know her. She is why I am bound for Prospa House. I have come to bring her home."

"No one gets out of Prospa House," said Amos. "Not alive, anyhow."

"Of course she is getting out," I said, jumping from the barrel. "I have been there before, I know where she is being kept and . . . she *must* be there." I was suddenly troubled by doubts.

"What will I do if she has been taken somewhere else?"

"You can bet she's still in Prospa House," said Amos firmly. "I have a friend who works in the city—he said the souls stopped coming a few weeks back. Justice Hallow wouldn't waste a remedy, even one who causes trouble."

"What color?" said Lily suddenly.

I frowned. "What *color*?"

"You said you have been to Prospa House," said the girl. "What color were the doors where they were keeping Rebecca?"

"Yellow. Why?"

"That's because she was a new soul," said Amos. "Remedies grow weaker with each healing—that's why they're moved to other floors." He looked down at his arm and touched the paste, which had started to dry and crack. "By now I'd guess she'd be on green. Or purple."

"How many colors are there?" I asked.

"Purple is the last," said Lily softly.

I thought of Mr. Blackhorn, whom I had discovered on my last trip to Prospa House. His room had been a vile shade of purple. "Prospa House is a wicked place," I declared.

"Yes," said Amos, "but the Shadow is worse."

"Papa was taken when I was just a baby, and Mama got sick last summer." Lily's voice quivered. "It showed on her hands first, the skin turning dark gray. Then it spread until her whole body was covered."

"I'm sorry," I said.

"She wasn't in pain," said Amos firmly. "The Shadow is lethal, but it doesn't hurt."

Then the boy stuck his arm in a bucket of water and washed off the paste. We all gathered around to look. Underneath my natural remedy, the wound had healed—it was still rather red, but the cut had closed and mended.

"How'd you do that?" said the boy, his face a mask of wonder.

"Who are you, Ivy Pocket?" said Lily.

I smiled. "One of a kind, dear."

"The Shadow took them all."

"Who?"

"The Queen and her kin," said Lily.

"Wiped out the whole bloodline," said Amos. "That's why

we have Justice Hallow and her kind running things now—been that way for two centuries."

"It's Justice Hallow who decides who can see the remedies," said Lily. "The healings are meant to favor neither rich nor poor, but it doesn't work that way. Not at Prospa House."

We had been walking for nearly an hour through the white woods. Amos and Lily thought it best to keep clear of the farmhouse, in case Miss Always came looking. I noticed a set of train tracks snaked through the forest, winding between the bare trees.

"Leads straight to the city," said Amos, pointing to the tracks. "If you want to reach Prospa House, that's how."

"She can't!" said Lily, her voice carrying across the woodlands. "Anyone caught riding the train without a ticket is executed. And even if she could get on board, they'd take one look at her and know she didn't have the Shadow—she'd be done for."

"Then she'd better not get caught." Amos flashed me a crooked smile. "Though be sure you're on the red train, *not* the white."

"What's the difference?" I asked.

"The red train carries the rich folk to Prospa House so they can be healed," said Lily. "The white train takes the sick away from the city so . . ."

"So they can die out of sight," said Amos bitterly. "It's against regulations to have the Shadow in the city—folks have to get on the white train as soon as they fall ill."

"There's a hospital in the highlands, and those with the Shadow are taken there." Lily pushed the hair from her face. "They don't ever come out."

Which was frightfully depressing, on the one hand. But thrilling news on the other. All I had to do was get on the red train, and it would take me straight to Prospa House.

"Where can I get on?" I said brightly. "Point me to the nearest station."

"The closest one is miles away," said Lily.

"That's monstrously inconvenient," I said. "How do you people get about?"

"Horses, of course," said Amos, looking slightly vexed. "Or on foot."

"The train line is only for the sick," explained Lily. "Besides,

Justice Hallow doesn't encourage the villagers to venture into the city."

"We're too scruffy for her liking," huffed Amos.

I let out a rather irritable sigh. "So how do I get onto the red train?"

"You can't, Ivy!" Lily looked as if she were about to burst into tears. "It's like I said, if you got caught, they'd——"

"It comes through these parts around three every day," interrupted Amos. "It slows down when it comes round the verge—if you're fast, I reckon that's where you could jump on." He looked at me with great interest. "Are you fast, Ivy?"

"Terrifically fast. Monstrously quick. I once ran out of options in two minutes flat."

The brother and sister looked at each other and shrugged. Probably a local custom.

With time to kill until the afternoon train, we had set off farther into the woods—bound for where, I did not know. Amos and Lily knew the forest well and were able to lead me through a web of thick scrub and rocky hills, until we reached our destination.

"This is how we earn our keep," said Amos proudly.

"It's tiresome work," said Lily with a sigh, "but it pays."

We stood on the edge of an enormous cliff, its silvery white stone sparkling under the midday sun. Across the canyon stood another cliff. And far below us, a river raged, separating the two. "It's very beautiful," I said, "but how do you earn money from such a place?"

Amos crouched down, pulling a small hammer from his pocket. He pounded on the rock at his feet. It crumbled easily. Then he picked up a few of the gleaming fragments and ground them in his hands. "These are called slumber rocks."

"The powder is used by physicians," said Lily. "A small pinch is enough to put a patient to sleep—for operations and that sort of thing."

"It's harmless enough," said Amos. "Just fogs the memory a little."

Of course! That must be the strange powder Miss Frost had blown in my face on the carriage ride to Weymouth.

"If you're *really* going to Prospa House," said Amos, walking over to me with his fist clenched, "then this might come in handy."

He opened his hand and let a handful of silvery slumber rocks slide into the pocket of my dress. I wanted to thank him. But didn't get the chance. For a figure now loomed before us.

"Goodness," said Miss Always, pulling a dagger from her belt, "what a lovely surprise."

"Leave her alone!" shouted Lily.

"Not possible." Miss Always waved the dagger in her hand at Lily and Amos. "I only want the girl. Give her to me, and I will let you live."

Lily, Amos, and I were corralled at the edge of the cliff. And Miss Always stood between us and the woodlands. To reach safety, we would have to go through her.

"I surrender," I told her. "Let them go and I will come with you at once."

Miss Always didn't looked entirely convinced. "Is that so?"

"Yes, dear, it is."

"Don't do it," whispered Amos. "I can fight—I know how."

"As can I," said Lily.

"That's very kind, but it's best if I give myself up. Miss Always is destined to outsmart me, I can see that now."

I walked toward the villainous hag. She was watching me cautiously. Her dagger still drawn. When I got close, her eyes danced. "You grow smarter by the minute, Ivy."

"I quite agree." Then I drew back and kicked her as savagely as I could in the leg. Miss Always howled like a wolf under a full moon and stumbled back. Which is when I pushed her over. "Hurry!" I called to Amos and Lily.

The pair started running, darting around Miss Always. I was already charging toward the woodlands when I heard Lily scream. I skidded to a halt and looked back. Miss Always had sprung up and had Lily in her grip, her arm snaked around the girl's neck, the dagger at her throat.

"What a clever trick, Ivy," said Miss Always, panting.

"Amos!" cried Lily.

"Let her go!" shouted Amos. He began walking slowly toward Miss Always, who was now backing away toward the cliff edge.

"I will let the girl go as soon as Ivy gives herself up." Miss Always turned her steely gaze upon me. "Understood?"

"Yes." And this time I meant it. Lily and Amos were not a part of this fight. Which is why I raised my arms in surrender. "I will go willingly. You have my word."

I was just a few feet from the murderous hag when Lily bit down hard on her captor's arm. Miss Always yelped and pulled her hand away. But it was a victory of the temporary kind. As Lily took off, Miss Always lunged for her, grabbing the back of Lily's dress. But her footing slipped on the sparkling rocks, and Miss Always staggered, dragging Lily back with her. The girl stumbled, rolled once across the white stones, and swept over the ledge.

"Lily!" shouted Amos.

Miss Always grabbed for the girl, grasping her hand. Amos and I ran to the cliff edge. The young girl had a look of terror in her eyes but made no sound. I saw the strain on Miss Always's face as she tried to pull Lily back up. Amos reached for his sister's arm. Together he and Miss Always began to pull her up. They were winning the struggle.

Lily's body inched up, bit by bit. Miss Always gritted her teeth and pulled with great force. Amos grunted. And Lily moved. But as she did, the brittle rock beneath her began to crumble. They pulled harder. But the ledge snapped, breaking off like a biscuit. Lily's arms slipped from Amos and Miss Always's grasp. And she fell.

Her scream tore across the canyon. I didn't watch. I couldn't. But I heard Amos begin to weep, and Miss Always let out a ragged breath. The shock, the horror, seemed to squeeze the very breath from my body. It was too awful! Too beastly!

I walked about for a moment. In a daze. But it was brief. For Amos lunged for Miss Always. But the wicked creature was too quick. She flung the boy across the bluff like a rag doll. "I had no wish to kill the girl," she said evenly, "and I have no wish to kill you—but I will if you get in my way. Ivy is the one I want, so let me pass."

In the distance I heard the roar of a steam engine and a whistle blowing. It distracted me for a moment, so I did not notice that Amos clutched a white rock. I turned back just as he threw it at Miss Always. It struck her in the head. She dropped to her knees and groaned.

The boy began to run, grabbing my arm as he passed. We

were now bolting into the woodlands. Through the trees I saw a dozen locks darting about.

"I will distract them," said Amos, his face ghostly pale and stained with tears. He stifled a sob, his whole body shaking, and pointed straight ahead—and I saw a red train snaking through the forest like a blood serpent. "It slows as it comes around the verge." His voice was rasping and faint. "I wish you luck."

"I'm so sorry about Lily," I called out. "If it weren't for me—"

"Run, Ivy," he shouted. "Run!"

So I did. Amos peeled away as two locks flew at us. I punched one in the head and then, jumping onto a fallen tree, leaped over the other. My eyes scanned the woodlands and quickly found the red train again. It had begun to slow. I quickened my speed. From out of nowhere a lock lunged, knocking me to the ground. Hissing violently, with talons unfurled, it flew at my neck. I rolled quickly, and the hooded fiend crashed to the ground. Then I jumped up and kicked it squarely in the chest.

I spotted the red train and took off. It had indeed slowed as it took the sharp rim of the mountain. I skidded down a ravine, my boots churning the dirt like a plow, and bolted straight ahead. By then the last carriage was roaring past me. I had no choice but to jump.

My hands gripped the railing as I found my footing on the metal steps. I climbed up and tried the door. It opened! With the wind roaring around me, I stepped into the carriage. Closed the door behind me. Lily. Poor Lily! The memory of her slipping from the cliff played over in my mind. But I knew that if I was to rescue Rebecca, I had to push such thoughts away. My plan was rather simple. To stay on the train until it delivered me to Prospa House.

But there were difficulties.

The first became clear when I looked through the glass doors into the cabin. It was quite a sight—plush blue chairs, overhead lamps, silver knobs, and thick carpet. All the seats were taken, save for the last one on my right. A woman sat there alone, reading a book. I was perfectly comfortable in my little alcove and could have stayed there for the entire journey. If not for the conductor. He was dressed in a dark suit with brass buttons and a regulation hat. And he held a clipboard and was going from seat to seat, checking off passenger names.

While the conductor didn't trouble me, the maid who appeared from the other end of the carriage certainly did. "Afternoon tea," she announced. "Afternoon tea will now be served."

The tea trolley was a terrific problem. For it was right beside me, the decanter puffing little clouds of steam that fogged up the window. The maid was nearly at the door when I dropped down. Parted the curtain around the trolley and crawled underneath. There wasn't a huge amount of room among the dirty teacups, stacks of plates smeared with cream and cake, and stained napkins. But I managed.

I heard the door open. Then the trolley lurched to one side as it was turned around and pushed through the narrow door. The maid moved slowly down the long aisle, dispensing hot drinks and desserts with good cheer. I peeked through the curtain and stole a look about. The passengers were smartly dressed. As rich and important looking as Lily had described.

There were a few people playing cards. Others reading. A girl played with a doll. While a boy busied himself with some paper and pastels. But what really caught my attention and made me shudder was how these finely dressed travelers *looked*—their skin was as gray as a thundercloud. An ashen shadow was cast upon their flesh. They weren't all the same—some were grayer than others. But all were marked by the Shadow.

"When you've finished serving," came a voice (I guessed it was the conductor), "make sure you give the trolley a thorough cleaning, top to bottom, you hear? It was in a shocking state last week, and I won't have it."

"Yes, Mr. Truman," came the meek reply.

Which was terrifically unhelpful. I would be exposed the moment she parted the curtain. Therefore I needed a way out. And being tremendously brilliant, a plan sprang to mind. It was frightfully last minute. And at its heart was the boy drawing with pastels. When the trolley passed by him—his mother ordered a cup of tea and a slice of cream cake for her son—I slipped my hand out rather swiftly and took a pastel from the folded table. If the boy noticed, he didn't sound the alarm.

When the maid reached the end of the aisle, I crawled out from under the cart and darted through the door. Crab walked straight toward the lavatory. Entered, locking the door behind me. Pulled out a handful of tissues from a lovely gold box. Turned on the tap. Plugged the sink. Then got to work.

It was really very simple. I dropped the gray pastel into the sink of shallow water and, using the end of a toilet brush, crushed it into a paste. Then used the tissues to smear the concoction over my face and neck, hands and arms. The experiment was a stunning success. In no time at all I looked just as afflicted as the rest of the passengers—my face a sickly gray, the dreaded stain of the Shadow upon my skin.

When I slipped out of the lavatory, I peered into the next carriage. It was full. So I headed back the way I had come. There was no other choice. By that time, the conductor was near the second-to-last row, clipboard in hand. I slipped past him, smiled at an elderly couple, and took the only spare seat in the carriage. Beside an elegant woman. She had dark hair and green eyes, and her skin was hideously ashen. She glanced up from her novel— but made no comment.

"Where did *you* come from?" It was the conductor. Eyeing me with suspicion.

"The lavatory," I said. "I get frightfully gassy on long journeys."

"What's your name?"

"What's your name?" I shrugged. "Haven't a clue, dear— though I'm suspect it's something like Wilbur or Bob."

"Very amusing," said the conductor. "What's your name? And I've no time for games."

"Well . . . my name . . ." Of course I could come up with a name, but the conductor certainly wouldn't find it on his list. I kept thinking of Lily's warning—the punishment for stowing away on the red train was death. "I . . . my name is . . ."

"Grace Havisham," said the woman sitting next to me. "I do apologize for my daughter—she has a habit of taking a joke rather too far."

The conductor frowned. "I thought we were one passenger down."

"Grace Havisham," said the woman again. "You will see it on the manifesto."

"Yes, well . . ." The silly man looked slightly bashful. "I was told the child died last night."

The woman touched her red lips. Glanced briefly out of the window. Then fixed the conductor with a calm gaze. "Does she look dead to you?"

The conductor looked disheartened. "Must be a mistake, I suppose."

"I'm sure it happens from time to time," said my glorious protector.

"Of course it does," I said, the relief washing over me. "Now shuffle off, you silly man, and leave us to suffer in peace."

When the conductor had departed, flicking through his clipboard, the woman smiled gently at me but made no further remark. I wanted to thank her, of course, but something in the way she turned back to her book told me not to. That I would be intruding.

I felt a chill in my bones, thinking of what lay ahead. It would not be easy. Instinct told me that finding Rebecca and bringing her home would require every ounce of strength, skill, and courage that I possessed. But at least I was on my way. Bound for Prospa House.

The whistle blew as the train roared through a tunnel

carved into the mountainside. The elderly couple sitting in front exchanged a few words—about the arrival time and whatnot.

"Not long now," remarked the old man to his wife.

I closed my eyes. The words repeating in my head. Not long now.

13 *

"Where are we going?"

"Don't you ever tire of questions?"

We were trudging through the snow between towering oak trees. My mother and I. She had ahold of my hand—hers felt awfully damp—and was striding just in front of me. When I looked up at her, the sun flared in my eyes, swallowing her face in a glaring light. I wanted desperately to see her—to see her and recognize her. But as we slogged through the thick blanket of snow, all I could manage were glimpses. The length of her nose, her cheek dripping with perspiration, the red blotches on her neck.

"Where are we going?" I asked again.

My mother's breaths were heavy, her chest rattled. "I don't know, Ivy."

"I'm tired," I groaned.

"Come now, a strong girl like you?" She wiped her eyes with the sleeve of her dress. "We'll find a place . . . somewhere to rest awhile."

The train rattled violently, and I woke gasping.

"A nightmare?" The woman sitting next to me smiled faintly. "My daughter, Grace, was the same—always dreaming of things that lurked in the shadows."

I yawned and stretched. "I was dreaming of my mother. Which is rather thrilling, as I know nothing about her. I don't even know what she looks like, and even in the dream it's proving rather tricky—but I feel a breakthrough is *awfully* close."

"Oh." A long pause. The woman glanced down the length of the carriage. "You are a stowaway, are you not?"

I nodded.

"It shall be our secret," said the woman. "I am Mrs. Havisham."

"Is your daughter . . . ? What I mean is . . ."

"She fought very hard but could not hold on." The woman's green eyes swept over my face. "How long have you had it?"

"Not long at all. It came on very suddenly and whatnot."

"It always does." She patted my hand. "I am very pleased that my daughter's place will not be wasted. Have you been to the city before?"

"Not really. What's it like?"

My traveling companion raised her gloved hand and motioned to the window. "See for yourself."

The woodlands went right to the city's edge. Then stopped. Not thinning out gradually—just stopping. One moment we were in the white woods, the next a vast city spread out before us.

We passed through a great avenue of pavilions that curved and then straightened and then curved again. The shop fronts sparkled like new pennies, all in yellow stone—some were bowed with timber slats, while others had windows that slid away (to where I didn't know), making the grocer or cobbler's store part of the footpath. Above the shop fronts were apartments, a few with birdcages out on the ledge; others hung tapestries from the windows depicting a large white building that I knew to be Prospa House.

While the shops were open, there were very few people about—a handful of women wearing bright dresses that showed their ankles. One pushing a stroller. A man walking a cat on a silver leash. What I *didn't* see were horses or carriages or carts.

"How do people get about?" I asked Mrs. Havisham. "Where are the carriages?"

"The city frowns upon such things," she replied. "All deliveries must be made before seven each morning or after ten at night. Walking is strongly encouraged."

"But why? And what if you have a sore leg, or no legs at all?"

"Justice Hallow believes in the value of exercise. In the villages and farms it is different, but *here* Justice Hallow prizes good health above all else."

The train swept past the pavilions, through an arched dome with four red marble pillars, and into an avenue dotted with enormous windowless buildings. "There is the city council and the bank," explained Mrs. Havisham helpfully. "And over there is the training camp for Justice Hallow's guards."

The buildings were made of pale brown brick with mirrored columns ribbed along the front, flaring madly in the sunlight. And at the sides of each building were brightly colored paintings and signs. The first showed a rather pretty girl with fair hair and a fetching blue dress. But she wasn't smiling. Instead, she was looking with much distress at a spot of gray upon her arm. And below her, blazed in thick white letters, VIGILANCE, ALWAYS.

Another contained no picture, just letters written black on white—

WATCH FOR THE SIGNS

Sudden Weariness

Chills

Gray Patches on the Skin

Proceed Immediately to the White Train—

Leaving Every Hour on the Hour

"Do not worry," said Mrs. Havisham. "Though it is an offense to be ill, we are here at the invitation of Justice Hallow."

"Why should a person be sent away just for getting ill?"

"No one really understands how the Shadow is spread, which makes people rather fearful. Those that are well live in mortal fear of the sick—even though there is no proof that the Shadow is contagious. Justice Hallow wishes to preserve the city as a jewel where the Shadow cannot trespass."

"Seems bonkers to me."

"You are not the only one who wishes things were different." Mrs. Havisham pointed to a building across the silvery boulevard. "These signs are popping up all over the kingdom."

I looked and saw a three-story building with lovely patterned ironwork. At the side was another WATCH FOR THE SIGNS poster. Except *this* sign had been painted over in red with the words THE DUAL IS COMING! Two men in matching orange overalls were already painting over the message.

"They cover them as soon as they appear," said Mrs. Havisham. "Some say it is a protest group, while others believe that the message is true. Either way, people are talking openly— though who is behind it, I cannot think."

Well, I could. For I knew *exactly* who was behind those signs. Miss Always. That mad cow was spreading the word that I had come to save the day. At one time I might have believed it myself. But now it seemed like dangerous nonsense. Rebecca was all that mattered.

Through the window I spotted a woman in an olive gown running at great speed. Running and pointing. Behind her was an elderly man. He was on his knees. Head bowed. Looking with horror at his hand—half of the flesh, from his fingers to his wrist, was a sickly gray. A few of the passengers muttered and shook their heads.

The train crossed a small bridge suspended by wire cables, then swung around a row of terraces before passing into a vast concourse paved in pale green bricks. On one side was an enormous white building ten stories high. Which caused a great deal of pointing and chatter.

"Prospa House," said Mrs. Havisham.

I had only seen the building from the other side, which is why I hadn't recognized it. There were massive columns, arched windows, and a vast terrace bordered by a set of stairs running the length of the building. At the very top was a clock tower capped by a spire.

At the end of the concourse was an immense lake, its emerald water sparkling. Dozens of copper water pumps were set into the stone border surrounding the lake. Neatly trimmed

227

trees flanked Prospa House and ran all the way to the water's edge. The trees had white branches. Bloodred leaves. And bright yellow fruit shaped like an oval. Many fruits had dropped and were scattered about. And a few of the well-dressed folk promenading were sweeping them up.

"What sort of fruit is that?" I asked.

My traveling companion gave me a strange look. "You don't know?"

"Of course I do—the name just escapes me at present."

Mrs. Havisham smiled kindly. "Ovid berries grow all over the kingdom. The taste is reported to be delicious, though eating them will cost you your life."

"Then why aren't the trees cut down?" I asked.

"As a reminder to be vigilant," came the reply. "Justice Hallow makes it the job of *all* who live in the city to keep the fruit far from the reach of children or animals or the great lake—as you know, the water there contains healing minerals and is prized throughout the kingdom." She sighed with little enthusiasm. "We must all play our part."

The train began to slow. I gazed out across the concourse and saw a large monument. It was set upon an octagonal platform towering so high above the city it seemed to touch the clouds. The statue was made of solid silver, and what it depicted made me gasp.

"I don't believe my eyes," I whispered.

Mrs. Havisham laughed. "Have you not seen pictures of the monument?"

I shook my head. There atop the statue was an enormous, glittering Clock Diamond. A perfect replica of the stone beneath my dress. I practically sat on Mrs. Havisham's lap to get a closer look as the train swept past. At the base, carved into the honey-colored stone, was the inscription BY THE STONE WE HAVE HOPE, BY THE REMEDIES WE ARE HEALED.

The carriage lurched sideways, taking a sharp corner. The engine hissed up a storm as we came to a stop. Mrs. Havisham closed her book. "We have arrived."

"Please do take a seat, ladies and gentleman, boys and girls," announced a bland-looking chap in a crisp black suit. "This will not take long at all."

We were in a rather plush waiting room—about seventy of

us. It had thick carpet, bleached paneled walls, a vaulted ceiling painted with half-moons. Black Suit went along checking our names and issuing each of us with a card. They were all about the size of a library card but not all of the same color.

I wasn't the only one who noticed.

"Why are these cards different colors?" said a middle-aged man whose skin was a deep gray. He coughed and clutched his chest. "I paid good money—"

"Now, sir, I must stop you right there," interrupted Black Suit. "Everyone is equal here at Prospa House. The remedies are all of the same high quality. The color system just ensures that you all get your turn."

The sick man looked doubtful. And thanks to Amos and Lily, so did I. The card I held in my hand was yellow (as was Mrs. Havisham's). That meant we were to be healed by a new soul. Which was terrible luck!

"Please come forward and stand behind the line corresponding to the color of your card," was our next instruction. I told Mrs. Havisham to go ahead. That I was tying my boots. But the truth was, I needed to think. I had a yellow ticket. But it was unlikely that Rebecca would still be considered a new soul. Green or purple—that was Amos's guess. If I had any hope of finding my friend, I would need to act swiftly.

A set of white doors opened, and the lines began to move. We entered a corridor and began peeling off into several different hallways—each a different color. I scanned the lines. Some folks clutched purple tickets, others blue, green, or yellow. It was a great risk—not knowing for sure what color Rebecca was now—but I was prepared to chance it. I did a quick sidestep and elbowed the sickly man who had asked the question. He held a purple ticket in his hand.

"It's all lies, of course," I said.

"What is?" he said, coughing.

"That the system's fair." I held out my yellow ticket. "I happen to know yellow is the pick of the bunch. Now, I only have a mild case of the Shadow, while *you* look like a man on the very brink of death."

His brow buckled. "What of it?"

"Well, I'd be happy to swap tickets." I shrugged. "Only if you wish to, of course."

He hesitated. Just for a moment. Then snatched the ticket from my hand.

"Follow me, please," said a fresh-faced young damsel in a plain dress. "It's rather a long walk, but there will be tea and refreshments at the other end."

The hallway was narrow and long, its lavender walls sweeping up to a pointed arch. Gas lamps, hung from chains, hissed above our heads. I was the last in a line of twelve or so. No one spoke. They just walked silently, perhaps filled with hope that their suffering would soon be over.

The young man in front of me wheezed a great deal. His shoulders were hunched. The back of his thin neck pallid and gray. At the end of the corridor, we passed into a comfortable chamber. The tall windows were of frosted glass, but the light poured in, making the space cheerier than it might otherwise have been. A dozen wingback chairs were arranged around a low table, filled with books, magazines, and newspapers. A large purple curtain covered the far end. A door in the corner seemed to be connected to some sort of pantry or kitchen. For as soon as we entered the room, two maids came out bearing pots of fresh tea and coffee.

As I sat down, I scanned the room. There was no sign of Rebecca or any other remedies.

"Good afternoon. I am Professor Finsbury." An older man strode into the chamber, wearing a pale lab coat. He had wispy

...Swap ticket...?

dark hair plastered to his pointed head, thin lips, and a mustache that lacked commitment.

He babbled on about the great work done at Prospa House, about their compassionate treatment of the remedies and how Justice Hallow was quite possibly the greatest woman who ever lived.

"Where are the remedies?" I said when he paused to take a breath. "I don't mean to hurry you, dear, but we're dying of the plague over here."

Professor Finsbury bobbed up and down on his feet. Tried to smile. "Your impatience is perfectly understandable, my young friend. There are just a few things each of you must be aware of before we can begin." He walked to the back of the room and stood with his finger poised on a shiny gold button set into the wall. "During the healings, there is to be no communication with the remedies. None at all. If you violate this rule, the healing will be terminated and the offender charged with crimes against the kingdom."

Which was rather harsh. I sat forward in my seat. Anticipating the moment the curtain would part and I would see the remedies. How I prayed Rebecca would be one of them!

"Do they suffer?" said a frail-looking woman sitting in the chair next to me. "I heard that the remedies find healing very painful."

"Incorrect," said Professor Finsbury. "It is true the remedies experience a *slight* stinging sensation during the process, but it is very mild." He cleared his throat. "Now, let us begin."

He pressed the button. A faint whirring sound rang out as the curtain rapidly parted to reveal the other half of the chamber. This is what I saw: two guards standing at the back, heads shaved, wearing ghastly orange coats. Batons and daggers at their waist. In the middle of the room was a row of six plain chairs. And in front of each chair was a contraption of iron and wood. It was rather like a table or a workbench with an embroidered screen blocking the view behind it—each tapestry depicted the white woodlands of Prospa. Cut into the bottom of the tapestry was an iron bracket held by a bolt. And shackled within each bracket was a hand. Just a hand. No sign of the person connected to it— for they were hidden behind the embroidered screen. I wanted to cry out. To tear down those tapestries. To bash Professor Finsbury in the head.

"I will select six of you to go first," announced the Professor. "Please take a seat at the healing table—you may sit anywhere you like, it makes little difference."

The remedies made no sound. I scanned the six hands, desperately looking for one that might belong to Rebecca. Which is why I didn't notice Professor Finsbury pointing at me. Not at first. I leaped up and hurried over. A few of the sick were already taking their seats. I peered intently at the disembodied hands. They were of different sizes and colors—the skin so thin and faded it was largely transparent. One was large and brown. Another thin and slender. Only one caught my eye. It was small. Lightly freckled. Trembling. Rebecca. It had to be!

There were only two chairs left. One in front of Rebecca's hand, and the other, a rather coarse and lumpy set of fingers. The sickly fellow I had been walking behind in the corridor was heading for Rebecca. I moved swiftly, knocking him with my shoulder and grabbing the seat. This elicited a few gasps from the others. I responded by poking out my tongue and discreetly blowing a raspberry.

"When I say the word," said the Professor, pacing back and

forth behind us, "you are to reach out with both hands and touch the remedy. There is no need to squeeze or press tightly—just touching the remedy is enough to begin the healing." He stopped at the back of my chair. "Do not move your hand from the remedy until I tap you on the shoulder."

I wanted desperately to call out to Rebecca. To know if it was really her on the other side of that screen. The shackle around her wrist was a problem. As was the bolt. My forehead began to perspire. So I wiped it quickly with the sleeve of my dress.

"You may now touch your remedy," instructed Professor Finsbury.

My fingers trembled as they moved toward the hand before me. I held my breath. Then touched the translucent flesh of her fingers. And I heard her gasp. Her fingers curled around mine. It was Rebecca, I was sure of it!

Around me there were a great many groans and moans. I glanced over and saw the man in the chair next to me shuddering. The gray of his flesh rippling like the surface of a windy pond. Then his ashen skin began to fade, washed away by a healthy glow. Behind the screens there were noises too. Shudders of pain. Stifled sobbing. Whimpers aplenty. If healing the sick was as painless as the Professor described, why did these poor souls sound like wounded animals?

"Help is at hand, dear," I whispered.

"Ivy?" came a fragile voice.

I felt a hand on my shoulder. Professor Finsbury was above me. Looking at my face with growing alarm. He tilted back my head, pulled out his pocket square, and wiped my cheek. Too late I glimpsed the gray smear on the sleeve of my dress from where I had wiped my sweaty forehead. The Professor's eyes bulged as he looked at the pocket square now streaked with gray. He thrust it into the air and hollered, "Guards!"

I jumped up before the Orange Coats reached me and gave Professor Finsbury a mighty shove. Then I ripped the tapestry down with my hands. And there was Rebecca. Fastened into that hideous contraption. Her skin glowed as if the faintest of light blossomed under her flesh. Her wavy blond hair was limp. Her brown eyes sad and vacant.

I pulled on the padlock shackling her arm. It didn't budge.

"She's gone mad!" cried one woman.

"I knew that girl was trouble," declared another.

"Watch out, Ivy!" shouted Rebecca.

I looked up. The two guards were upon me. I ducked, slipping underneath them with great skill—possessing all the natural instincts of a jailbird—and took off. But one of them grabbed a clump of my hair. Pulled on it savagely. Suddenly I reeled back. His fist pulled so tightly on my hair, I feared he would rip it out. Which is when I threw my elbow back and struck him in the belly. He grunted loudly. So I thumped him a second time. He groaned and I pulled free, charging toward the table and picking up a stack of books. Then threw them savagely. I hit the female guard in the face, which was glorious. And got the other one right where it would hurt him most.

The Clock Diamond began to glow beneath my dress, throwing orange about the room. This caused a few more gasps and comments. But I ignored the stone (while the Clock Diamond might allow me to leave Prospa, I had no idea if I could help Rebecca as well).

I turned back and grabbed the biggest book in the pile. Then charged. Kicking one guard in the shin (a personal favorite of mine) and bashing the other in the side of the head with the book. As he fell against the wall, I heard the jangle of the keys at his belt.

"Call for more guards!" shouted Professor Finsbury to a maid. "Now!"

The Professor grabbed me by the neck, squeezing rather savagely. So I elbowed him viciously—landing right in the ribs. He howled, the feeble buffoon, and I thumped him with the book. Then reached for the guard's keys, pulling them from his belt.

"Somebody grab her!" shouted an older man, sick and gray.

"Not me," replied a gangly boy, shaking his head.

"Quick, Ivy!" said Rebecca.

My hands trembled as I fumbled, trying several keys in the thick padlock. At last I heard the magnificent snap of the lock. The bolt popped open. I pulled Rebecca's hand free, and the girl leaped up. "Come, dear!" I shouted.

"Stop them!" cried a maid, clutching a teapot.

We were racing across the room by then. "Just you try," I declared, "and I'll knock your block off."

"Follow me, Ivy!" Rebecca ran through the back door. Into a

kitchen, where a cook and a few maids were milling about. One of them gave a startled cry. But we bolted through in a flash. Rebecca led the way through a series of small hallways, then down a set of metal stairs.

"Where are we going?" I called after her.

"To the very bottom," she called back.

Down and down we went. How many floors I couldn't say. Nor did I understand how Rebecca seemed to know exactly where she was going. All I knew was that we were breaking out of Prospa House. I had found my friend, and we were going home!

As we rounded the small platform between two floors, a guard flew out. Grabbing each of us by the arm. She was a frightfully ugly creature, with a ferocious grip and a snarl upon her lips. "Thought you'd get away, did you?" she hissed. "Thought it was that easy to escape Prospa House, did you?"

Rebecca began to weep. Shaking her head. "Please don't take me back."

"Not your lucky day, is it?" Then she glared at me. "And there's worse in store for you."

"It does sound tempting," I said brightly, my free hand

slipping into my pocket. "But as it happens, I've made other plans." And with that I lifted my fist and blew a handful of slumber rocks into the guard's face. She coughed exactly once, then had the good sense to tumble to the ground. But there was little time to bask in our victory. Up above we heard a great many boots pounding the metal stairs. So we took off again.

"Where are we?"

Rebecca led the way down three more flights. Through two corridors. And finally a spiral staircase concealed behind a wall hanging. We emerged into a windowless chamber. It had lime floors and an arched ceiling made of brick. Stone pillars flanked each corner. Bare walls, moss clustered between the cracks. At the far end were steps leading down to a pool of water—the liquid glowed a vivid gold as if it were lit from within.

I walked to the edge. Looked down. Small ripples brushed the surface, making it hard to see clearly—but there was something at the bottom. It was flesh colored. And large. Bubbling with great regularity, each puff breaching the surface in a little cloud of steam.

"This is how I got here," said Rebecca. "This is where

everyone who wears the Clock Diamond comes out."

"Through the water?"

Rebecca nodded. "I'm not sure what it is exactly, but the first thing I remember after putting on the stone was being pulled from that water."

How wondrously strange!

"I escaped once before," said Rebecca faintly, rubbing her wrist still marked by the shackle. "I managed to trick a guard into letting me walk about the hallway to stretch my legs. Somehow I found my way down here." She pointed to an arched doorway in the far corner. "The passageway leads out to the woodlands. I made it out, Ivy, I was free until . . ."

"Yes, dear, I know." And I did. For Amos and Lily had helped to hide her. Until the locks swept the forest and dragged her back. "Come, let's get out of here before we are discovered."

I ran toward the arched doorway. But Rebecca did not.

"Where will we go?" she asked mournfully.

"Home, dear," I said. "I will take you home."

"I can never go home."

"Says who?"

"Justice Hallow," came the faint reply, "and Professor Finsbury."

"These fatheads lie about everything, don't you know that? Why do you suppose they are telling the truth about this?"

Rebecca thought on that for a moment. "Oh, Ivy, do you think it's possible?"

"I know it. I'm not certain about all the details—though I'm confident the Clock Diamond will provide the solution. We just need to get far from this house of misery first."

Rebecca smiled—the first smile I had seen on her face since Butterfield Park. We joined hands and ran toward the passageway, toward freedom. But the sound of voices coming from that very place sent us racing back. Without a word we flew to the farthest pillar and cowered behind it.

Peeking rather artfully, I saw two Orange Coats come through the arched door, followed by a figure in a dazzling silver cape, embroidered with an intricate pattern of swirls and loops. The figure threw off the cape as she walked. Beneath it was a much simpler dress of brown muslin.

"Justice Hallow," whispered Rebecca timidly.

"Two girls were able to outsmart and outflank my royal guards?" said Justice Hallow, her voice rich and pleasant. "Search this house until you find them—then bring the intruder to my chambers."

"Yes, Justice Hallow," the two brutes said in perfect unison.

Justice Hallow was tall and solid. Her gray hair was shorn close to her head just like the guards. She had piercing blue eyes. Large cheekbones. As for her age, it was impossible to say—her neck was rather wrinkled, yet the skin on her face was as smooth and fair as a butter bean.

The guards marched toward the spiral stairs—terribly close to where we were cowering. Rebecca and I shifted around the side of the pillar to stay out of sight. Which was a grave mistake. For Justice Hallow had slipped quietly behind us. She tapped Rebecca on the shoulder, causing her to cry out as if in pain.

"How lovely to see you again, Rebecca." Justice Hallow allowed a thin smile as she gazed at us both. "Tell me, dearest, who is your friend?"

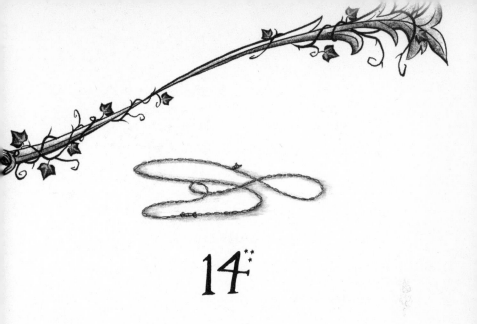

14

The room was beastly and dim. Neither a bed nor a chair. Just four walls. A bucket of water. A tall cabinet in the corner. And a door. The guards had separated us. Rebecca was marched up the stairs, screaming my name. Her cries a hammer to my heart. How close we had come to freedom! I was taken to the first floor and led into a sparsely furnished room. Then locked in this horrid cell.

I did a great deal of yelling. Making threats and such. Demanded that they bring Rebecca to me that instant. They didn't. I slid down the wall and sat. Time slowed to a trickle. I may have dozed. I'm not certain. But a key in the lock roused me. The door opened, pale light spilling across the floor of the dim cell. Then Justice Hallow walked slowly in.

"This cell is connected to my private quarters," she said. "That makes you rather special. I do hope you are comfortable?"

I stood up. "Oh yes, frightfully content."

"That will be all," said Justice Hallow to the guard at the door. When he was gone, the imperious woman came to a stop just inches from my face. "The whole of Prospa House is talking about you."

"Can you blame them? Now I really must insist that you bring Rebecca to me—I want to see that she hasn't been hurt."

"Hurt?" Her chin lifted proudly. "Remedies are revered in this house. They are treated with the greatest kindness and respect."

"Is that why they groan and sob during the healings?"

"I offer hope in a hopeless world," said Justice Hallow calmly.

Then she pulled a cloth from the sleeve of her dress. Walked over to the bucket and dunked it. Then returned to my side. "My guards report that you had a strange glowing object beneath your dress." Justice Hallow began wiping the gray paste from my face rather gently. "I assume it was the Clock Diamond?"

I tried to look baffled. "What on earth is a Clock Diamond?"

Justice Hallow smiled. I thought of Anastasia Radcliff—her very own daughter. Did I dare to mention her name? Something flared inside me like a warning. Telling me to keep quiet. Justice Hallow wrung out the cloth. Then set about cleaning my neck and hands. "I know you have the stone," she said softly, "and I know where you are from. We cannot have you slipping back to your world, now can we?"

She dropped the cloth and felt around my neck for the Clock Diamond—finding only a silver chain and nothing more. When she realized it wasn't there, something wild flashed in her eyes. She proceeded to search my pockets. And my boots.

"Where is it?" she said at last.

"Where's what, dear?"

"Things will go much better if you cooperate."

"I want to see Rebecca."

"She is resting, Ivy."

"How did you know my name? Do you know me?"

Justice Hallow pressed her hands together as if she were praying. "Should I know you?"

"Hard to say—I'm frightfully well known in England. Also Paris and certain pencil shops in Istanbul. Your guards seemed to know who I was the last time I was here."

"Now that *is* strange." She turned and walked to the tall cabinet in the corner. Pulled a key from around her wrist and unlocked the top drawer. Pulled out a small bottle of purple liquid. Slipped it into her pocket. "Who sent you here, Ivy? Was it Miss Frost? Miss Always?" She released a low chuckle. "There was a time when they answered to me—but these days they do as they please."

"Frost and Always?" I shrugged. "Never heard of them."

"Miss Frost and Miss Always have certain *abilities*," said Justice Hallow. "They can travel between worlds under the right moon, and Miss Always can summon a small army of tiny foot soldiers as easily as opening her mouth—these things must seem very impressive to someone from your world." A smile played on her lips. "But the powers they have come from the portal. Did you know that, Ivy? Without it, they would be ordinary women."

I ignored her and tried to look as bored as possible.

"Many years ago, Prospa was a kingdom that indulged in

dark magic," she said, looking around the cell as if it fascinated

her. "The Shadow is proof of how horribly it can go wrong. Ivy, I will ask you one more time—where is the Clock Diamond?"

Being a remarkable sort of girl, I'd had the good sense to hide the stone as soon as I was locked in that tiny chamber— removing the diamond from the chain and slipping it beneath the top of my braid. There was a slight bulge, but nothing that called attention to itself. As hiding places went, it was rather perfect.

"I want to see Rebecca," I said again.

Justice Hallow made no reply. She took a long, calm breath, smiled warmly, and walked from the cell. The door swung shut behind her. I was once again in darkness.

The house was dark and grim. No lights burned in the windows. We stood in the bitter cold looking upon it. "Come, Ivy, we . . ."

My mother coughed violently, doubling over. Drops of blood fell from her mouth into the crisp white snow. She covered her face with a tattered scarf. "It's not the prettiest house, but it will do for the night. I . . . I must rest awhile."

It was a horrid place. Broken windows. Marks on the

walls. Rooms without doors. There were vagrants fast asleep. Men drinking. A woman with no teeth sitting on the stairs, shouting at someone who wasn't there. The smell was simply awful.

We found a room upstairs. There was no fire in the room, and it was bitterly cold. We huddled together beside the cold hearth. My mother kept the scarf pulled up around her cheeks. "I know it's grim," she said, her breaths heavy and slow. She pulled a note from the top of her dress and slipped it into my pocket. "We'll find somewhere better tomorrow. Somewhere nice."

I nodded. But I did not believe her.

A bright light suddenly flashed in my face—and the dream was over. I blinked. Bringing a hand up to shield my eyes. Between my fingers I glimpsed Rebecca standing in the doorway.

"Ivy, are you all right?" The girl rushed into the cell and pulled me to my feet. Hugged me rather feverishly. "Did they hurt you?"

"No, dear, not a bit. How . . . I did not think they would let me see you."

"Nor did I," said Rebecca, the faint glow of her translucent skin throwing light upon the walls. "They woke me up and said we were to go."

I was frowning now. "Go where?"

Two guards marched into the cell, each orange coat cinched at the waist with a thick belt holding two daggers. They grabbed us and marched us from the cell.

"Where are you taking us?" Rebecca asked.

"What is going on?" I demanded to know.

The guard pulling Rebecca looked at us with cool indifference. "You'll find out soon enough."

"Justice Hallow's orders." That's what I heard one of the guards mutter as we were hurried down the spiral staircase. We found ourselves back in the same windowless chamber where we had first been captured. The same lime floors and arched brick ceiling.

"Don't drag your feet!" said one of the guards, pulling Rebecca ahead of me.

"Stay close, Ivy," said Rebecca meekly. "Stay close."

"Don't worry," I called back. "I'm right behind you!"

"Shut up, both of you!"

We were practically pulled through the dank chamber. There was barely enough time for me to glance at the one part of this underground room that had captured my interest. The pool of water. But as we swept past, headed for the arched doorway, I saw that the water wasn't the same vibrant gold. Now it was a murky lilac. And as it bubbled it released a hideous odor—a cross between rotting fish and Mother Snagsby.

"We don't have all night!" said my guard, pushing me through the doorway.

We were marched down a dim passageway. Then out through a thick metal door that led to a walled courtyard, glistening under the emerald moon. There were two carriages waiting by a set of iron gates. Blackened windows. Bolts on the doors.

"They are going to separate us," said Rebecca anxiously.

"Yes, dear, I'm afraid you're right."

But we were both wrong. One of the guards went to the front carriage. The other bundled Rebecca and me into the back carriage—together. The door was shut, and I heard the bolt sliding into place. Then one of the guards gave the word. I heard the carriage in front begin to drive off, and a moment later we followed suit.

There was no light in the cabin, so it was rather helpful that Rebecca gave off a faint glow. In the half light, I could see the uncertainty and the weariness on my friend's face. And I knew that her head was swimming with bad thoughts.

"This is a good thing, Rebecca," I said.

"It *is*?"

"They have taken us together. Is that not a stroke of great fortune?"

But fear pierced the girl's dark eyes. "Why were there two carriages?" she asked. "Where are we going? What are they going to do with us, Ivy?"

"Not a thing," I replied with supreme confidence. "For we are never going to reach our destination."

Rebecca was frowning. So I explained my plan. Then some time flew by. Roughly half an hour. We waited patiently. Finally, with a nod to Rebecca, I began pounding on the roof.

"Please help! Please help!" I hollered as convincingly as I

could (which was *thoroughly* convincing). "Rebecca is dead! She is dead!"

I heard the driver pull up the horses. The carriage slowed. A set of boots hit the road beside us. Then the squeak of the bolt being slid back. The door opened.

"What are you on about?" said the guard.

"Look at her, you neckless fathead," I sobbed wildly. "She was perfectly fine and then she . . . she wilted and fell against the window." I bawled like a troll whose bridge had collapsed. "My dear friend is dead as a doornail!"

Rebecca was perfect. Crumbled in the seat. Utterly still. Eyes closed.

"If she's dead, why's she still glowing?" snarled the guard.

"What's going on down there?" called the driver.

"Nothing at all," shouted the guard. "Just two brats taking us for fools."

Which was the exact moment I swung my leg and kicked him in the chin. Then unfurled my fist and blew the last of the slumber rocks in his face.

I pulled Rebecca up, and we had leaped from the carriage

even before the guard hit the ground. There was a great deal of ruckus and carry-on. The driver cursed us like a drunkard. I saw him jump from the carriage and holler to the carriage in front. But by then we were running like the wind.

The woodlands. We were deep in the woodlands, the white trees standing like an army of ghosts guarding the night. Rebecca and I charged through the moonlit forest. I was in the lead— with no idea where I was going. We just had to get away. Find a place to hide.

Behind us, I heard the driver shouting our names. And a few more voices calling to one another. "Look over there." "They can't have gone far." "Justice Hallow will cut our throats!"

"Why are we stopping?" said Rebecca, panting madly.

I pointed to the tree behind her. It was as white and majestic as the rest. But it had great streaks of black upon the bark. And the trunk was hollowed out. Dead. And a perfect place to hide. For Rebecca, at least.

"What about you, Ivy?" said the girl when I ordered her inside.

She stepped carefully into the hollow. The cavity was small so she had to crouch down. And though she didn't entirely disappear—her skin was too luminous for that—the shadow of the darkened tree trunk made her difficult to spot.

"What about you, Ivy?" said Rebecca again. "Where will you hide?"

"Nowhere, dear. I'm going to circle around and steal the carriage right from under that driver's nose. I recently had cause to steal a wagon, and I'm rather good at it. I will drive back this way and collect you."

"Be careful," said Rebecca. "Oh, Ivy, be careful!"

I nodded and took off. Making a wide loop around the stationary carriages. I pulled up behind a tree. Looked about. The driver was nowhere to be seen. The guard still unconscious on the ground. Just up ahead, the trees thinned out into a clearing. There was a low stone fence. And a millhouse. I saw the guard from the first carriage stalking about. He kicked his unconscious coworker in the leg and cursed his name. Then he climbed onto the carriage and signaled the driver. "We best get on," he grunted, "before we lose *this* one as well."

Something in what he said pulled at the knot already in my stomach. And brought a tingle to my flesh. I cannot say why exactly, and I knew it wasn't the time for such things, but I felt utterly compelled to see who was in the back of that carriage.

The driver whipped the horses, and the carriage took off at speed. I sighed—there was no way I could leave Rebecca and start running after it. Besides, in a short time it would be too far down the dirt road to catch. Except that it wasn't. The carriage turned toward the millhouse.

I glanced around for any sign of our driver. There was none. So I darted through the trees, dropped down, and crept toward the stone fence. The carriage had stopped a few feet from the front door. I peeked over the fence just as the guard jumped down. He unbolted the carriage door. Opened it. Then climbed inside and, a few moments later, climbed out again. Only this time he was carrying something. It was wrapped in a blanket and was about the size and shape of a child. Or a small adult. Were they dead? If so, why would they be locked in a carriage?

The impulse to jump the low fence and take a closer look was overwhelming. But I did not. I simply watched as the guard carried the body toward the house. As he climbed the three steps leading up to the porch, he stumbled. The side of the blanket slipped, revealing a girl—the glow of the green moon a spotlight on her face. And it was all I could do not to cry out. For the girl was me.

15

"She looked just like you?" Rebecca was frowning up a storm. "How can that be possible?"

"It puzzled me too," I replied. "Though the explanation is simple enough. I'm frightfully certain you could travel to a thousand worlds and there would be an Ivy Pocket in each of them—a girl like me is *essential* to civilization."

When I returned to the second carriage, the driver was there—loading the sleeping guard into the back before taking off. It seemed that searching the woodlands for two runaway girls wasn't his cup of tea. So our escape would have to be on foot.

I had run back to collect Rebecca. The girl's skin was so faint I could see the veins, like tiny rivers, tracking over her cheeks. She looked as weary as I felt. But we had little choice but to start running. The driver was certain to sound the alarm, and the woodlands would be swarming with Orange Coats.

As we bolted, I told Rebecca about the girl I had spied being carried into the millhouse.

"Now I understand why those guards recognized me when I first came to rescue you," I said as we ran up the side of a shallow gorge. "They thought I was the girl in the blanket."

Rebecca slowed her pace. "But it does not make sense," she said. "Why would they be keeping someone who looks exactly like you in Prospa House? And why were they moving her tonight?"

We crossed a moonlit road, the bright green moss scarred by carriage wheels. "I'm sure the explanation is monstrously straightforward," I said. "They usually are."

The sound of horses coming down the road sent us both scurrying behind a tree. I heard the galloping hooves slow as they passed by. Then stop. Neither Rebecca nor I was game to sneak a look.

"Ivy Pocket, we know you are out there," shouted a woman. "We work for the Mistress of the Clock, and we have come to bring you to safety."

Rebecca grabbed my arm. "Who is this Mistress of the Clock?"

I smiled brightly. "Miss Frost."

We journeyed on horseback, Rebecca and I each sitting behind a rider. Both were fierce-looking women—one dark, one fair—in brown pants and black coats. They did not say much at all, but they rode with great skill. Jumping two fences and passing through a ravine, the water up to our knees.

Our destination was a weather-boarded farmhouse. Rather modest. A maid greeted us, and we were ushered upstairs to a small chamber—it had whitewashed walls, a bed, a chamber pot, and a great many knickknacks.

"Sit and rest," I told Rebecca, pointing to the bed.

The girl did as I suggested. Taking a seat on the bed. She looked up at me and managed a smile. "Thank you, Ivy," she said. "Thank you for coming even when I told you not to."

I was about to say something terribly modest when a rather unhappy creature marched into the room. "What have you to say for yourself, Miss Pocket?"

Miss Frost regarded me as one might a triple murderer.

"Well, hello to you too, dear," I said.

"I instructed you to stay at the cottage in Weymouth." Miss Frost was pacing about the room in her gray dress, her bright red hair pulled back in a bun, her pale face a mask of ill humor. "So imagine my surprise when I discovered you had fled in the night like a *thief*."

She was referring to the fact that I had dug up the Clock Diamond—the very stone she had hidden from me—and taken it with me. Hideous dingbat!

"It's a good thing I did escape," I said rather proudly. "For Miss Always came that very same evening looking for me. Poor Jago was captured, probably cut up into at least four pieces by now. I wanted to rescue him, but there wasn't time."

"Don't be absurd," said Miss Frost. "Jago fought bravely and managed to escape into the tall grass, where he hid until Miss Always and her henchmen departed."

Which was thrilling news! "When were you there?" I asked.

"I returned from your world just a few hours ago." Miss Frost frowned at me. "You look rather sickly, Miss Pocket."

I practically ran toward the tomato-headed warrior. "Did you see Anastasia? Was she there? Did she——"

"Anastasia and Bertha reached the cottage," interrupted Miss Frost. "As for how she is—fragile is the word I would use. We . . . I spoke at length to her, and I feel sure that in time she will recover." She paused. Sighed. "Rescuing Anastasia could not have been easy. You did very well."

As Miss Frost gave out compliments like a starving man gives out chocolates, I wished to bask in the glow of her approval. But there wasn't time. For I had questions aplenty. "How did you find us?" I dug the diamond out from under the top of my braid and threaded it on the necklace, then fixed it around my neck again. "How did you even know where I was?"

"Bertha told me your plan." Miss Frost did not ask anything

at all about my ingenious hiding place for the stone. Which was infuriating! "As for how we found you, I have an informant at Prospa House who sent word that you had been captured and were being moved tonight." Miss Frost glanced briefly at Rebecca. "Though I am not at all clear why you were *both* moved. I suspect Justice Hallow wished to use your friendship as a bargaining tool."

"A tool for what?" I asked.

Miss Frost started to speak, then stopped herself.

"The water," said Rebecca faintly from across the room.

It took a moment for me to understand what the girl was talking about. "Oh, yes," I said, sitting down on the bed beside Rebecca. "The water in that strange underground chamber stank to high heaven."

To my complete surprise, Miss Frost practically ran at us. Her face knotted most anxiously. "What color was the water?"

"Lilac," was my reply.

Miss Frost began pacing again. Muttering to herself. Something like "What has she done? Could it be true?"

"What are you muttering about, woman?" I demanded to know.

"That pool of water is the portal that allows passage between our worlds," she said. "It was created using an enchanted sun diamond centuries ago, and it is alive. It is alive, Miss Pocket, and as such it can be killed."

"You think the portal is dying?" said Rebecca.

Miss Frost nodded. "I believe it may have been poisoned."

Which reminded me of something. I told Miss Frost about the small vial of purple liquid that I had seen Justice Hallow slip into her pocket. This caused Miss Frost's eyes to narrow and her lips to purse even more violently.

"Then it is true," she said. "I suspect she used the sap of the jugular tree—there were only six of these trees in the entire kingdom, and all were destroyed when dark magic was banished from Prospa centuries ago. But there have always been rumors that Justice Hallow inherited a small bottle of the poison when she became chief justice. It is the only toxin strong enough to kill something as mighty as the portal."

Which suddenly made me think of my conversation with

Justice Hallow. "I have it on good authority that you and Miss Always *need* the portal," I said. "Is that true?"

Miss Frost nodded. "Many moons ago, a royal alchemist discovered that injecting the blood of the portal into your veins gives the user certain *abilities*." She glanced out the small window overlooking the moonlit yard. "If the portal dies, so too does my work as Mistress of the Clock."

"Well, thank heavens for that!" I declared. "Now no one else will have to suffer like Rebecca and all of those other poor souls."

"I . . . I think I might lie down," said Rebecca quietly.

I helped make the girl comfortable. Fluffed the pillow. Wiped her brow. I would have stayed by her side, but Miss Frost practically pulled me away.

"Have you no sense at all, Miss Pocket? Without the portal, our worlds will be split forever. The stone's power comes from the portal, and without it, you will not be able to cross back—you will be stranded in Prospa forever. If there was any way I could stop the portal from dying I would, but there is no antidote to the jugular's poison."

"Then I will take Rebecca and leave now," I said quickly.

"After all, I only came for her, and now we can go home again."

"Are you really so foolish?" snapped Miss Frost. "Rebecca cannot return to your world, not in the way you imagine. I *tried* to make you see sense, but you never listen. Further, the Clock Diamond allows you to travel at will, but it will not work for Rebecca. She would need to use the portal, and even then . . ."

I looked over and saw that Rebecca had fallen into a fitful sleep.

"If that is true, then Rebecca and I will simply sneak back into Prospa House and be on our way."

"You think it is that easy?" Miss Frost crossed her arms. "Prospa House, indeed the entire city, will be swarming with guards."

"Then we will go tomorrow," I said, crossing my own arms.

"It might be too late," said Miss Frost, her voice softening. "Miss Pocket, while we cannot know exactly when Justice Hallow poisoned the portal, I believe that its death, while slow, would take less than a day. Prosparian folklore talks of a hunter who was poisoned by the jugular's sap at sunup and was dead by sunset." She put a finger under my chin, lifting my head. "Use the Clock Diamond and return to your home. There is no hope for Rebecca—accept that and go while you still can."

"Stuff and nonsense!" I whispered. "She is coming home with me."

"Her soul has faded. It fades still. Even if she never performs another healing, she will only last a few weeks. That is the price, Miss Pocket. That is the bargain."

"Rebecca made no bargain," I declared. "She wore the Clock Diamond in order to see her mother again." I turned my back in a dramatic fashion and looked again at Rebecca. "We will cross together *before* the portal dies, and that is that, Miss Frost."

The infuriating redhead left the room and returned some time later with a glass of milk and a rather delightful cookie. "Miss Always has been rather busy," she said. "Word is spreading throughout the kingdom that the Dual will appear tomorrow." She sighed. "Justice Hallow has declared her an enemy of the kingdom."

As I munched the cookie, I wandered about, looking over the tabletop and chest of drawers. It was a plain room, with books on Prospa history and a collection of wooden soldiers. "Whose house is this?"

"It belonged to my uncles. I grew up here."

I reached for a small portrait. In it were two girls and a boy— the boy and one of the girls had bright red hair; the other girl was rather mousy with spectacles. And I recognized them instantly. Well, two of them anyway. "That is you and Miss Always," I said.

Miss Frost nodded curtly. "We went to school together."

"Who is the dashing young fellow standing between you?"

"My brother." Miss Frost snatched the picture away. "Enough questions. Let us focus on the problems before us— first, you need to change out of that ridiculous ball gown."

Which was monstrously unkind! Miss Frost pulled a box from under the bed, looking for a dress I might wear. As she foraged about, a strand of red hair came loose and fell in front of her eyes. For some reason, this made me think of *her*.

"I have been dreaming of my mother," I said. "Just in the last week or so."

At that Miss Frost looked up. "Did . . . you have seen her then?"

"Not fully. The sun is always in the way." I frowned. "Why do you ask?"

"Miss Pocket . . ." Miss Frost paused and looked rather lost for words. "I know this probably isn't the right time, but I have something—"

"I have not told you the strangest thing," I interrupted, stunned at my forgetfulness. "Tonight I saw a girl with my face."

"What did you say?"

I repeated myself. Which felt unnecessary.

Miss Frost demanded all the facts. Which I gave in thrilling detail. When I was done (and I had changed into a hideous auburn dress), Miss Frost said, "This millhouse where the girl was taken—could you show me the way?"

I huffed indigently. "Well, of course I could! I'm not some silly—"

"Wear this coat." Miss Frost practically threw the dusty relic at me. She was already halfway out the door by then. "And do hurry, Miss Pocket."

Miss Frost regarded me as one might a triple murderer

The carriage charged through the woodlands. Miss Frost and I were in the cabin. One of her women drove up front. Another hung from the back, a sword and dagger at her belt. On the lookout for any sign of Justice Hallow's guards (or Miss Always and her locks).

"Who is this girl that looks like me?" I said for the sixth time. "You must have *some* idea. Otherwise we wouldn't be roaring through the forest in the dead of night."

Miss Frost smoothed down her dress. "When you wore the Clock Diamond for the first time on the boat from Paris—you lived. You lived when you were not supposed to."

"What has that to do with me having a double?"

"Your soul was meant to pass into Prospa through the portal," continued Miss Frost. "But instead you stayed stubbornly in your world, though with certain changes."

I nodded. "I can't get hurt, I have no blood in my veins, I can heal people from your world."

"Correct."

"I used to believe I couldn't get sick either—but I've been

violently ill of late. Brink-of-death stuff. And the Clock Diamond stopped working."

"Yes, Bertha told me." Miss Frost sighed, but it was out of frustration, not weariness. "I think it is all linked, Miss Pocket. When you wore the Clock Diamond, you did indeed stay in your world, but I believe that a part of you passed through the stone and arrived in Prospa like every other soul does."

I gasped. "And that is what I saw?"

"I think so. I cannot say for certain, but I suspect this girl, this part of you, would also be different from other souls— my informant at Prospa House tells me that her skin doesn't glow and that she has been in some kind of stupor since she arrived. The mere presence of a girl like that would have intrigued Justice Hallow." She looked out at the darkened woods. "When you told me the guards at Prospa House had recognized you, it confirmed my own suspicions. After I left you in Weymouth, I returned to Prospa, hoping to find your other half and return her to your world. But retrieving her proved impossible—she is watched by a dozen guards around the clock."

Which was most unexpected!

"Despite your new abilities," said Miss Frost, "you fell ill because half of you is dying—and I am certain your illness is the reason the stone temporarily stopped working."

"Blimey." I frowned. "Am *I* dying?"

"When the split happened, you got the better part of the bargain, Miss Pocket." Miss Frost allowed a faint smile. "The girl you saw tonight is something of a remnant—while you gained strength and immunity from wearing the stone, she passed into Prospa a mere shadow of you. Think of it this way: without her, you are weakened, but without *you*, she cannot survive."

We hit a pothole and were jolted around.

"If Justice Hallow was hiding this *other* me away, why did she not recognize me when I was captured?" I asked.

"She is playing games," said Miss Frost crisply. "I am confident that tonight she planned to bring the *two* Ivy Pockets together."

I shot up in my seat, nearly hitting the roof of the carriage. "Is such a thing possible?"

The millhouse was in sight, and Miss Frost signaled through the window for the carriage to stop. "That is what we are about to find out, Miss Pocket."

Breaking in was a violent business. Miss Frost felled the guard standing by the Prospa House carriage. One of her associates picked the lock on the front door with ease. Then the other took on the pair of guards in the kitchen, thumping their heads together. Miss Frost ordered her associates to sweep the other rooms downstairs and check the basement. While I followed her up the stairs.

We trod lightly, though the boards did a great deal of snapping and creaking. At the top was a narrow hall. Three doors. A guard was snoozing heavily on a chair outside the last one.

Miss Frost ordered me to stay where I was. Then she walked furtively toward him. Tapped him on the shoulder and blew a handful of slumber rocks in his face. He slid from the chair and landed in a heap on the floor.

"Come," whispered Miss Frost, her hand upon the door.

By the time I got there, Miss Frost was already inside. Standing by a bedside. She seemed lost for words. I hurried over, and saw what had startled her. There was girl upon the bed. She was . . . she had my face. Except hers was awfully thin. Cheekbones sunken. Dark circles tracked under her eyes. Skin as pale and washed out as a bedsheet. The Clock Diamond sparked to life, warming the top of my dress like a furnace.

"I cannot believe it," I said softly. "She is *me*."

"Yes. But after so many months in this stupor, she is wasting away." Miss Frost pointed to a chair against the wall. "Get me that blanket."

I did as she asked. Miss Frost wrapped the girl—*me*—in the blanket and picked her up with ease. "Let us go before the guards find their feet again."

We were nearly at the bedroom door when we heard a loud commotion downstairs. Grunts and groans, breaking furniture and rattling pans. Then we heard one of Miss Frost's women cry out. Then an awful thumping sound. Then feet pounding on the stairs.

Miss Frost darted quickly behind the bedroom door.

She gestured toward the bed with her head. "Take her place, Miss Pocket," she whispered. "And do not open your eyes."

I could hear the footsteps hurrying toward us. So I ran to the bed. Dove on my back. Shut my eyes. And tried to calm my rapid breaths. I heard the guard enter the room. "She's still here!" the brute hollered. "Keep your eyes peeled down there—you can bet there's more of them about."

"Yes, sir!" came an equally loutish voice from downstairs.

The guard's boots clipped upon the floorboards. I smelled the sourness of his breath, close to my face. "When I find your *friends* I'll break their necks," he whispered. "Can't think what Justice Hallow would want with an ugly runt like you."

Which was simply too much to take. My eyes flew open. "You're not exactly portrait material yourself, dear."

Then I punched him right in the nose. He yelped. His puffy face red with rage. Then he grabbed me by the throat and thrust me against the wall. "They're your last words," he hissed. "Hope they were worth it."

I felt my throat being crushed. The air sealed off. But I managed to say, "Justice . . . Hallow won't be happy."

He smiled wickedly. "Accidents happen."

"Unhand her!" said Miss Frost, stepping out from behind the door. "Or do you only fight children?"

The brute turned. And seemed stunned to find another Ivy Pocket in Miss Frost's arms. I looked about and glimpsed the water jug by the bedside. Grabbed it. Then smashed it over the swine's head. His grip on my throat slackened as he moaned and held his head. I followed up with a swift kick to the stomach.

"Well done, Miss Pocket." Miss Frost glanced out into the hallway. "His accomplice is sure to have heard the commotion. Let us go."

"Where?" I whispered. "Won't he see us coming?"

There wasn't time to respond. As we ran out of the bedroom, the brute was already charging down the hall toward us. "Hurry, Miss Pocket!" shouted Miss Frost.

We flew down a set of rickety back stairs. The guard bore down on us, hollering abuse and gaining ground with every step. "I'll break your necks when I get my hands on you!" he grunted.

I scurried after Miss Frost. Praying the violent brute never got the chance.

16

"**D**o something, Miss Pocket!"

"Like *what*, you unreasonable redhead?"

He was still pounding the stairs behind us. And as Miss Frost was carrying my other half, it fell to me to bring him down. I leaped down the last three steps. Grabbed a broom that was leaning against the larder door. Slipped it between the rails. The rotter took flight, sailing through the air, bulging arms flailing about. He landed on his head, somersaulting across the drab kitchen.

We charged out into the night and ran toward the carriage.

Miss Frost's two associates had recovered, though one had a nasty gash on her forehead. They were already taking their positions at the front and back of the carriage. I was still climbing into the cabin when the horses took off at speed.

"Close the door, Miss Pocket," ordered Miss Frost, carefully unloading her cargo on the seat beside her.

"I'm trying!" I shouted back.

With great skill, I gripped the side of the carriage, swung out, and pulled the carriage door shut. I landed in a heap. Opposite me, Miss Frost took the blanket from around my other half. The girl was slumped against the window, her face ghostly white, her dark hair plastered against her hollow cheeks.

"Well," I said, "now what?"

The answer came before Miss Frost could reply. The Clock Diamond came alive beneath my dress again. And the cabin began to shake as if we were driving over a valley of rocks. The air thickened and hummed. I pulled out the Clock Diamond, crimson light spilling out. It was suddenly impossibly hot, the carriage crackling and fizzing as if we were inside a furnace.

Miss Frost must have seen the uncertainty on my face. "Relax, Miss Pocket. I had hoped that having both of you in such close proximity would quicken the process of unification, and it seems I was correct."

Two things happened next. The first, I felt. An unseen force seemed to swirl around me, catching me in its grasp and pulling me toward my other half. The second, I saw. The other Ivy Pocket awoke with a rather violent start. Looked about and quickly spotted me.

"I'm not surprised," was the first thing she said. "I always suspected I was a twin. Separated at birth, possibly at the hands of a witch or a double-crossing pixie. All very tragic."

Despite my predicament, I couldn't help sighing. "Wouldn't that be *lovely*?"

Miss Frost was having none of that. "You are two halves of the one exasperating whole—so stop fighting it and come together."

"Who are you?" said the girl, looking rather doubtfully at Miss Frost. "Are we in London? The last thing I recall was being on the *Britannia*—it's a perfectly glorious ship and I'm in first class, as you would expect. But I'm keeping very much to myself, quiet as a church mouse and whatnot. You see, I'm on a mission for the Duchess of Trinity—she was a wondrous fatso, stabbed brutally in the heart. The murderer is still lurking about, which is rather thrilling." She gasped and pointed at me in a most accusing fashion. "That's my necklace! Give it back, you—"

"Oh, do shut up!" I thundered.

My body began to slide off the seat toward her—pulled as if by a gigantic magnet. It felt awfully wrong. As if I were being sucked into a void from which there would be no return. So I thrust out my leg, pressing it against the seat opposite to halt my progress.

"Miss Frost, what is happening?" I asked.

"Do not fight it, Miss Pocket." Miss Frost was now perched on the edge of her seat, watching the process with great interest. "Let go. Let go, Miss Pocket."

"Don't be ridiculous, woman!" I shouted. "This girl talks a huge amount of nonsense—we are *nothing* alike! This could be some wicked plot to steal my soul."

My other half was feeling the same pull. She had her hands on the back of the seat, trying to hold on for dear life. "I had a great-uncle who had his soul stolen by a pickpocket," she shouted through gritted teeth. "Poor fellow ended up locked in my grandmother's basement eating candle wax."

"That's not even *slightly* true!" I bellowed.

"Who can say?" she shouted back.

By now my knees were buckled, straining against the unceasing pull. My other half had her nails dug into the seat cushion and was gripping most violently.

"Miss Pocket, if you have ever trusted me before, then trust me now," said Miss Frost. "Let go, and you will be whole again."

"*Never* trust a redhead," my other half shouted at me. "Have you no sense, dear?"

I fixed my gaze upon Miss Frost. "If you're wrong, I will box your ears!"

Then I let go. What happened next took mere seconds. My body lifted from the seat and flew at the girl. As it did, the scarlet light flaring from the stone became a golden orb that swelled, reaching out and enveloping the other me. She gave a startled cry.

Her skin took on a heavenly glow, and she was pulled from the seat. Shooting straight at me. No, not at me. At the Clock Diamond. We collided in an instant. The shimmering girl was swallowed into the stone, her nightdress falling in a heap on the chair.

I heard Miss Frost call my name.

My head began to churn. The cabin swirled. A great light filled my eyes.

When the dazzling light cleared, I was somewhere else. A desolate room. Bare walls. An empty hearth. A broken window, the snow billowing in. I was bundled in my mother's lap. Puffs of mist slipped from my mouth and curled into the cold air. I looked up—she had a scarf pulled over her face. She wasn't moving. Her eyes were open, though she appeared not to see me.

I touched her hands. They were ice cold.

"Mama?"

No reply.

I reached up and pulled the scarf from her face. Looked upon it properly for the first time. It was plain but sweet. There were lines upon her forehead. Her skin dry and mottled. Her lips dry. No puffs of steam escaped from those lips. Then I looked in her eyes and realized they were not looking back. I touched her face and noticed the mark under her eye. It was small and looked just like . . . like a cloud.

The door flew open, and a woman in a yellow bonnet stalked into the room. Marched toward us. Crouched down. Then sighed. "You are not who I have been searching for."

She stood and walked about. Then asked me my name. I gave no reply. I burrowed into my mother and turned my back on the woman.

"Your mother is dead," she said softly.

I felt her searching my mother's coat. Then my own. She pulled out a piece of paper. "Is Ivy your name?"

I stayed silent. She scooped me up in a bundle.

"Come, Ivy," said Miss Frost. "We must find you somewhere more suitable to live."

And I began to scream.

"It's all right, Miss Pocket." Miss Frost's voice was calm and crisp. "You are safe."

I felt her hand wiping tears from my face.

"How do you feel, Ivy?" said Rebecca.

Opening my eyes, I saw that I was back in Miss Frost's house. She was sitting on the bed beside me, Rebecca standing over her shoulder. Both looked rather concerned.

"Well, Miss Pocket?" said Miss Frost.

I went to speak, but nothing came out.

"You said she would be stronger," said Rebecca to Miss Frost. "Why does she not answer you?"

And I *did* feel stronger. Utterly wretched, but stronger than I'd felt in a long time.

"Now that Ivy is whole again, all should be as it once was." Miss Frost reached down and pulled a small dagger from her boot. "But there is only one way to be sure."

"What are you doing?" said Rebecca anxiously.

But I knew. For Miss Frost had done this once before. So I didn't flinch or call her a mad cow when she sliced the blade down my arm. And this time, instead of dark smoke coiling up, blood oozed from the wound. I was fully human again.

"Is she . . ." Rebecca did not seem to have the words to finish the question.

Miss Frost nodded, and put her hand over my wound to quell the bleeding. "There will be no more falling down stairs or leaping into fires. Miss Pocket can now be hurt like anyone else from your world."

I looked squarely at Miss Frost. "The dead woman you found me with all those years ago—she was McCloud, the Dumblebys' maid."

If my declaration stunned her, she did not show it. Perhaps she had already guessed that the truth was dawning on me. "I think so," she replied.

"Who is McCloud?" said Rebecca.

"Miss Butterfield, would you be so kind as to fetch some more water?" said Miss Frost.

Rebecca took the hint and scrammed. When she was gone, Miss Frost stood up, her arms folded. "I didn't know it at the time, of course," she said calmly. "I believed I was on the trail of Anastasia and her child and was rather disappointed when I came upon you and McCloud. You wouldn't speak, but I found a note in the pocket of your dress. It had the name Ivy scrawled on it. When I took you to the orphanage and they asked for a name, I gave it as Ivy Pocket. As for Anastasia, I just assumed my information had been wrong. Until . . ."

"Until I told you that the Dumblebys had given Anastasia's baby to McCloud."

"Yes." Her voice had softened. "If I had only known . . ."

"So I am her daughter?"

"Anastasia Radcliff?" Miss Frost took a deep breath. "Yes, I believe you are—which explains a great deal about your bond with the Clock Diamond."

I felt a ripple of anger surge through me. "Why didn't you tell me?"

"I did try, Miss Pocket." She turned to the window, the morning sun washing in. "The truth is, I feared you would do something foolish—such as returning to Lashwood in search of Anastasia. You might recall we had rather a lot to deal with at the time."

I had a mother. It didn't seem real. Or true.

"She didn't know me," I heard myself say. "I was with her, in the very same room, yet she didn't know who I was."

"Anastasia survived by blocking out the real world and living inside her mind," said Miss Frost. "She did not recognize you because she couldn't see you. Not really."

"Perhaps she will never know," I said faintly.

"Actually, Miss Pocket, she already does."

I sat up in bed, looking thoroughly stunned. "Explain yourself!"

"As you know, I ventured back to your world not long after you arrived in Prospa," said Miss Frost. "I went to the cottage in Weymouth to check on you, and found Anastasia instead."

"And?"

"While still deeply troubled, her mind was beginning to clear—despite the great torment she suffered, I believe that we with Prosparian blood recover more swiftly than those from your world."

"And?" I said again, barely able to contain myself.

"I told her what I believed to be true. That you were her daughter."

"Did she . . . did she say anything?"

Miss Frost paused for a moment. Touched her chin. "She wept, Miss Pocket. She wept."

I leaped up. Fished the Clock Diamond from under my dress. "I must go to her at once. Have a family reunion and whatnot."

Rebecca returned with a jug of water, placing it on the bedside table.

"Rebecca, dear, I suggest you jump on my back like a bear cub clutching its mother. For we are about to return home."

"That won't be possible." Miss Frost pointed to the stone. "Take a closer look, Miss Pocket."

I did as she said. And what I saw was a very different diamond—the stone was splintered inside, and black as night. "Is it . . . ?"

"Destroyed? Quite so." And despite my shock, my sorrow, I saw the melancholy flickering in Miss Frost's eyes. As Mistress of the Clock, her very life had been the stone and its grim work. "The mere fact that you have the blood of our two worlds in your veins explains your rare connection to the stone. But the force that brought your two halves back together was more than the Clock Diamond could take. Its magic is gone, Miss Pocket."

"And so is its curse," whispered Rebecca.

I thought then of Justice Hallow's words about dark magic in the kingdom of Prospa. "Is it true that the Shadow was caused by dark magic?"

"Perhaps." Miss Frost rubbed her brow, looking thoroughly exhausted. "Several centuries ago, the Queen's daughter used a magi's curse to kill her mother—the magic summoned was dark indeed, and took the Queen's life within hours. When she was found, her body was utterly gray. Her ashen skin looked as if a shadow were passing overhead."

"That is how the Shadow started?"

"Many believe so," said Miss Frost. "The curse had great power, great wrath, and it did not stop at the Queen. It quickly spread throughout the castle and then the kingdom." She cleared her throat. "After that, all magis and their kin were slaughtered, and magic banished from the realm—but by then it was too late."

I thought of the man I had seen from the train, looking down at the patch of gray on his skin. And the faces of the sick at Prospa House. "Was there no way to stop the curse?"

"The best minds in Prospa tried everything to defeat it," said Miss Frost faintly, "but nothing worked. We still do not understand how people are infected. The Shadow does its work without detection, infecting all but those who are immune from its deadly grasp."

Which raised an interesting question. "Does that mean *you* are immune?"

"So it would seem." Miss Frost closed her eyes briefly. "Immunity is an inexact science, Miss Pocket. Survival is the proof, showing itself when a person remains healthy even as their entire family or village is infected."

"Is . . . is that what happened to you, dear?"

"Correct." She folded her arms. "Aside from the Shadow, the portal is all that remains from that time. It was created by the Queen's sorcerer after Her Majesty grew bored with palace life and demanded access to other worlds. Prospa House used to be the royal palace, so the portal was brought to life under the Queen's private chambers. But it proved something of a disappointment. The poor fools sent to test it were destroyed in the void. All that came back were a few severed limbs and a head."

"How wondrously awful!" I declared.

"Once the Shadow began to spread, the first Chief Justice ordered the portal be destroyed, along with every other vestige of magic in Prospa. Luckily, a brilliant professor by the name of Peggotty Spring urged her to reconsider. She had unearthed a rather exceptional diamond in the deserts of the northern border, which she believed had the necessary power to get her from our world into yours."

"The Clock Diamond," I said.

Miss Frost nodded. "Professor Spring hoped to find a cure for the Shadow in your world. She was granted permission to experiment with the portal, and the rest is history. Once the Chief Justice learned what the stone could do, she created the roles of gatekeeper and Mistress of the Clock to ensure the necklace could do its important work."

"Stealing souls," I said with a satisfying scowl.

"*My* role was to monitor the Clock Diamond's use and ensure its survival, so that some of my people might be saved from the Shadow," said Miss Frost rather crossly. "It fell to Miss Always, as gatekeeper, to bring a steady stream of remedies through the gate. But over the years, Miss Always discarded the rules governing the stone—she did not want to limit herself to capturing the souls of the dying and the elderly. In fact, she began to see herself as the natural leader of Prospa, using her role to undermine Justice Hallow. As such, she fell afoul of your grandmother and was declared an enemy of the kingdom."

"I don't think Granny's very fond of you either, dear," I said helpfully.

Miss Frost huffed. "Justice Hallow is as corrupt as she is devious. I saw how she was profiting from the Shadow— selling access to the remedies among the rich and powerful. I told her that if she didn't stop, I would do it for her." The redheaded warrior shrugged. "She didn't like that very much, and sent an army of her guards to assassinate me. Fortunately, the portal's blood gave me the ability to fell those bloodthirsty goons."

"Doesn't that make you some kind of witch?" I shook my head knowingly. "I'm almost certain it does—you have the hideous clothes, the foul temper, the whiskers."

Miss Frost bristled. Her nostrils flared. Things might have gotten physical if one of her associates hadn't come to the door with a note—which Miss Frost read, then slipped into her pocket. I thought of how much sorrow and pain that stone had caused. But I also knew that it was a symbol of hope for the people of Prospa—the only chance those suffering from the Shadow had of surviving. And now it was gone.

"I'm not sorry the Clock Diamond will never steal another soul," I said, walking over to Miss Frost, "but if there is any way that I might be what Miss Always *thinks* I am—that I might be able to stop the Shadow for good, then—"

"I believe in facts," said Miss Frost coolly, "not myths. And the facts are that the Clock Diamond is no more, which means your only hope of getting home is the portal."

"But the portal is dying," said Rebecca.

"Which is why we must find a way to get Miss Pocket to it before it shuts down completely—though I fear the crossing will be rather treacherous." Miss Frost looked at her watch. "The note I received was from my informant at Prospa House. He tells me that Justice Hallow was seen heading down to the

underground chamber around midnight last evening. If she poisoned the portal at that time, then I believe we have less than four hours until it closes."

Which was a shocking thought. If I couldn't return to my world, how would I ever be reunited with my mother? Which led to another shocking thought.

"Justice Hallow is my grandmother!" I said, spinning around. "It's true that she seems slightly malicious, but I'm certain that would change once she knew that I was her very own flesh and blood!"

"You are quite wrong," snapped Miss Frost. "Justice Hallow does not entertain tender feelings, not for anyone. While I cannot know for certain why she has poisoned the portal—the remedies are her source of power, so it is most odd—it does speak of a desperate woman. And desperate people are not to be trusted."

"Miss Frost is right, Ivy," said Rebecca. "When I first arrived at Prospa House, Justice Hallow visited my cell and asked many questions about the Clock Diamond. She seemed to know that you had worn the stone, and I could see how desperate she was to learn more about you." Rebecca shook her head. "I didn't break, Ivy. I told her nothing."

I smiled warmly. "Well done, dear."

But that did not prove that Justice Hallow knew I was her own flesh and blood. Perhaps dear Granny was a *touch* ruthless. But then, her daughter had run away to another world and left her alone. It made sense that her heart had shriveled like a raisin. But once she learned who I was, all that would change. Her heart would melt, her eyes would water, and we would embrace like two explorers lost in a blizzard.

"Granny just needs to know the truth," I said brightly. "Then she'll gladly let Rebecca and me return home before the portal dies."

"Do you think so?" said Rebecca hopefully. "Oh, do you really think—"

"Don't be foolish," said Miss Frost most cruelly. "I suspect Justice Hallow knows *exactly* who Miss Pocket is. We must find a way to reach the portal without detection. This will take some thinking."

"Where is the lavatory?" I asked, heading for the door.

"If I wasn't such an upstanding girl, with my very own lodgings in Berkeley Square, I'd tell you that I'm positively bursting."

Miss Frost's sigh was full of reproach. "It is downstairs, past the kitchen."

There were four of Miss Frost's associates milling about downstairs, a pair each guarding the back and front doors. So I darted into a small library off the sitting room and climbed out the window—bound for Prospa House.

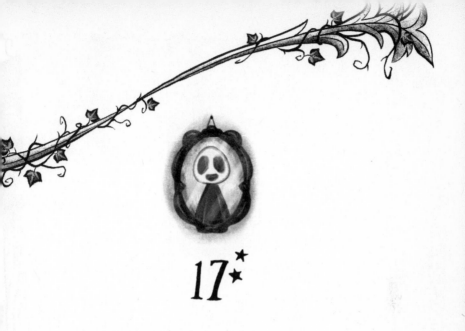

17

Escaping is a tricky business. Which is why I was cowering behind a rather unruly shrub, cursing Miss Frost. For the outside of her house was as heavily guarded as the inside. I had jumped from the window and landed among a wall of bushes. Quickly spotting one of Miss Frost's cronies, I ducked down. She passed by, then turned and walked the other way. So I darted out and crawled along the ground, hiding beside a barrow filled with turnips.

I heard chatter. Then the sound of boots marching back toward me. A few feet away was a maple tree with a rope ladder hanging from it. With few options—and no powers of invisibility—I dashed over and scurried up the ladder. At the top was a rather delightful tree house. All wood slats and rusty nails. I crawled in, heading for a small square cut into the wall opposite. My eye was drawn to a pair of initials carved into a heart—G.A. and E.F. But only briefly. I peered out and saw a horse and rider galloping into the yard. The woman wore the familiar brown pants and black coat. She tethered the horse to a branch right under me and jumped off, dashing into the house.

When she was gone, and with the two foot soldiers deep in conversation down by the stable doors, I made my move. Climbed out the window. Found my footing on a thick bough. And jumped. I landed rather skillfully on the horse's back. There was some buttock pain, I won't lie. As I unthreaded the reins, I heard a great commotion coming from the house.

"She cannot have gone far," Miss Frost called out from one of the front windows. "Search high and low!"

I tugged on the reins, and the horse galloped from the yard. We flew like the wind spiriting away from the house at great speed. The breeze untangled the braid from my hair, my locks billowing out behind me. It was a glorious getaway. Until

I spotted four dark carriages charging along the road not thirty feet away. I recognized the drivers' orange coats and shaved heads—Justice Hallow's guards. And they were hurtling toward Miss Frost's house.

I quickly turned off the road and flew into the thick woodlands. I didn't go back. There wasn't time—the portal would be closed in just a few hours, and with it, any hope of seeing my mother again. I felt utterly certain that Miss Frost and her cronies would make short work of those Orange Coats. And besides, I was confident the whole silly business would be cleared up once Justice Hallow learned who I was. She would agree to let Rebecca and me return home.

So I flicked the reins hard and galloped on.

Prospa House was eerily quiet. Marvelously deserted. Hardly any guards about that I could see—though I felt certain they couldn't *all* be at Miss Frost's farmhouse getting pummeled. I had followed the train tracks all the way, jumping from the horse on the outskirts of the city—much better to go on foot, what with horses and wagons being forbidden during the day.

When I reached the bridge, I circled around the back of Prospa House.

A guard stalked about, hands behind his back. He appeared to be patrolling the entire perimeter, quickly vanishing around the corner. So I ran like the wind. Turned down the silver stone path surrounded by bloodred hedges. Flew past the plaque that read PROSPA HOUSE. Slipped inside the building, utterly unseen—having all the natural instincts of a foul odor.

The place was empty. No maids milling about. No sign of any guards. The grand staircase loomed before me, so I charged up, heading for the first floor. That was where they had taken me after Rebecca and I were captured. While I couldn't be certain, instinct told me that Justice Hallow's quarters *must* be nearby. After all, she had kept the vial of poison in the cell where I was locked.

At the top of the stairs was a large portrait of Justice Hallow looking frightfully regal, surrounded by an array of regimental flags. The hall split off, left and right. I chose the left. There were a great many doors. All were open, revealing a series of empty offices and a large library. All except for one. Which was *terribly* interesting. So I opened it and entered.

The room was vast and airy. Lined with white bookcases. A large desk in the middle with a high leather chair. A fireplace of dark stone and the words VIGILANCE ALWAYS carved above it. At the far end were a set of large copper doors etched with hundreds of little Clock Diamonds. I walked over for a closer look, and as I did, I felt the ground tremble and shift beneath me. Just for a moment.

The doors were rather glorious. On either side were tall windows. Looking out, I instantly recognized the vast terrace, the wide steps, the concourse leading down to the great lake, the Clock Diamond memorial. It was just as I had seen it from the train. Apart from a few differences.

The first was a large platform sprouting up from the middle of the lake with a red throne upon it. The second was the great crowd milling about on the concourse and around the water's edge. A great many were marked by the Shadow, their skin ashen and sickly. And the guards from Prospa House were shouting at the people and pointing in a rather fierce fashion.

"You came back."

I jumped, startled. Turned around to see Justice Hallow

standing in the doorway. She wore a plain brown dress. No jewelry or adornment.

"Yes, dear," I declared. "I had to, for I have the most fantastical news."

Justice Hallow walked toward me. Then, without a word, she reached for my throat. Her cool eyes sparkled when she felt the stone. She pulled it out. Looked at it, cracked and dark.

"It is as I expected," she said. "Why don't we talk in my private quarters?"

Which was a splendid idea! Justice Hallow led me through a door set into the bookcases. I followed her into a room that I instantly recognized. It was connected to the cell where I had been kept. Very simple. A few wooden chairs. A bed in the corner. A table and an oil lamp. A faded tapestry of the great lake on a wall.

"This is your chamber?" I said.

Justice Hallow looked about. "The people of Prospa do not expect their leader to live as a queen—she must be as humble and unassuming as a peasant."

Then she turned. Walked to the wall tapestry. Lifted the edge.

Behind it was a door, which slid away as soon as she touched it. Justice Hallow passed through it, and I quickly followed. Finding myself in a *very* different sort of apartment. This one had a carved oak roof, with a glorious lantern hanging from the center. Rich woven carpets upon the floor. A canopied fireplace carved with daggers. Heavy furniture covered in red and black silk. The whole room smelled of peaches and oranges.

"This is my little secret," said Justice Hallow. "Every great leader has a few of those."

Along one wall was a long row of glass cabinets bursting with objects both beautiful and strange—hand-painted vases, a dark sceptre sparkling with green stones, and ivory statues stood alongside shrunken heads, bones that appeared to have been dipped in gold, and glass bottles filled with what looked an awful lot like *tongues*. I looked at my granny with a certain amount of confusion.

"Prospa has a dark and fascinating history," she said softly. "I am a keen collector of remnants from that time. The tongues belong to royal subjects who displeased the Queen." She strolled to an ornate desk and sat down. Motioned to the chair opposite her. "Now, what is it you wished to tell me, Ivy?"

I hurried over and launched into the story. Told her everything as briefly as I could—given that the portal was dying and time running out. When I was done, I ended with a few poetic words, "Now I am almost certain, dear Granny, that you will wish to have me around forever, shower me with hugs and kisses, cash and cake. Which is awfully sweet—but quite impossible. For I already *have* a home in London and, as it turns out, a mother. She's your daughter, so you've probably met."

Granny said nothing. Just smiled silently.

"You're overwhelmed," I said brightly. "The shock and whatnot."

She opened a drawer, took something out, and slid it across the table toward me. It was a photograph (in *color*, no less). Of a girl. A girl who looked remarkably like me.

"That is a photograph of my sister, Florence," said Justice Hallow. "She died a few days before her fourteenth birthday. There is quite a resemblance between the two of you—don't you agree?"

So Granny had known who I was all along. Miss Frost's hunch had been right. Which was infuriating. And rather confusing. "I don't understand," I said.

"Don't you?" Justice Hallow sat back in her chair. "When your other half first came through the portal, it was plain to see that she was no ordinary soul. Her skin did not glow, and she looked exactly like my sister. As impossible as it seemed, I knew that this girl could not be anything less than my daughter's child. And as my daughter's child, you had both Prosparian blood and the *other* kind. I also understood that there was a real chance you might find your way here—indeed, I hoped you would come." Justice Hallow waved her hand in my general direction. "And here you are."

There was a knot in my stomach now. A growing dread. "Why did you poison the portal, Granny?"

"To sever the ties between our worlds forevermore," she said simply. "That chapter in Prospa's history is over."

The floor shook again. A low, deep rumble. A painting on the wall wobbled. The windows rattled. Justice Hallow noticed it too, a frown carved in her smooth flesh. But I had more important matters to discuss. "But what about the Shadow and the remedies? Without the portal, they—"

"The remedies have been moved for their own safety."

She motioned to the window and the concourse below. "The gatekeeper has raised my people's expectations about you, Ivy—they are going to be sorely disappointed. That is why my guards are attempting to clear the city and send them all home."

"But the sick will die without the portal," I said. "I think it's a beastly business, stealing souls, but are you not meant to help your people?"

My granny looked at me in silence. Her blue eyes were stunning, but there was a great coldness there. I still had questions . . . but I suspected I would not like the answers. "Why did you move us last night—Rebecca and the other me?"

"Rebecca was a tool, something I could use to ensure you didn't slip back to your world using the Clock Diamond. While I was unable to locate the necklace, I knew you would have it within reach. And I also knew that you couldn't take Rebecca with you using the stone. As for your other half, the plan was always to reunite the two of you." She sighed. "After all, I couldn't kill you until you were whole."

I stood up. "Well, it was lovely meeting you, Granny. Do let's keep in touch. If you'll excuse me, I need to go back and collect my friend. Now you mustn't go to any trouble—a farewell luncheon or bunting. We will just slip down to the portal and be on our way."

"That won't be possible." Justice Hallow stepped out from behind the desk, and I saw that she held an elegant silver pistol. "My daughter is dead to me, and as her child, you are little more than proof of her betrayal. She ran from me as if I were a monster. I didn't think I could despise a human being more than Anastasia, and then *you* appeared."

Which was monstrous. "Let me return home, and you'll never have to see me again."

"Anastasia had no need for a mother," she said calmly, "so why should you?"

And at last I truly understood. "You poisoned the portal to stop my mother and me from being together." I was shaking my head. "It is vengeance."

"It is justice!" Granny pushed the pistol against my heart. "In another life I might have admired a granddaughter who didn't cower in the face of greater strength. Who was brave and loyal. But we must accept the times in which we live. Even if you weren't my granddaughter, you are a threat to the one thing in this world that makes my heart sing."

"Power," I heard myself say.

She didn't deny it. She didn't have to. It was there in her proud, bald head. And in her hidden apartment, fit for a monarch. And in her ravenous eyes. Being Justice of Prospa was everything—all else was a hindrance to be disposed of.

"I would shoot you," she said, "but there is the mess and the noise to consider."

"Terribly sporting of you, Granny."

Using the pistol, she forced me back until I hit the glass cabinets. "Might I suggest death by cold porridge? Or possibly a firm talking-to and straight to bed without supper?"

I swung quickly, hitting the wicked creature's arm. My plan was for the gun to go flying across the room. But Justice Hallow barely flinched. She brought the pistol right back to my chest—and cocked the hammer. "I am stronger than I look," she said.

"Crazier too," I added.

But I was trapped and we both knew it. With a satisfied smile Justice Hallow opened one of the glass doors and turned a small ivory statue of a woman holding a fob watch. As she did, I heard a hissing sound. Then the cabinet lurched forward as if it was being pushed from behind, and slid open. Revealing a small room just wide enough for a person to stand.

"This little chamber is lined with steel and, once closed, is utterly devoid of ventilation." She indicated with a wave of her pistol that I was to step inside. "I thought suffocation was the best option."

"Whereas *I* thought we might talk things through, agree you were a monstrous fruitcake, then go our separate ways."

Justice Hallow grabbed my arm and pushed me into the small space. It was so snug the walls seemed to press in, holding me like a vise. I attempted to jump out. But the pistol quickly forced me back in.

"It's not the noblest end to your journey," said Granny, "but there is a certain beauty in locking you away in my cabinet of curiosities."

"Wouldn't it make more sense to stuff me and mount me on the mantelpiece?" I said, gulping up a storm. "Let's head to the nearest taxidermist and work out the details."

"You should have stayed in your world, Ivy, and left mine alone."

Justice Hallow reached for the ivory statue. With a simple turn, she would seal me in. And my life would be over. She clasped the statue. As she did, a gloved hand snaked around her neck. A dagger flew to her throat. Behind her a figure loomed, wearing a wicked grin.

"Hello, Ivy," said Miss Always.

Stepping out of my tomb felt glorious. Miss Always pulled the pistol from Justice Hallow's hand and pushed her away. Glanced at the hidden chamber.

"I'd heard rumors about your nasty little vault," she said, "but I thought it was a fairy tale."

"The tomb has been a great comfort," said Justice Hallow, lifting her hand and stroking her crinkled neck. "I've only had need to use it once or twice—the threat is usually enough."

"But not today." Miss Always pushed the spectacles up her nose, and I noticed the scar on her forehead from Amos's rock. "While killing Ivy has a great deal of merit—I once planned to do it myself—I came to see that she has a *higher* purpose. You knew she had survived the stone, that she might be the one we were looking for—yet you were going to kill her?"

"I *will* kill her," said Justice Hallow calmly. "Miss Always, you don't suppose that either of you are getting out of here alive? My guards will—"

"Your guards are outside trying to stop the revolution," interrupted Miss Always.

"And the rest are getting thrashed by Miss Frost even as we speak," I chimed in.

The ground shook again. This time more violently. The cabinets rattled, the glass doors swung open, and many of Justice Hallow's ornaments tumbled out. Miss Always's eyes darted about. Then returned to Justice Hallow. "What have you done?"

Granny sighed. Said nothing.

"She poisoned the portal," I declared. "I'm not sure if that's what is making the whole place shake, but the portal is closing this very moment and I *must* cross back to my world before—"

"How could you be so foolish?" hissed Miss Always. She lunged at Justice Hallow, pressing the dagger's blade to her throat. "You want to kill the girl so she can never be the Dual. And kill the portal so it cannot bring back souls to heal the sick. Do you not want to stop the Shadow? Do you not care?"

Granny met Miss Always's gaze and did not flinch. "I am the Chief Justice. I know what is best. The portal will close in one hour, and that will be an end to it."

Miss Always shook her head in wonder. "And what will you tell your people?"

"I will tell them that the gatekeeper stole into Prospa House under the cover of darkness and poisoned the portal."

Miss Always looked more impressed than upset. "Blame it all on me? Clever."

"When they discover that you have not delivered the Dual, that there is no such girl, they will be ready to believe the worst of you," said Justice Hallow, her eyes sparkling with feverish excitement. "And I will be there to carry them through this great tragedy. The sick will perish and the well shall rebuild. A way to start again—with my guiding hand."

"You're off your rocker, dear," I said helpfully.

The floor shook again. The walls trembled. I heard a violent crack up above; then the lantern dropped from the ceiling, smashing just a few feet away.

"Prospa House was built over the portal," said Miss Always. "It will not survive what you have done."

"You are wrong," said Justice Hallow. "The portal will be dead soon enough. Prospa House can survive a few tremors."

"It won't," said Miss Always sadly. "It is happening already."

Justice Hallow paled then. I saw it. "You are wrong," she repeated, though she no longer sounded sure.

"What a miserable end for the *great* Justice Hallow," said Miss Always, the sharpness returning to her voice. "By the end of today, this house will be in ruin and Prospa shall have a new queen."

I knew what she meant. That I was the Dual. Justice Hallow knew it as well. Which is why she flew at Miss Always, pushing her back. Miss Always stumbled. Justice Hallow reached for the gun. Miss Always spun around. Throwing a kick. Justice Hallow was flung against the cabinets with force. Glass shattering around her. My evil granny let out a painful groan.

"Well done," I said, clapping my hands.

Miss Always didn't respond. She charged at Justice Hallow

and practically threw her in the vault. I ran over. Put my hand on the ivory statue and twisted it. In an instant, the cabinets were sliding together. "Lovely to meet you, Granny!" I said, giving a parting wave.

The tomb slid shut, sealing her in. Miss Always threw the pistol into the fire. Looked about and took a deep breath. I was already hurrying from the room. "Thank you, dear. Couldn't have done it without you. Now if you don't mind, I have a friend to collect and a portal to pass through. Clock's ticking and all of that."

Miss Always stepped in to my path. Pointed the dagger right at me. "Time to meet your destiny, old friend."

18

The dress was white and rather pretty. Miss Always threw it at me and insisted I change before my grand entrance. Before taking leave of Prospa House, we went down to the portal—Miss Always wanted to see it for herself. The ground trembled again as we entered the chamber. The air was positively rank, and the dark water bubbled furiously.

Miss Always looked upon it with something like sorrow. "It is truly dying."

"How long until it closes?"

"Hard to say." She looked at her watch—it was just after

eleven. "Justice Hallow said an hour. I suspect she is right."

"Which is why I must go and fetch Rebecca." I took off toward the tunnel. But I didn't get far. For Miss Always grabbed the collar of my dress and yanked me back.

"Your future is here in Prospa, Ivy." Then she pushed me rather roughly toward the spiral staircase. "No more games. It's time."

Miss Always had been rather busy. Spreading the word throughout the land. She was responsible for the signs and the pamphlets scattered all over the kingdom, telling her people that the Dual was coming today. Inviting the sick and dying to defy the law and Justice Hallow's guards—and flood the city to witness the end of their torment.

And they had come. Thousands of them. As we came through Justice Hallow's office, passing through the brass doors and out onto the terrace, I gasped. Truly gasped. Down below, the concourse was positively heaving with people. A great ocean of them, women and children, men and old folk, swarming around the concourse and the great lake.

"They have all come for you, Ivy." Miss Always was behind

me, the dagger pointed at my back—handily concealed in the sleeve of the red cloak she was now wearing. "Today you make history."

"How do you suppose I'm going to do this?" I said, unable to take my eyes off the crowd. "Wave a magic wand and cure them all? Well, I don't have a wand, you beastly rotter!"

Miss Always pointed to the great lake and the platform in the middle, suspended over the sparkling water. "*That* is how," she declared eagerly. "The legend of the Dual prophesizes that water will be the agent of healing—and the water here is something of a mystery. Beneath the lake is a dry clay bed, yet for centuries fresh water laden with healing minerals has bubbled up without explanation. Don't you see? This *must* be the place."

"You're at least two chickens short of a picnic, dear." I looked at the masses milling about the dozens of water pumps around the great lake. Many in the crowd had empty buckets and jars at the ready. "These poor creatures will tear us limb from limb when they discover I'm *not* the girl they think I am."

Was I the Dual? I truly didn't know. But now that I was fully human again, it didn't seem possible. Or rational. All

I could think about was the portal. And the time. So I pulled away, ready to bolt. But Miss Always grabbed my arm and held it tightly. "Your options are death or glory," she said. "Which do you choose, Ivy?"

"I want to go home," I said.

"You *are* home."

It was true in a way. My mother was from here. I had Prosparian blood in my veins. Yet my home was in England, with her.

But Miss Always cared nothing for my heart's desire—which is why she was marching me down the stairs. As we stepped onto the concourse, the crowd began to part. Muttering and pointing and gasping. "It's her!"

"There she is!"

"Little, ain't she?"

"We're with you, Ivy!"

"God bless the Dual!

While there were some finely dressed folk, most looked like farmers and villagers—plain dresses and worn suits. Many had the dreaded mark of the Shadow. A great ocean of gray faces and hollow eyes. I learned from Miss Always that they had come by the hundreds in wagons and on foot. Defying the ban on horses and carriages, they had swarmed into the city. All in hope of a cure.

Justice Hallow's guards were hideously outnumbered and had retreated inside Prospa House—though a few stayed outside to watch the spectacle with the rest of the kingdom.

Some of the crowd called out to the gatekeeper, thanking her for delivering the Dual. Miss Always lapped it up like a kitten to milk. "I have done what any gatekeeper would do," she said grandly. "Ridding Prospa of the Shadow is all the thanks I need."

"Horse poop," I muttered to her. "Lily is dead because of you."

"Who is Lily?"

We passed the concourse and were walking around the side of the great lake, the crowd swelling by the minute. "The poor girl who fell from the canyon, you hideous hag!"

"Oh." She sighed. "That was unfortunate. It wasn't my intention to kill her."

"Maybe not, but killing is a sport for you. Look at poor Mr.

Banks and the Duchess of Trinity."

"I made sure the stone was able to do its work," she said, smiling madly at the passing crowd. "Ensuring a regular supply of souls is my sacred mission, and I have done it proudly."

"You're a monster."

"I am the gatekeeper."

A wooden gangway had been set up, leading to the platform in the middle of the great lake. It was clear that this was where Miss Always was leading me. We were nearly there when I heard a familiar voice call my name. I looked across the way and saw a boy. He was holding a box, with a strap around his neck. His face was ashen, the skin a light gray. It was Amos. I pulled away from Miss Always.

The boy sidestepped a sickly looking woman holding a baby and hurried to my side. "You're really the Dual?" he asked, rather stunned.

I didn't reply. My eyes dropped to the box he was holding—it contained rows of small jars filled with a red substance. There was a hand-painted sign hanging from it. IVY POCKET'S MIRACLE CREAM—ONLY FIVE CLIPS A JAR. The boy saw that I was baffled.

"Your remedy worked so well on my arm, I decided to make

up a big batch and sell it." He looked at me bashfully. "Hope you don't mind."

"Of course not, dear." Then I noticed that his gray arm was covered with the red paste. Which was odd. "Your cut was healed, was it not?"

Amos nodded. Stepped close to me. Winked. "Customers like the personal touch—it's good for sales."

Just then the ground shifted beneath our feet, lurching from side to side. It was brief. But everybody noticed and began to mutter. Though I had other things on my mind. "When did you get sick, Amos?"

"Came on during the night," he said, looking down at his hands as if he no longer recognized them. "By morning it had spread all over—never heard of it coming on so fast." He offered me a crooked grin. "Guess I'm special too."

"I'm awfully sorry."

He shrugged. "The Shadow took my parents—always knew it might come for me."

Miss Always appeared beside me. "Keep moving!" she whispered, gripping my arm again.

When Amos saw Miss Always, his eyes blazed with hatred. He went to lunge at her, but stopped himself. I thought of all that the boy had lost.

"About Lily," I said quickly. "I know that if it wasn't for me, she wouldn't be—"

"It's *her* fault, not yours," he said, staring daggers at Miss Always.

"Walk, Ivy," said Miss Always, ignoring the boy. "Everyone is waiting."

He reached out and grabbed my hand. "I hope it's you, Ivy. I hope you're the one."

I nodded. Squeezed his hand. "Amos, you mustn't get your—"

Miss Always pressed the dagger to my back. I felt the blade pierce my dress and then my flesh. I could offer Amos little more than a parting wave as I was marched away.

Thirty minutes. Thirty minutes until the portal closed forever. From my position on the platform I had a perfect view of the clock tower atop Prospa House. It had just struck eleven thirty.

The portal would be dead by noon. Yet instead of racing down to the underground chamber and jumping in, I was stuck in the middle of the great lake—just me and Miss Always. And a rather large red throne on a platform behind us.

It felt bonkers. Unreal. Impossible. Yet here I stood. The sparkling blue lake beneath us, and a crowd of thousands around the water's edge watching me with bated breath—waiting for me to lift the curse of the Shadow from their lives. I looked at the clock again. Twenty-nine minutes left. Miss Always stepped forward and welcomed the crowd.

"This is a great day," she declared, her voice carrying across the water. "The Shadow is a thief. It steals lives and dreams, and from the very moment it began to spread through our people, over two hundred years ago, we have lived with but one promise—the Dual. The girl who would come from another world and banish this plague from our homeland."

The crowd began to cheer and whistle and cry out—a great wave of sound. And there was something else rippling through the crowd, through the air, that I couldn't name. But it was there.

"Ivy will now take her place, and we shall begin!" cried Miss Always.

A great cheer went up again. And Miss Always came to my side. Before me were three steps leading down to the water. "Take your place, Ivy," she said with a rare smile. "Place your hands in the water, and the rest will take care of itself."

A red velvet pillow lay at the water's edge for me to kneel upon.

"No," I said.

"Yes," said Miss Always.

"I don't want to be the Dual. I don't want to be the Queen— yes, it would be lovely to wear a crown, chop people's heads off, and eat cake all day, but that is not the life I want." I looked at Miss Always as earnestly as I knew how. "I want to be with my mother. I want to go home."

"We don't always get to choose our destiny, Ivy," she said, and though her voice was firm, I was shocked to hear tenderness there. "Do you think I chose this life? The Shadow took everything from me—my parents, my grandparents . . . my husband."

"You had a husband? Are you sure, dear? I'm almost certain you're a crazed spinster."

"We were not married long at all," she said softly. "After he was taken from me, I swore that I would do *whatever* it took to stop the Shadow. That is why I became the gatekeeper, and it is why I have hunted you across this world and yours." She pointed out to the thousands of gray faces surrounding the great lake. "Look at them, see their suffering. Can you really walk away? Can you really not try?"

I didn't reply. Of course I wanted to help them. To take away their suffering and lift the death sentence from all those dying of the Shadow—including Amos. But in saving their lives, I was destroying mine. I wasn't sure I had the courage to do that.

The crowd had begun to murmur a great deal. And I saw the worry on their faces. They were starting to doubt me. As they should. Miss Always bent down and met my gaze.

"Sometimes you must give up what you think you want, for something that matters more. Ivy, can't you see that this matters more?"

I looked out. At the faces. And it was then that I understood what I had felt rippling through the crowd that I couldn't name—faith. The people, *all* of these people, had come here on the promise of something of which there was no proof. They had all made this journey, and stood up to Justice Hallow's guards, on the promise of a brighter day. They believed in me, a girl they didn't know, for no other reason than it was something to believe in. Was it true? Were they right? In the end, there was only one way to find out. And despite how much I longed to be with my mother, I knew that I owed it to them—and to me—to find out.

I walked past Miss Always to the end of the platform. Down the three steps. Knelt at the water's edge. The crowd had fallen silent. I looked up and out. And what I saw there made my heart sing. Miss Frost and Rebecca were standing on the terrace of Prospa House. They had made it! Next, I glanced up at the clock tower. Twenty-two minutes until the portal closed.

Suddenly I knew just what to do—I would cure the plague, and *then* Rebecca and I would race to the portal and go home. It was perfect! I took a deep breath. My eyes fell to the sparkling blue water. I placed my hands out in front of me, palms down, and lowered them into the lake. They breached the surface and slipped under, the water icy cold.

I held my hands there. Waited. Hoped. Prayed. It seemed the whole of Prospa was holding its collective breath. All was still and silent. Then I felt my fingers tingle—starting at the tips and rushing up. A charge began to ripple from under the water, causing tiny waves upon the surface. Without warning, the chain around my neck snapped. The Clock Diamond unspooled, plunging into the lake. As it sank, the lake began to bubble and glow—the blue liquid swallowed by water so golden and bright it stung my eyes.

The crowd gasped as one. Miss Always was suddenly by my side. "It is happening!" she shouted. "It is happening!"

A great roaring cheer went up. I pulled my hands from the water. The lake shone like a radiant, liquid sun. I sat back on my heels. Watching as the people huddled around the water pumps and began pulling on the levers—great torrents of glistening honey-colored water pouring out.

"Drink it," instructed Miss Always. "Drink it, splash it on your skin, and be healed!"

Which is exactly what they did. Gulping it down. Splashing

it on their gray flesh with abandon. Several minutes passed. Miss Always and I watched from the platform, and what started to happen all around us was . . . nothing. Not a thing. The gray faces stayed gray. No one was even *slightly* cured. The murmurs of disappointment and anger began almost immediately. People wondering aloud what foolishness this was. Yes, the water had glowed wondrously, but it had not done a thing to wipe the Shadow's ashen mark from their flesh. I glanced up at the clock tower. Nineteen minutes left.

"Give it time!" shouted Miss Always. "It might not happen straightaway!" But I could hear the doubt in her voice, and so could the masses.

"It's a trick, that's what it is!" cried a man.

"I spent forty clips to get here," shouted another, "all for nothing!"

"The Dual is a fraud!" shrieked a woman.

"That's frightfully harsh!" I called back. "I never said I was her!"

It had been a mad dream. A fool's errand. I looked to Miss Always. She was pale. Probably thinking that the crowd would savage us the moment we stepped from the platform. Then a voice called out above the tide of discontent. A boy. And his cry was this: "It's gone! It's gone! She's done it!"

We all looked at the same time. The crowd parted to give the boy room. And I saw that it was Amos. He was pointing at his arm, for some reason. Pointing at where my healing remedy was smothered on his skin. I took off down the gangway, and Miss Always followed right behind me.

When we reached Amos, people around him were beginning to shout and cheer. And we quickly saw what was generating such excitement. When Amos had splashed the water from the pump on his skin, nothing had happened. At first.

Then he noticed that on the part of his arm where the water had washed over my natural remedy, the foul-smelling red paste had begun to blister and sizzle. Before sinking into the pores of his skin as if it were a sponge. Then that patch of his arm began to change color, the sickly gray fading, leaving in its wake a healthy glow. And it spread like a virus, bleeding up his arm and down his hand—until his entire body was as flushed and healthy as an infant.

"It's Ivy's remedy that did it!" he shouted. "She is the Dual!"

Amos ran over and kissed me on the cheek. Then began passing out the jars of Ivy Pocket's Miracle Cream—the crowd grabbing for the little crimson pots rather desperately.

"The combination of that ridiculous remedy and the energized water unlocked a cure," muttered Miss Always. "Incredible!"

"Not really, dear. My natural remedies are legendary."

"Don't worry," shouted Amos to the swelling crowd. "We will make a huge barrel, hundreds of them if we have to—everyone will be cured! The Dual is real!"

A deafening roar exploded up from the crowd, starting near us and sweeping back toward the concourse. It made my bones rattle. They gathered around me, grabbing and touching and clasping my hand. Miss Always pulled me back up the gangplank. "The prophecy has been fulfilled!" she shouted, with an arm clasped tightly around my shoulder. "The Dual has come!"

Another great cheer went up.

"We have seen the end of the Shadow," continued Miss Always. "And in keeping with the prophecy, Prospa has a new queen!"

Again, the crowd went thoroughly berserk. Chanting, "Queen Ivy! Queen Ivy!" Which was awfully thrilling. And frightfully bonkers. Miss Always lowered her arm, and I felt the blade at my back.

"But we must not forget that our new Queen is just a child, and the burden of the throne is a heavy one," she continued. "Therefore Ivy has asked me to become her new Chief Justice— we will perform the coronation immediately, and then I will take charge of the day-to-day operations." She threw out her arms like a lunatic. "Today is not just a new chapter in Prospa history—it is a new book!"

"Miss Always?" I said loudly.

The dreary villain was grinning like a lunatic. "Yes, Your Majesty?"

"You seem rather overheated. Fortunately, I have an excellent remedy."

Then I pushed her with great force. She spun over the railing, the dagger flying. Then she plunged into the water. There was a moment of utter silence. The crowd looking at one another, bug-eyed. Then Amos began to laugh heartily—and soon the

343

entire crowd was joining in. By the time Miss Always was being pulled from the water, she had become a laughingstock.

All the jars had been passed out. Dozens and dozens of people had smeared a few drops on their hands, then hurried to the water pumps and let the liquid splash over my natural remedy. And within moments, the gray flesh had washed away and they were utterly healed.

Amos had scribbled down a list of ingredients. Wagons took off for the local dairy to bring back milk to be curdled in the sun, while others went into the woodlands to collect tree sap, wildflowers, and moss. But I was no longer looking at the great sea of hope and joy churning around me.

As I hurried from the gangway, the ground shook again. This time most violently. People stumbled. Some fell. Then a horrible rumbling could be heard under our feet, like the growl of a lion. A great cry went up from the concourse. I looked over just as a great crack split the front of Prospa House. Chunks of stone hurtled to the ground. Windows shattered, shards of glass raining down on the crowd. Some began to run and scream. But most were too elated to really care about what was happening.

I was running now, barely noticed by the swarm of people. I looked at the clock tower. Fifteen minutes left. Then my eyes slipped down to Miss Frost and Rebecca on the terrace—I wished to wave and let them know I was coming. Only they no longer stood there alone. Guards flanked them at either side, gripping their arms. And a woman stood before them. Somehow she found me among the crowd. Looked right at me. Justice Hallow smiled, beckoning me like an old friend.

Waited. Hoped. Prayed.

19

"Attention, good people of Prospa!" thundered Justice Hallow.

I was bounding up the stairs as she began to speak. Her voice carried over the great lake. Some in the crowd booed her. Others hissed.

"You said there was no Dual!" barked one irate woman.

"Justice Hallow takes care of the rich!" shouted a man. "The farmers and their clans never got near the remedies!"

But Justice Hallow simply lifted her hands into the air rather majestically—as if to tell the good people of Prospa to shut their pieholes. Which, strangely, they did. "Today is not about recriminations," she declared. "This is a day of great joy—a day I have dreamed of since I was a little girl. A new dawn for Prospa."

Which was unexpected. And complete nonsense. When I reached the top of the stairs, I noticed that Professor Finsbury was lurking nearby. I headed straight for Miss Frost and Rebecca— but a guard fell in beside me, and I was marched over to Justice Hallow. I stood just behind her, looking down on a great sea of faces, crowded around the Clock Diamond monument and stretching out to the farthest corners of the great lake.

"But this shining hour, this greatest of days, is not about me," said Justice Hallow, shaking her head humbly. "It is about the girl who came to our world and defeated the Shadow—my *own* dear granddaughter . . ."

There were gasps and murmurs of surprise from the crowd.

"Her royal highness *Ivy the First!*"

The crowd erupted in a stupendous cheer. I glanced at my watch. Ten minutes left.

"Prospa has not had a queen for more than two hundred years," announced Justice Hallow, "but today we pass the ancient sceptre from the old royal line to the new."

Justice Hallow turned and gave the signal. Instantly one of her guards emerged from Prospa House carrying a white cushion with a sceptre lying upon it.

"How did you get out?" I whispered to Granny.

"Professor Finsbury saw you and Miss Always leaving my private quarters. He suspected foul play and came looking for me." She smiled faintly. "And as my second-in-command, he knew just where to look."

When the guard reached Justice Hallow, the ground rumbled and shook. The terrace seemed to be sliding under us. Granny lost her balance, saved from falling only by clutching the guard's arm. The stairs below were rippling like a heaving tide. A loud shudder came up from deep under the ground; then the stairs split down the middle. On the concourse, the impossibly tall clock tower monument was swaying from side to side.

"What's happening?" someone cried out.

"It's the Shadow seeking vengeance!" shouted another.

"You are wrong," said Justice Hallow. "A crime of the gravest kind has been committed, and that is why Prospa House is falling." She bowed her head slightly and turned to me. "I will

let our new Queen tell the sorry tale."

Justice Hallow turned her back on the crowd and picked

up the sceptre. It was the one I had seen in her cabinet of

curiosities—a black staff, carved with gold coronets, a large

green stone capping either end. "Do you wish to go home, Ivy?"

she said softly.

"Of course I do, you murderous medusa!"

"Then tell your people that Miss Always poisoned the

portal—tell them you saw her do it with your own eyes. Tell

them you cannot be their queen, as you wish to return to your

world. Tell them that you are passing the throne to your beloved

grandmother."

"Why would I do that?"

"Because if you don't, my guards will make sure you never

get home." She pushed the sceptre at me. "And I will have

Professor Finsbury put a bullet in Miss Frost."

I looked behind me. Saw Professor Finsbury standing by Miss

Frost with a pistol at her back.

"I may lose the war, Ivy," whispered Justice Hallow, "but I

win the only battles you seem to care about—your friends and your mother."

"Don't listen to her, Miss Pocket," said Miss Frost, defying the pistol. "I can take care of myself. Do what you know is right."

"You wouldn't shoot her," I said to Justice Hallow, "not here in front of the whole kingdom."

"What have I to lose?" said Granny, her eyes dancing. "These wretched fools would kill me if they knew what I had done. I am offering us both a way out. Go home and leave Prospa to me."

"And what of Miss Frost?" I said.

"I will make sure no harm comes to her. You have my word." Justice Hallow glanced back at Rebecca. "As for the girl, she is far too weak and would not survive the crossing. I will ensure that she has every comfort." She pushed the sceptre at me again. "So, Ivy, what's it to be?"

"Say yes," said Rebecca, her voice ringing with urgency. "You must be with your mother, Ivy, for nothing else matters." She nodded. "Accept the offer and go home."

"Listen to the girl," said Justice Hallow.

I took the royal staff from Granny's hand. The crowd let out a mighty cheer. I checked my watch. Seven minutes left. Then I stepped past my grandmother and stood at the edge of the terrace. The boisterous throng fell quiet.

"The portal has been poisoned," I said loudly.

The crowd erupted in furious chatter. Then Justice Hallow lifted her hands, and they fell silent. I looked down and saw Miss Always, dripping wet, standing by the monument. I thought in that moment of my mother. Of going home. Of old friends. And finally, of doing what I *had* to do—no matter the consequences.

"Miss Geraldine Always is the poisoner," I declared. "I saw her do it."

The gathering exploded with a wail of righteous anger. The mob turned on Miss Always, pointing, pushing, and shouting. Miss Always looked up at me in bewilderment. I glanced at Justice Hallow and saw the wicked delight on her smooth face.

"At least, that is what my grandmother wanted me to tell you," I said next, using the sceptre to point at the old rotter. "But the truth is, it was Justice Hallow who poisoned the portal!"

"Well done, Miss Pocket!" cheered Miss Frost.

Gasps and cries of disbelief rang out across the great lake. I glanced down at Miss Always—she offered the faintest of smiles and a small clap.

Justice Hallow was now at my back. "Do not do this!" she hissed.

"The reasons why are rather ugly," I continued, ignoring the villain, "but the only way I can really explain it is this— she wished to punish her daughter. My mother ran away from Justice Hallow, many of you must know that. And why does a child run from her mother right when she needs her the most? Because her heart was cold. Because her heart was closed."

I saw heads bobbing. And murmurs of agreement. I looked at my watch. Four minutes left.

"The girl is a liar!" thundered Justice Hallow.

"Earlier today, Granny tried to kill me," I said just as loudly, "so that I would never be able to rid you of the Shadow—which I did rather brilliantly, you must admit."

"God bless you, Queen Ivy!" shouted a delightful young girl. And others soon joined in. Wonderful peasants!

"What I do now," I said next, "I do for the good of Prospa and its people." Then I spun around and threw the sceptre as hard as

353

I could. It twirled through the air and hit my target in a brutal fashion. Professor Finsbury cried out as the gun was knocked from his hand and flew across the terrace. He clutched his hand, whimpering like a hungry puppy.

"Get her!" barked Justice Hallow to her guards.

One guard lunged at Miss Frost—but she made short work of him, clocking him in the face, then sweeping him from his feet. Then the other guards did something astounding—they stood down. Refused to attack Miss Frost or me or Rebecca.

"Traitors!" spat Granny.

"Miss Pocket, watch out!" cried Miss Frost.

I turned just as Granny charged toward me—she had pulled a dagger from one of the Orange Coats and had it lifted, poised to strike. Her face glowing with rage and hatred. I froze in that moment. But Rebecca didn't. She was already running. Diving to the ground and catching Justice Hallow's leg. Granny stumbled. Which gave me time to twist around, thrusting my boot into her buttocks—sending her tumbling down the cracked stairs. Granny landed facedown. But quickly rose to her feet, a large gash on her cheek. The crowd closed in around her, calling her a host of rather unpleasant names.

"You wretched fools!" she hissed at them. "I have kept the best of you alive, and this is my thanks?"

Miss Frost picked up the sceptre. Handed it to me with a bow of her head. "Queen Ivy."

"For my first and last ruling as monarch," I said, turning back to the crowd, "I pass this glorious stick to Miss Frost and declare that as I must return to my world. She is now the Queen of Prospa. Long may she reign and whatnot."

The poor woman looked positively stunned. I practically had to force the sceptre into her hands. "Are you sure?" she said faintly.

I shrugged. "You can't be any worse than Granny."

A tremendous roar, a great wave of joy, swept up from the concourse. It was so loud I almost didn't hear the clock tower chiming the hour. It was noon.

"Ivy, you have to go!" shouted Rebecca.

"It is too late," bellowed Justice Hallow, pointing at me. "You will never get home! You will never know your mother!"

I met her gaze and held it. "Just watch me, you mad cow."

But she never got the chance.

I heard startled cries. Then saw Miss Always leaping out of the way. I wasn't at all sure why. Then the solid silver statue capped by an enormous Clock Diamond came down. Right on top of Granny. The poor fossil had just enough time to twist around and throw up her arms. Then the stone smashed into the ground with her underneath, cracking the green bricks on every side. Then the cheering began. But it was brief, as the ground shuddered violently. One of the pillars holding the roof above our heads split open, sending great clumps of stone to the terrace floor.

"Come, Miss Pocket!" shouted Miss Frost.

I might have felt a tinge of sorrow for my dead grandmother. For how she hated me so very much. And what a waste all that bitterness was. But by then we were running at speed into Prospa House—the terrace crumbing behind us.

"It is noon," I shouted. "The hour is up!"

"As long as the tremors continue, the portal is still alive," said Miss Frost.

We tore down the hallway. Prospa House trembled. Walls

were cracking. Windows shattering. Plaster dropping from the ceiling. The portrait of Justice Hallow lay in ruin on the dusty carpet. We rushed down the back stairs. Through the labyrinth of corridors. Then down the spiral staircase and into the darkened chamber. The windowless vault smelled stupendously awful.

Rebecca ran first to the pool of murky water. Miss Frost and I were by her side in seconds, followed by two guards now loyal to the new Queen. The water was a sickly purple. Only the odd bubble rising from below. "Is it still alive?" I said. "Is it still open?"

"I believe so," said Miss Frost. "But not for long."

Rebecca clutched my hand. "Oh, Ivy, we are going home!"

"Didn't I say that we would?" I said brightly.

The walls groaned and shook. Therefore I got straight down to business.

"There is a boy called Amos Winter," I said, turning to Miss Frost. "He is a young man of great courage and spirit who had brains enough to bring my natural remedy to the city today. I would like you to take him under your wing."

"I will see what I can do," said the ginger queen.

"Now to Miss Always." I thought of everything that had

happened today. All that I had learned about that evil librarian. So I said, "She was married?"

"Briefly," said Miss Frost. "The marriage was conducted at her fiancé's sickbed—Edward died that very night. I don't suppose Miss Always ever recovered."

I suddenly remembered the picture at Miss Frost's house— of Miss Frost and her brother and Miss Always. And the tree house with the initials carved into it. "Was the young man she married your brother, dear?"

Miss Frost nodded. Closed her eyes briefly. "As for Miss Always's fate, it was her perseverance and belief that proved you were the Dual. Her contribution should be honored *and* her cruelty punished."

"How?"

"Since Miss Always has an appetite for power, I shall make her my minister for waste disposal."

I frowned. "What on earth is *that?*"

"The sewerage plant on the outskirts of the city. The conditions are rather grim."

"Just to be utterly clear," I said hopefully, "you *do* mean poop, don't you, dear?"

Miss Frost allowed a faint smile. "She will hate every second of it."

It's entirely possible that I squealed then. But not for long— as the curved ceiling began to crack. A handful of bricks dropped like rain. I wondered if the entire city would fall in a heap. Miss Frost read my mind.

"The ground will settle once the portal is closed," she said.

"The remedies!" I shouted, ashamed that I had not thought of them sooner. "Justice Hallow had them sent away—we must find out where they are so that they can cross back with us!"

Miss Frost was shaking her head. "They were taken to an infirmary several hours from the city. It is too late to bring them home, Miss Pocket—in your world their bodies are gone, and they would be no more than a soul." She saw me looking thoroughly outraged and lifted a hand. "But as they will no longer be needed as remedies, I *promise* you they will spend whatever time they have left here as honored citizens. We owe them that."

And I knew she meant it. But it took a moment for Miss Frost's words to truly sink in. When they did I was frowning, looking at Rebecca in bewilderment. "If you return to our world, you will not be alive," I said, still unable to believe it. "You will only be a soul."

"I know," said Rebecca softly.

I gasped. "Then why do you wish to go?"

The girl looked at me. Her eyes welling with tears. And I knew. *Of course* I knew. It was the reason she had put on the Clock Diamond in the first place. "Your mother," I said.

Rebecca nodded. It was a grim choice. But a noble one too.

Miss Frost bent down and put her hand in the water—it was thick, oozing between her fingers. "The crossing will be treacherous," she said, standing up. "The portal is in its death throes and will not provide safe passage as it usually does. Once you pass through it, you will find yourself in the void. This is a most dangerous place, and without the portal guiding the way, there is a real possibility you might get blown off course." She shifted her gaze between Rebecca and me. "Find the scarlet light and go toward it. Understood?"

I looked down at the poisoned water. Then at Miss Frost. "Will I see you again?"

"Once the portal dies, the link between our worlds is severed forever. Hurry, and remember—head for the scarlet light. That will lead you home."

I waited for a speech. Declarations of undying gratitude. Great puddles of emotion. She'd never forget me. Loved me like a sister. Or an aunt. Or at the very least, a slightly repressed second cousin. Instead she lifted my chin with her finger and said, "Thank you, Miss Pocket."

Which was rather perfect. Miss Frost and two guards took off toward the arched doorway, bound for the tunnel that led outside. Rebecca and I walked to the edge of the pool. Without a word we linked hands, squeezing tight, and dove into the water.

Thank you, Miss Pocket.

20

My eyes stung. My lungs hurt. My skin tingled as if it were being pricked by a thousand needles. Particles swirled through the purple liquid like a tempest. Having a dead girl with me was a great help—Rebecca's shimmering skin bloomed within the murky water like a lamppost.

The portal was easy enough to find. A large and dark mass pulsing down at the very bottom of the pool. I kicked my legs, feeling Rebecca beside me. The far wall was covered in rock and barnacles and seaweed. And set into the bottom, among the heaving weeds and the gnarly shells, was our destination. The portal was large, plump tendrils covering its flesh, and in the center was a tunnel—though it was nearly closed. It pulsed, but just faintly, barely a bubble or two rising from within it. I went first, kicking my legs and pushing my way into the portal.

Inside was a long, narrow membrane—rather like the underside of a mushroom. The walls of the tunnel groaned deeply, like the last gasps of a dying giant, pressing in on me. I wanted to look back to check that Rebecca was close behind, but there wasn't room enough for me to turn my head.

The farther in we went, the tighter the membrane grew. I heard a great shudder. And though I could not look back, I felt Rebecca at my feet and knew the portal was collapsing behind us. I kicked hard, pushing at the fleshy walls in the mad hope I could keep the portal open until we reached the void.

There was no air left in my lungs. Yet all I could do was kick and hope we would make it out in time. I felt a great surge from behind, pushing me forward. And just when I felt as if my chest would bust—a mighty wind was hammering my face. I gasped and took in a wondrous breath. Then looked back and saw Rebecca flying out as the dark and festering portal shriveled into a tight knot behind her.

"Ivy, help me!"

My eyes flew up as Rebecca spun wildly above me. I reached up and was able to grab her arm. Pulling her to me. It is rather difficult to describe a void. All I can say is that this place was empty and full at the same time. An endless landscape with nothing. It had color—the palest of blues. And it had weather— mighty winds that screamed in rage, churning and swirling and battering.

"Where do we go?" screamed Rebecca.

I looked about. Searching for any signs of a scarlet light. Far off in the distance was the faintest, the softest, of glows. Was it red? I couldn't be sure. The whirlwind roared so furiously it made seeing terribly difficult.

"This way!" I shouted, pointing toward the faint glow.

Rebecca nodded her head and gripped my hand. "Don't let go, Ivy," she cried. "Promise you won't let go."

"Of course not, dear!"

But it was a promise I should not have made. For just at that moment a violent gust of wind hit me from below and sent me reeling.

"Ivy!" cried Rebecca.

My hand was pulled from hers. I tried to use my arms and legs to stop my rapid ascent. But I was a leaf in a tempest, and the more I struggled, the farther from Rebecca I flew. In seconds she was little more than a dot in the great emptiness of space.

"Foolish child," whispered a voice in my ear.

Then I felt myself being swallowed. The wind sealed off. The great wall of furious noise silenced. It was as if I was inside a ball—or a fat ghost. The Duchess of Trinity took off, flying me back toward Rebecca. "What wonderful timing you have, dear," I said. "For once, I'm actually pleased to see you."

"You have no business being in this void," she sang. "Did I not warn you about meddling?"

"I'm practically positive you didn't," I replied.

"Foolish child," she growled again.

I put my hands on the sides of her luminous flesh and looked down. Rebecca was in sight! She was being blown about, but when she spotted me zipping through the air inside a ghostly bubble, she began to sob madly—with relief, I assume. The Duchess did not slow when we reached Rebecca. For a moment I was terrified that we were going to fly right past her. Instead, the ghost opened her big mouth and gobbled the girl up.

"Who is she?" Rebecca asked as I pulled her upright.

"Just a chum," I said brightly. "Slightly murderous, but awfully good in a pickle."

The Duchess flew through the swirling winds, right toward the scarlet light. The faint glow began to brighten into a deep shimmering red the closer we got. It was shaped like a teardrop, great blooms of crimson mist rising out of it.

When we were a short distance from the light, the ghost stopped. The winds around us were pounding the Duchess on all sides. I heard her groan and noticed fragments of her luminous aura lifting off and flying away.

"What is happening, Duchess?" I said.

"Mind your own business." The ghost's voice sounded strained and weak. "The winds here are ferocious—crawl through the tunnel and do not look back."

"What tunnel?" I said.

"Ivy, look!" shouted Rebecca.

The Duchess's blue blubber began to stretch out in front

of us, making a perfectly round channel leading to the light. We took off, crawling on our hands and knees. I made Rebecca go first so I could keep an eye on her. We were just a few feet from the scarlet teardrop when the tunnel tore open. The winds encircled the Duchess like a pack of rabid dogs. Rebecca and I were spat back into the void—and almost immediately my friend began to blow away.

"Ivy, what is happening?" she cried.

Salvation was within reach. I grabbed Rebecca by the arm and pushed as hard as I could, throwing her into the scarlet light—she gave a faint cry and was swallowed within it. I felt a current at my back. I turned and saw that the Duchess of Trinity was blowing me toward the red hollow. "Are you not coming?" I shouted.

The winds had savaged her—fragments of light tore from her flesh. The ghost shook her head. "There will be nothing left in a moment or two." She blew again, and I flew closer to the light. "Good-bye, child."

"How did you find me here?" And in that moment, the answer dropped into my head, and I understood. "This was your last great mission—wasn't it, Duchess?"

"I made my choice, and I am not sorry." Starlight flew from her until I could barely make out her ghostly glow. "Rebecca will return to the place where she departed. With enough headwind, so will you."

She gave one final breath, and I felt the warm light at my back. The wind raged, and the Duchess of Trinity, that marvelous and murderous creature, was carried away like dust on the wind. I turned and plunged into the hollow.

My landing wasn't as dignified as I would have liked. I was spat out, tumbling across the floor. But I recovered well and climbed to my feet. Found myself in a narrow corridor—dirt floor, brick wall. I got up, dusted off my dress, and pushed on the door. The glass panel opened silently, and I found myself in the darkened ballroom. It looked rather less chaotic than when I was last there. The red velvet curtains were drawn. The place silent and still. I broke into a run, heading for the door.

Finding Rebecca wasn't difficult. I suspected she was close when I passed through the drawing room and saw a maid shrieking about ghosts and running for her life. Rebecca was in the great hall. And she wasn't alone. Lady Elizabeth sat on the steps of the grand staircase, looking at her granddaughter, her weathered face a mixture of wretchedness and wonder.

"I . . . I do not believe it," she muttered to herself. "My granddaughter has come back."

The dead girl now glowed blue, as the Duchess had. Her skin threw off an icy light, her dark eyes danced. But she was a ghost on the hunt. Her brow was knotted, darting from room to room and returning each time to the great hall. And I understood why.

"She will come," I told her with certainty. "Your mother will find you here."

Rebecca threw her arms around me. "You made it, Ivy! Oh, I was worried that you would be lost in that awful void."

"Yes, I made it," I said softly. "Though I cannot say the same for the Duchess."

But Rebecca's thoughts were elsewhere. "Do you really think she'll come, Ivy? Oh, but how will she know where I am?"

"She watches you, dear. Trust me, she will come."

Lady Elizabeth got to her feet with some effort. Leaning heavily on her cane, she walked toward Rebecca, her beady eyes roaming her granddaughter's ghostly glow. "You have come home, Rebecca," she said.

"Yes." Rebecca shook her head, starlight leaping from her hair. "No. I am waiting for my mother."

"Oh." Lady Elizabeth let out a faint huff. "I thought you had come to haunt me. . . ."

And the old bat sounded disappointed. I was struck by the silence in the vast house.

"Where is everyone?" I asked.

"Most of the servants gave notice after the calamitous ball," she said. "Some claptrap about Butterfield Park being cursed." She huffed again. "Idiots!"

"Where is Matilda?" asked Rebecca. "Perhaps I could say hello—and Lady Amelia, is she about?"

Lady Elizabeth rested both hands on the top of her cane. "They are gone." She let out a shallow breath. "Set sail for Australia."

"You are here alone?" said Rebecca.

The old woman ignored the question. "When your mother died," she said, her wrinkled face a mask of torment and shame,

"I did what I thought was best. I wanted you to get *on* with things, to stop being so glum—but I did not behave as I should have. I was cruel." She nodded her head. "Yes, cruel . . . and I am sorry."

"It doesn't matter now, Grandmother." Rebecca touched the old woman's cheek. "If it's forgiveness you seek, I give it freely."

With these words, a great sob flew out of Lady Elizabeth. It was deep and long buried and rather beautiful.

"She is here!" cried Rebecca, pointing at the window.

I looked out and saw Rebecca's mother. She was standing out in the meadow by the schoolhouse. Her glowing blond hair falling about her shoulders. A marvelous smile spread across her face. Lady Elizabeth gasped. I waved. Rebecca's mother waved back—lovely ghost!

Her mother's presence seemed to answer all of Rebecca's doubts. All her fears. Before she departed, Rebecca turned and kissed her grandmother.

"You better get going," I said as brightly as I could. I was determined not to howl like a girl who was saying good-bye to the best friend she had ever had. It wasn't a complete success.

We threw arms around each other and embraced. I felt the

coolness of her skin against my own. Then I felt her kiss my cheek. "You brought me home, Ivy."

"Be a shiny bright star," I whispered, squeezing her tight. "A shiny bright star, so I'll always know you're there."

I don't recall exactly what happened next. One moment Rebecca was with us in the great hall, and the next she was a shadow slipping through the door. Lady Elizabeth and I watched as she flew toward her mother. When they came together, it was as if they merged—Rebecca's light and her mother's spilling into each other. Then washing away, leaving a hazy afterglow that splashed briefly over the wildflowers and was gone.

Some time passed before anyone spoke. I turned around and regarded Lady Elizabeth. She was a broken woman, made humble and frail by loss. I didn't *want* to feel sorry for her—she had been thoroughly wicked to me. But somehow it didn't much matter anymore.

"Well," I said brightly, "I suppose you'll beg *my* forgiveness now—cry buckets, kiss my feet, butter my toast and whatnot."

"You?" Some of the old spark crackled in her eyes. "Never!"

"Well, then, you might at least take my advice—unless you

want to die all alone in this beastly house of yours."

She huffed, but her heart wasn't in it. "I'm listening."

"Fix things with Lady Amelia and Matilda," I said. "Go and make it right. You are a horrid old bat, but I'm almost certain you didn't start out that way. Lady Amelia deserves your respect and Matilda needs your example—show her that being hateful and vengeful and cruel makes for a lonely life. Let her see that you are trying to change, and then she might too."

The old bat thought on this a moment. Then she gulped. "Australia?"

I nodded. "Afraid so."

She huffed again. Tapped her cane on the floor. "There are *worse* places, I suppose."

"Not really, dear—but that's the spirit!"

Lady Elizabeth had a note sent booking a berth on the next ship sailing for Australia. She offered me an iced tea and a raw potato, but I told her it was time that I departed. She was kind enough to give me five pounds for the train. We were not friends—how could we be after the wretched things she had done? But without saying it aloud, we both understood that whatever had happened between us, we were leaving it there in that hall. I slapped her on the shoulder and headed for the door. I was almost there when she called my name.

"Where will you go, Miss Pocket?" she asked.

I thought of my destination. And who would be waiting there. "Good-bye, Lizzy."

Moments later, as I walked down the gravel drive toward the train station, I looked back at the great house and saw in its grand splendor a kind of emptiness. It was beautiful, yes, but how little joy I had seen within its walls. I couldn't say whether Lady Elizabeth would return with Matilda and her mother. Or if the mansion would sit empty for the next hundred years. I only knew that Rebecca was now somewhere far away. Blissfully happy and at peace. And that my part in the story of this sad place had reached its end. And I was glad of it.

"It's good to see you, miss," said Bertha for the seventh time. "I was awful scared you'd never set foot in England again, and that's a fact!"

I had sent word from the train station at Butterfield Park that

I would be arriving in Dorset the following day. Bertha and Jago were there to meet me—Jago shook my hand in a most vigorous fashion, Bertha wept like a burst pipe. As I had no luggage, we headed straight to the wagon and set off for Weymouth.

There was a great deal to discuss. My adventure, of course. I gave them all the particulars. Jago was rather glum when I mentioned that Miss Frost would not be back.

"She's as tough as old boots, Miss Frost," he said, his voice ringing with admiration. "Doesn't take any guff neither."

"Very true, dear, and well said." I bumped his leg in an encouraging fashion. "You have a marvelous way with words. Have you ever thought of giving English a try?"

Jago burst out laughing. Then Bertha joined in. Which was confusing, but really rather nice. There were other matters to talk over—Mrs. Dickens was still at the apartment in Berkeley Square, awaiting our return.

"She sent a box of your things, pretty dresses and such," said Bertha cheerfully. Then she snorted. "Though I can't think why she included a battered old clock. Her note said you would understand."

It must be Rebecca's clock. And the thought made me smile despite the sadness. Bertha prattled on a little longer, declaring that Mr. Partridge had written several letters. But really there was only one topic that mattered to me.

"How is my . . . how is Anastasia?"

"She's getting stronger every day," said Bertha.

Jago turned the horses and we left the main road, rolling up a prairie bursting with tall grass. "All she did was hum and shake that first night," he said. "But after Miss Frost called at the cottage, your ma was a different person. Let Bertha clean her up and started eating and talking some. This morning she was singing as she dug in the garden."

"She has a lovely voice, your mother," said Bertha.

I saw the little cottage as we crested the hill. My mouth went dry. A knot pulled in my stomach. I don't believe I've ever felt so ill. Despite my mad wish that the dirt road would stretch on for a thousand miles, we were there all too soon. Jago pulled the horses up in the yard. "Are you ready, chatterbox?"

It seemed that I had been on this journey for an age and that here, at last, was the destination. So why was I not leaping from the wagon and bounding into my mother's arms? Perhaps it was travel sickness. Or scurvy.

"It's going to be grand, miss," said Bertha gently.

"Blimey, she's lost for words!" said Jago.

"What a horrid thing to say!" I declared.

In the end, it didn't matter how I felt. There was only one thing to be done. So I stood up, ignoring the uncertainty and doubts whirling through my head, and jumped from the carriage.

21

She was waiting for me in the garden. Standing beneath an elm tree, the ocean at her back. It was a great shock to finally see who was behind that curtain of matted hair. She wore a pale green dress. Her dark hair glistened in the sun, flowing down her back with no bands or ribbons. Her face was scrubbed clean. Bright blue eyes. A fetching smile. Her hands were clutched together.

Bertha and Jago stopped at the back door. I did not mind that they were there. Perhaps I had imagined my mother would run to me and bundle me up. But she didn't. She lifted her hands to her chest as I walked the length of the yard. When I stopped in front of her, there was a brief moment where I worried she was about to start humming. But then something warm and tender bloomed on her face.

"You have come a long way," she said.

I nodded.

"How are you, Ivy?"

"Utterly stupendous, dear," I replied. "There have been a great many thrills and spills—life on the line and whatnot. Your mother's something of a nutter, but I expect you know that already." I sighed. "Most ordinary girls would have curled up like kittens and sobbed for days. But not me. Yes, there was danger at every turn and a great many people trying to get me. But I didn't flinch. Bashed people left and right. Rescued Rebecca. Pushed Miss Always into the great lake. Cured the Shadow. Became Queen. Met my other half—the mad cow could talk underwater—and then became a whole girl again." I sighed once more. "So you see, dear, it's been a rather marvelous adventure."

Anastasia Radcliff crouched down, her eyes level with mine. She lifted her hands and cupped my face. "How are you, Ivy?" she asked me again.

"How *am* I?" Had she not heard me the first time? Was my answer not thrilling enough? Had I not dazzled and amused her? Yet there was such tenderness in her lilting voice that it nearly took my breath away.

And I saw that she was asking something completely new of me. Something of which there was no need for tricks or games. In her face and in her question, twice asked, this strange woman was asking me to take a leap of faith and speak of something true and unvarnished and as real as the heart pounding in my chest. She wished to know how I was, *who* I was . . . and although a part of me raged against offering this part of myself, I ignored it and set the words free.

"Scared. I'm scared."

"Scared of what, Ivy?"

"A great many things. I'm scared that this isn't real. That you are just a dream. I'm scared that if you *are* real, you won't like me. I'm rather a lot to take, you see. And I'm scared that even if you wish for us to be together, that it won't work. That I will wear you out and you will send me away. Or you will leave a note on my pillow and flee into the night."

My lips had a mind of their own and were trembling madly, tears congregating in my eyes with no regard for my dignity. But I was glad of it. For so long I had used my imagination as a place to hide. But now all I craved was something real. Something true.

"Before you knew I was your mother," said Anastasia, still holding my face in her hands, "when I was just a lunatic in a madhouse, you cared enough to help me. I spent twelve years humming to you, day and night, dreaming of this day—and as you walked toward me just now, I was terrified that I would disappoint *you*. Ivy, my love is nothing you need to wish for. I am your mother, I will stay by your side come feast or famine, and I will remain there until my last breath. If you have faith in nothing else, have faith in that."

I found myself nodding—for I believed *every* word. I don't recall flinging my arms around my mother, but I must have. We hugged for the longest time, and I don't think either of us wanted to let go. I heard Bertha sniveling in the background. And Jago telling her to blow her nose.

When you meet the person to whom you are a link in the same chain, there is a great deal to talk about. We ended up in the kitchen, eating crumpets with honey and speaking of a great many things. Bertha brewed a pot of tea. Jago watched in wonder. Words tumbled out one atop the other. People spoke at once. Things were repeated and repeated again.

My mother told me about Sebastian Dumbleby, my father. She said he was a dear man with a good heart and that he was overjoyed when I was born. She spoke of Justice Hallow, of growing up at her knee in Prospa House—and how she escaped her cruelty, changed her name, and fled into our world.

"I suppose I am Ivy Radcliff," I said, finishing off a delectable crumpet. "Or is it Dumbleby?" Then I gasped. "Estelle is my *aunt*. How beastly!"

"Hallow was my mother's name," said Anastasia. "And Radcliff was the surname of the nurse who took care of me—I always wished that I was her daughter, so I took her name. As for Dumbleby, I think that family has caused us enough pain." She leaned across and placed her hand on mine. "Pocket is a fine name, and I would be honored to take it—if you agree?"

"Of course she agrees!" said Bertha, sobbing into her crumpet.

I thought that was a glorious idea.

"Still hungry, chatterbox?" said Jago, offering me the last crumpet.

"Famished," I replied.

"Bertha, sit down and drink your tea," said Anastasia. "You'll wear yourself out."

"I don't mind, miss." The kindly lump sat down and looked about. "Not so long ago I lost my poor mother and had nowhere to go—now look at me!" She smiled and shook her head. "Life has a way of surprising, don't it?"

Bertha's words hit me as I took a bite of fresh crumpet, the honey drizzling down my chin. The events of the past year *had* been thoroughly gobsmacking. But then, my story had always been certain to involve breathtaking adventure, bone-shattering courage, and frightful danger. And it was destined to end in a homecoming of the most wonderful kind. I had found the one person in the whole world who yearned for me as I had yearned for her. Somehow, some way, we had found each other again. Which was hardly a great shock when you think about it—for I have all the natural instincts of a happy ending.

Epilogue

"Goodness, Ivy, I *do* hope it goes well."

I peeked through the curtain and looked out. People were streaming in. Taking their seats. Talking eagerly. "It will be a raging success, Ma. We're practically sold out, after all."

"Ten minutes until curtain up!" cried Bertha, hurrying past. "Jago, where is the sheet music?"

"I just gave it to Mr. Spencer," said the boy. While his voice had gotten deeper, his grin was as mischievous as ever. "Unless you or Mrs. Dickens want to play the piano?"

"Not me, lad," said Mrs. Dickens, rushing from the dressing

room. She had a needle and thread in her hand and a dress flung over her shoulder. "Two girls with uneven hems—I'm run off my feet, I am!"

Two years had rushed by in a wondrous blur. After a few months in Dorset, we had settled into the apartment in Berkeley Square; me and Ma, Mrs. Dickens and Bertha, and of course Jago. We were a family in every way that mattered. With some of the money from Mr. Banks, Ma had opened a music school in Hampstead—Pocket's Melodies. Ma taught piano and singing to girls and boys from all over London.

"The children are rather nervous about singing in front of their families." Ma had her hands clutched together like she did when she was fretful. "Oh, Ivy, it's our first big concert. Do you think we are ready? Perhaps we haven't rehearsed enough or spent enough time—"

"Your students are ready, and so are you," I said, gripping her arm. "Everybody knows their part, they will sing their hearts out, and the whole concert will be a smashing success."

Ma was like that at times. Fretful. Anxious. Usually she was strong and sure—but not always. Some nights her dreams were bad. She would cry out. About Lashwood. And my father. And the years we had lost. But I always told her that what we have now is so stupendous because it took two worlds, one necklace, and a great deal of calamity and good fortune to get us here.

Some others hadn't been as lucky. A few months after the ball at Butterfield Park, Mr. Partridge got word that Estelle Dumbleby's family fortune was gone—stolen by an underhanded banker who spent every pound Estelle had to pay for his gambling habit. The grand house in Highgate had been sold, and Estelle was last seen at a dress shop in Mayfair, begging for employment. Which was glorious!

Countess Carbunkle had fared even worse. After her humiliation at the Butterfield Park anniversary ball, Miss Anonymous wrote a wondrously snarky story under the headline COUNTESS CATASTROPHE STRIKES AGAIN! The story was printed in newspapers far and wide. Utterly humiliated and a worldwide laughing stock, Countess Carbunkle had purchased a lighthouse off the coast of Alaska, vowing never to show her face in public again. So good news all around then!

"Are you as musical as your mother?" said Mr. Spencer, combing his unruly hair.

Mr. Spencer was not our usual piano player, but as Mrs. Harding was out with the flu, he had stepped in. "Can you sing?" he asked me, slipping the comb into his coat pocket.

"No, dear—I sound like three cats in a meat grinder. Though I did once burp 'God Save the Queen.'"

Mr. Spencer let out a wistful sigh. "I do love Queen Victoria, such dignity. It can't be easy, can it, being a queen?"

"Actually, it's really not that difficult," I said brightly. "I admit, I was only Queen Ivy for about five minutes, but still—"

"Ivy." Ma was shaking her head.

"*Queen* Ivy, you say?" said Mr. Spencer, bug-eyed.

I groaned cheerfully. "Forgive me, Mr. Spencer. I talk a great deal of nonsense, being an odd sort of girl with an intriguing past."

All talk of Prospa was forbidden outside the house. On account of people thinking we were bonkers and locking us up. Ma had had her fill of madhouses. As had I.

"Girls and their tall tales," muttered Mr. Spencer as he set off for the piano.

Ma laughed and kissed my cheek. "Wish me luck."

I did. And she kissed me again. Then she began rounding up her students, putting them in position on the tiered platform. The concert hall was nearly full. I saw Mr. Partridge sitting up front—dressed in a fine white suit, his top hat in his lap. Mr. Partridge had taken quite a shine to my mother, though she was usually too shy and quiet to give him much encouragement. Ma had that way about her, though. You just wanted to be near her.

"Remember, children," said Ma, taking her position in front of the choir, "big voices, big smiles!"

She signaled to Jago. The boy pulled on the cord, the curtain parting. As it flew open, I looked out into the crowd again, delighting in their faces as they began to clap and cheer. Which is when I saw her. She was standing at the back. Dark dress. Flaming red hair. It was Miss Frost, stern and dignified. She looked at me, gave a slight nod of her head. I was too stunned to nod back. A man rushed in front of her to take his seat. When he had passed, Miss Frost was gone. My eyes roamed the hall, looking for any sign of her. Had it *really* been Miss Frost? Wasn't the door between our worlds shut forever?

Ma swooshed her arms through the air, and the choir began to sing. It sounded heavenly. I didn't keep searching for Miss Frost in the crowd. I had seen her, and she had seen me—that was enough. Was it her? How could it be? The whole thing was frightfully unlikely, yet I refused to fret or wonder too deeply about it. For if my life had been a school, it would have but one lesson. *Anything* was possible.

THE END

Acknowledgments

Oh, dear. How awkward. As this is the final book in Ivy's adventure—wasn't it grand?—now is the time to scatter thank yous and high praise like confetti. To declare my undying gratitude far and wide. Perhaps now you see my problem? Oh, well. Let's get it over with.

My literary agent, Madeleine Milburn, has been a bright light in the literary fog these past three years. Her wisdom, loyalty, and negotiating savvy are masterful and I thank her. A tip of the hat to Thérèse Coen for handling foreign rights with ease and Haley Steed for being terrifically helpful.

Thanks to the folks at Greenwillow Books, especially Virginia Duncan, Sylvie Le Floc'h, Katie Heit, and Tim Smith. I remain in awe of Barbara Cantini's incredible talent and whimsical illustrations.

I'm almost certain I was cursed at birth. Possibly by a witch. Or an ill-willed librarian. Despite my wretched fate, life has offered the odd ray of sunshine. My nephews and nieces, for example. Not to mention my mother and father, who have been hugely supportive

over the years. Honorable mentions to Carol, for friendship, humor, and countless movies. Also, Christine for encouragement and a sympathetic ear. And Paul for printing and computer-related stuff.

Well, dear reader, that brings our adventure to a close. Let's not get sentimental; that's not our way, is it? The ending was marvelous and you're sorry it's over, we can all agree on that—but there are other books out there, other characters. No, it won't be the same, but what ever is? As I need to keep myself in eggs and bonbons, I shall continue to write books about interesting children—but I suspect that none will be as infuriating, incorrigible, or offensive as Ivy Pocket. Nor will they be such glorious fun to write. It's been a hoot. Now shuffle off, I'm tired.

Caleb Krisp

a prized stallion

a junior Sherlock Holmes

a prima ballerina

a Buddhist monk

"For I have all the instincts of . . ."

a writer of penny dreadfuls

a stockbroker

a princess in a tower

a five-star general

a coffin maker's daughter

an assistant librarian

a physician

a sedated cow

a caterpillar

a postmaster's daughter

a highland hermit

a secret agent

a startled rabbit

a lion

a trapped miner

a cheese maker's niece

a startled rabbit

a lion

an assistant librarian

a five-star general

"For I have
all the instincts of . . ."

a Buddhist monk

a junior Sherlock Holmes

a highland hermit

a prized stallion

a cheese maker's niece

a sedated cow